COPYRIGHT

TABLE OF CONTENTS

CHAPTER 1

CHAPTER 2

CHAPTER 3

CHAPTER 4

CHAPTER 5

CHAPTER 6

CHAPTER 7

CHAPTER 8

CHAPTER 9

CHAPTER 10

CHAPTER 11

CHAPTER 12

CHAPTER 13

CHAPTER 14

CHAPTER 15

CHAPTER 16

CHAPTER 17

CHAPTER 18

CHAPTER 19

CHAPTER 20

CHAPTER 21

CHAPTER 22

CHAPTER 1

"You can't be serious?" Erich said, eying the ignition switch in his hand dubiously.

His 'customer' for the morning was a failed super villain. Or would-be supervillain, if the half-built exo-suit now cluttering up Erich's shop was any indicator. Could he still be considered a villain if he had never got around to committing any crimes?

At least, not any serious ones, he thought as he eyed the track marks running up and down the addict's arms.

"It's proof! Proof I'm good for it. I'm not about to leave my *baby* behind, am I?"

Erich supposed that even if the cobbled together power armor hadn't given away his powerset, the way the man's eyes flitted spasmodically between various bits of tech around the garage would have. Artificers fresh off the Event tended to have tics like that. Likely a byproduct of all that crazy new technology in their head searching for an outlet.

"Sir," Erich said, running a tired hand through his hair. "For the last time, this isn't a pawnshop, it's a repair shop. I fix things. I build things. I sell things. Sometimes I even design things. What I don't do is take on suits of half-finished power armor as collateral for loans."

Especially not suits as poorly designed as the specimen in front of him.

"Can't you see the opportunity here?" The would-be villain whined, "As soon as I get the money for more parts, I'll need somewhere to finish off my suit. This could be that place. Your shop could be the birthplace of the 'Crusher'"

Ah, now he knew why the addict had targeted his store rather than a pawnshop. He probably couldn't afford to store the unfinished suit wherever he'd previously been keeping it.

"This store could be the base of operations for my new faction!"

Headache already forming, Erich was about to take deep breath before thinking better of it. The guy opposite him looked like he hadn't seen a shower in days, if not weeks.

"I fail to see how having my shop tied to the origins of a Meta-human criminal would improve my business. Now, I'm sorry, but unless you have some *proper business* for me, I am afraid I must ask you and your suit to leave. You're getting in the way of real customers."

Even as he said it, he knew it was a lie. His shop wasn't empty because it had a drug addled supervillain in it. It was empty because it was always empty. The drug dealer in the alley next to his store saw more business than the store itself.

To make matters worse, it was nearly the end of the month, and Hard-Light's goons would be expecting their cut. He *needed* to make some proper cash, or failing that, find *something* to tide the man over...

"Hey," He said, cutting off whatever the addict had been saying, "I think I will take you up on that deal."

"Really?" The man looked overjoyed, completely missing the way that Erich's eyes were roaming over the machine. Or rather, the two B-Class power cells sitting in the suit's chest compartment. Even if he wouldn't get anything for the suit, the raw components that made it up would be worth something.

"Sure." Erich nodded, a smile stealing over his face, "how could I pass up the opportunity to be a part of the birth of the Crasher?"

"The Crusher."

"The Crusher." Erich corrected seamlessly. "I just want to make one slight alteration to the deal."

For the first time in their conversation, something akin to wariness peeped through the drug induced haze the man was under. "What?"

"A change in date." The young store keeper suggested, "Rather than have the debt default on the second week of the coming month, I would prefer to have it occur - which we both *know* it won't -two days before the end of this month."

That wouldn't exactly give him any time to strip and sell the hunk of junk for parts, but it would give him something to show Hard-Light's goons that he was good for the money.

Most of it at least.

And who knew, the crazy junky might even manage to drum up the cash in time. He wasn't counting on it, but he supposed stranger things had happened.

"That's not a lot of time," The junky murmured, unconsciously scratching at his scabbed elbow with a filthy fingernail as he eyed the exo-suit to his right. "I don't know..."

"It's a sure bet though, right? You have a tip." Erich pointed out, in a sudden role reversal.

Fortunately for him, it seemed that whatever substance the Meta-human was on, it wasn't conducive toward long term planning or risk assessment, because the reminder of his 'sure fire tip' had the
man grinning like a loon.

"Yeah." He grinned. "I do have a tip, don't I?"

"That you do." Erich nodded insincerely as he started to count out cash from the register.

△△△

Naturally, the debt defaulted. The junkie's 'hot tip' turned out be hot air.

The would-be supervillain showed up at his store not even a day later. The guy whined, cajoled and begged, but Erich was unyielding. The 'contract' had been clear. Ultimately the junky left in defeat, leaving Erich with half a ton of Artificer designed power armor.

Not that he cared about its current configuration. In fact, he considered it something of an eye-sore.

No, it was the materials that made up the suit that held his interest. He could flip those power-cells for a few grand each, maybe more if he was smart about it. It would take a little time, but he would have his money in the end.

So, he figured he could be forgiven for feeling cautiously optimistic when Hard-Light's goons stepped into his store.

That feeling promptly vanished when he saw who was leading them.

In another organization it might have been considered beneath the boss's daughter to go around shaking down small businesses for protection money, but given the relatively small size of Hard-Light's gang, it was pretty much an inevitability that even his daughter
sometimes had to partake of the 'menial' tasks.

"Sarah, you look as beautiful as ever."

"Why thank you, Erich" The woman in question grinned in a manner that exposed far too many teeth. "You always know how to brighten a girl's day."

"Why, I'm simply stating the obvious my dear." He wasn't even lying. The blonde woman was just as gorgeous as all Meta-humans tended to be.

Of course in this case, she was beautiful in the same way that particularly venomous plants could be. Eye catching and colorful, but virulently deadly to anyone that got too close.

An example of which could be seen in the way that electricity started to visibly arc along her fingertips as she sighed. "Of course, the reason you're always so free with a compliment is because you never have Daddy's cut ready."

Erich struggled not to wince as the acrid stink of ozone filtered through the air.

"Which is a shame." She said, "I actually enjoy visiting you, Erich. It's nice to deal with a man with a little class. Doubly so when he's a cutie like you." She winked.

"I have three thousand." Erich grinned weakly, sweat beading on his brow as the crackle of the woman's power grew in intensity.

"Only three thousand." She pouted, "That's not nearly good enough, Erich. The rules say five thousand, and I can't give you a pass this month. Sorry lover, but Daddy's starting to wonder if I'm going soft."

She didn't even blink as behind her, one of her goon's shoved over a display, sending electrical components clattering to the floor as it came down with a crash.

"I have something else though!" Erich shouted, before the carnage could begin in earnest. For just a moment he feared the goons would trash the place anyway, but Sarah held up a hand for them to stop just as one was about to tip over another display.

"Oh?" The woman tilted her head.

"It's in the back." He said hurriedly, "I'll show you."

"Stay here boys" The woman called, "I'm going to see what dearest Erich has to show me. And it better be good." She added for Erich's benefit.

"It is." He nodded as he strode toward the garage, keeping the fear from his voice through sheer willpower. "You won't be disappointed."

The pair stepped into the garage, and Erich reached over to flip the light switch. He nearly stumbled though, as the mob boss's daughter hugged him from behind.

"Alright Erich, you've got me all alone." She whispered into his ear. "I'm guessing you want to come to some alternative form of arrangement?"

"No!? I..." He started to say, flushing as the woman's hands roamed over places he most assuredly did not consent to. In the end, he was reduced to helplessly pointing in the direction of what he brought her in here to show her.

"Oh?" She murmured, releasing him as she saw the half-baked suit. "I reckon the old man would give you about two hundred thousand
for that. Finished, of course. He probably wouldn't give you a dime for it as it is now."

Erich froze partway through rezipping his fly. He almost couldn't believe his ears.

She... she wanted it? Whole? But it was awful? The power couplings were spaced too far apart. The synth-muscle was too loose. Hell, even the structure itself was configured sub-optimally. He hadn't even considered selling the thing because... well... it was illegal, he supposed - but more importantly, who would want it!?

"I need more parts." He said, mouth moving before his brain could catch up.

"Figured as much. Most Artificers get about halfway through a set of power-armor before realizing just how expensive they are to make." Sarah said, pulling out her omni-phone to flash a few pictures of the suit. "Whatever you need will come out of the final price. And while Daddy won't gouge you for the parts, he definitely won't be giving you any discounts either."

"That's fine." He said, still a little stunned by the sudden change in his fortune. Had it really been that easy?

She turned back to him, "So, how long will it take you to finish it?"

For something as crude as this? "A few weeks. Maybe less if you can get the parts to me quickly."

She nodded. "What kind of performance are you expecting when it's finished?"

"Class-Four Bruiser." He murmured, "As well as a Class-Two Shooter if I fit it out with some decent guns. Might even get it as high as Three if I can get some force projectors instead."
Puny numbers as far as he was concerned, but going by the way Sarah's eyes widened, she was impressed, even if she was quick to downplay it.

Were the standards of the local gangs truly so low?

More importantly, had he really been that blind? He'd been scraping by, fixing cars, toasters and air conditioners for the last year, when he could have been making real money working on cheap knock-offs of Meta-Tech weapons and armor.

"That shouldn't be a problem." Sarah said. "Not if you can de-liver on your promises."

He resisted the urge to huff. He could deliver on a promise like that in his sleep.

"But before we get to that though, I want you to look at something else for me."

Even with the thought of a possible payday in his near future, he still felt wariness well up in him as the woman reached behind her back.

He sincerely hoped she wasn't about to continue what she had started when they walked in here. Not that he didn't find her attractive. She was. Very much so. He just made it a habit not to get involved with women who could fry him alive with a flick of their wrist. A rule that went double for women who were also psychotic criminals with a long history of violence.

Which was why he felt relief wash over him – along with some muted disappointment he didn't read too much into – as the woman set down a large laser pistol on his worktable.

"Think you can do anything with this? I'm getting tired of having to
get the barrels replaced after they melt."

He didn't bother to hide his scowl as he looked the device over. It was classic Artificer work. Brilliant, bold, and criminally inefficient. The focusing lens was too small, the power-source too big, and the wiring was a complete mess.

"Where'd you get it from?" He asked, mentally resisting the urge to fling the insult to engineering into the nearest trash can.

"Daddy made it."

Well it was a good thing he hadn't immediately acted on his desire then. "I can see a few places I might be able to make some improvements. At the very least you won't have to worry about the barrel melting anymore."

"Great." She beamed, "Well, you can consider that your test

run."

"Test run?" He said, looking up from the gun.

"You didn't think we were just going to start handing you those parts willy-nilly did you?" She asked as if he were a particularly slow student.

Yes. That was exactly what he thought would happen. Which must have shown on his face, because Sarah became exaggeratedly smug.

"Oh honey, that's adorably naïve." She grinned. "Unfortunately for you, Daddy didn't get to where he is today by handing out loans to every Artificer with a big idea that came across his path."

"Right." He ground out, fighting down indignation.

"Don't worry, I'll be sending someone I trust tomorrow to pick up
your first project. If she likes what she sees, then we can start talking about getting that suit of yours up and running."

"I'll be looking forward to it."

And he was.

He was going to show this low-level rent-a-goon just who she was dealing with.

ΔΔΔ

Erich woke with a start. Disorientated, he looked around for a few seconds before realizing where he was.

"Fell asleep at my desk, huh?" He murmured, a small smile stealing over his features. "It's been a while since I've done that."

"Well, I wouldn't get back into the habit. Does terrible things to your posture." A voice to his left called.

Startled, he nearly tripped as he jumped up from his seat.

A woman was standing in his workshop. More to the point, she was holding the laser pistol he had spent almost all of last night working on.

"Who the hell are you? How did you get in?" He demanded, grabbing the first thing that came to hand.

The black woman raised an eyebrow at the screwdriver being waved threateningly in her direction, her eyes moving between it and the primed pistol in her hand.

"Really?" She asked.

Erich did not relent. "Who and how?"

"You know I have a gun, right?"

"An unfinished gun." Erich responded, "I was still resetting the focusing lens when I fell asleep. If you try and fire it now you'll be lucky if all you lose is a hand."

The woman looked at the gun in her grip, before shrugging and carelessly aiming at the wall.

"I told you the-" Erich jumped as she pulled the trigger and a strobing beam of red light lanced through the air.

"Impressive increase in power." The woman said, admiring the bubbling superheated stone now oozing out of the newly formed hole in Erich's wall. "Intuitive new design too. It only took me a few minutes to finish installing the lens."

Erich had already dropped the screwdriver and was in the process of getting ready to run when a belated thought hit him.

"Sarah sent you didn't she?" He sighed as he slumped back into his seat, trying to ignore the acrid stink coming from the newly formed hole in his wall.

"Hard-Light sent me." The woman corrected, as she put the gun down. "Important distinction. And, if you're curious, I got in because you left the front door unlocked."

Of course he did. Of all the stupid oversights he could have made.

If he was brutally honest, he was lucky it had been Hard-Light's underling that had strode into his store, and not some other lowlife looking to make a quick buck. Or worse.

"Yep," the woman said, as if reading his mind – which wasn't impossible given who she worked for. "If you're going to start working for Hard-Light, you need to start being smarter about your security."

"You like the gun then?" He asked, hoping to turn the conversation away from his embarrassing mistake. "Miss?"

"Call me Gravity." The woman said in lieu of a real name.

"Gravity then." Erich said, wondering whether that was a Cape name or just a nickname. Given just how far Cape culture had infected mainstream consciousness, it really could be either.

"And yes, I like the gun." The woman continued, "I'm just curious as to how much your little alterations have driven up the cost in components."

Erich shook his head. "Everything I put into that gun you could find at the local hardware store for about twenty bucks." Which hadn't been an intentional design decision on his part, but rather an inevitable result of his own severely lacking funds.

Gravity's eyebrows rose. "Impressive. Hard-Light will be happy."

"Happy enough to pay me to finish up that." Erich gestured at the exo-suit.

"He is. The boss liked the pics Sarah sent him. He's already getting the parts you listed together. They should be here by tomorrow at the latest."

Erich was stunned. "But you only just looked at the pistol?"

The woman shrugged, "I don't think you realize how much the boss wants to get his hands on that suit. This little test was more of a
formality than anything else."

Great. So he'd basically spent all night working on a laser for no real benefit.

"But what if I hadn't been able to deliver?" He couldn't help but ask.

"Then I've got another far more conventional pistol in my bag."

He deliberately tried to ignore the sudden dryness of his throat. "Right, so about payment?"

The woman gestured to a briefcase sitting by her legs. "Fifty thousand dollars in cash. You get what remains of the next fifty after expenses, when you finish the suit."

The sight of the briefcase full of money did more than make him forget about the danger, it left him feeling positively giddy.

"Right, well Ms. Gravity, I'll be waiting on that shipment of parts with bated breath." He grinned, "I'll also need to know how often you'll be needing updates on the suit's progress, and what number I should call to get in contact."

"I wouldn't worry too much about that. You won't need to call anyone because I'll be sticking around until you're finished."

Erich froze in his tracks. "But that could take weeks?"

"Yes," Gravity nodded. "During which time I will be watching over Hard-Light's investment. Day and night. But I wouldn't worry about it. I'll grab the couch and you'll barely even notice I'm here."

CHAPTER 2

"Put a damn shirt on woman!" Erich shouted after glancing up from the display in front of him.

Gravity, the woman in question, huffed but made no move to cover her nudity as she broke the tab on a cold beer. "A lot of men would pay good money to see what you're seeing right now."

Erich's scowl was audible even through the suit's speakers, "A lot of men aren't in the process of learning how to operate half a ton of power-armor while you flash them."

Any other time he might have been fascinated.

He would freely admit that Gravity was an incredibly well put together young woman. Her chocolate colored skin tone was only accentuated by the low light of the garage. Under the artificial light source, she all but glistened; a thin sheen of sweat coating her athletic form.

In all likelihood, she had just finished her usual morning workout.

Sighing, Erich gave up on trying to get the criminal to clothe herself properly and returned his attention to the task at hand.

Figuring out how to walk in a suit of power-armor was proving to be surprisingly difficult. Not only was he suddenly a good foot taller, but the suit had a momentary delay between sensing his input and the synth-muscles acting on it. That meant he had to plan every movement he was going to make a few microseconds in advance, which was harder than it sounded.

"I see you lowered the output on the synth-muscle again." Gravity said as she scooped up a nearby omni-pad.

"It was either that, or risk having my arms torn off every time I instinctively try to balance myself." Erich explained as he carefully brought one leg up, slowly shifting his weight in time with the whirring of the suit's pneumatics. "I figure I can start gradually increasing the strength again once this thing is closer to being calibrated."

"I suppose that's one way of doing it." The woman murmured as her fingers flew over the display. "The right knee still looks a little stiff when you move. Want me to increase input sensitivity there again?"

Erich flexed the resistant joint himself a few times before nodding.

Gravity tapped the screen a few times, "Alright, try it now."

This time when he moved it, it felt far more natural than it had a few moments prior. It still felt like he was moving through jello, but that was a hell of a lot better than moving like a jerky marionet.

"Better?"

He nodded. "Much."

He had to admit, occasional bouts of exhibitionism aside, Gravity was proving to be a competent assistant. In some ways she was even better than some professional assistants he had worked with in the past. The more he worked with her, the more he came to realize that her work with the laser pistol the other week hadn't been a fluke. She wasn't brilliant by any stretch, but she was quietly competent.

Listening to her observations - while determinedly keeping his eyes elsewhere - he methodically ran the suit through a series of simple motions, and the end of it the whole thing was moving much more smoothly.

Of course, there was still a world of difference between 'more smoothly' and 'smooth'.

"Alright, I reckon that's all were going to get with you standing in place like that." The woman said as she took a sip of her beer. "You're going to have to start moving around if we want to get the walk cycle down."

"I know." Erich groused, ignoring the undisguised anticipation in the woman's voice.

Taking a deep breath, he stepped forward.

Almost immediately he overcompensated the swing of his right arm, overbalancing himself as the errant limb shot out wildly. Synth-muscle whirred loudly around the suit as the whole system tried to compensate for the change in balance. Erich didn't try to fight it. Instead he watched on with depressed resignation as the suit slowly began to tilt.

The fall wasn't physically painful. The suit had ample padding to protect the pilot against far worse than tripping. That was not to say that Erich was unharmed. The damage to his ego was catastrophic.

It was only made worse by Gravity's great guffaws of laughter echoing around the shop.

"First walk cycle trial was a failure." He ground out from his position on the floor. "Please don't tell me you're going to be reduced to hysterics every time this happens?"

If she was, then they were going to be here a while. Erich would count himself lucky if they managed to get the walk cycle ironed out within the first few hundred attempts.

Gravity shrugged, wiping a stray tear from her eye, "Not every time. The first few dozen though? Definitely."

"Great." Erich groaned.

There had been a reason he used to leave this sort of thing to one of his assistants. Hell, he would have had Gravity do it if he thought he could convince her to get in the suit. Unfortunately for him, the woman was far too canny for that.

Groaning, he tried to get a leg under him; wincing as the sparks flew out from where the limbs dragged along the ground.

"Well, it's a good thing I'm planning on putting the paint on last." He muttered.

Entering into something that might optimistically been called a crouch, a grim smile appeared on his face.

That momentary sensation of success proved to be his undoing.

Overconfident, he made the fatal mistake of trying to straighten his legs and back at the same time, resulting in the powerful leg muscles outpacing the hip ones. Like an ungainly toddler trying to stand for the first time, he overbalanced once more, only this time he had the distinct sensation of vertigo that came with falling from a standing position straight onto one's back.

Like a trust fall, but with no trustee in attendance.

"Wait. Wait." Laughed Gravity. "I need to get my phone before you try the next one. I have to record this."

For one brief moment, Erich wished he had installed the force blasters onto the suit first. He could almost imagine the targeting reticules being superimposed over his assistant's back.
"One hundred thousand dollars. One hundred thousand dollars." He repeated over and over.

ΔΔΔ

Erich was really beginning to question whether a mere hundred thousand dollars was worth it.

"I don't do parties." He repeated for what felt like the tenth time that night.

In the driver's seat of her car, Gravity sighed, already beyond sick of hearing it. "You didn't do parties. Then Hard-Light asked you to attend one. Now you do parties."

Yes, well that was one of the reasons why he very specifically didn't want to attend this party.

...Hard-Light.

The crime boss for the local area, and a Meta so powerful that both other criminal factions in the city refused to move against his tiny gang for fear of his response. Not because they couldn't take him, but rather because of the sheer amount of damage he would do to their own organizations before he was brought down. Hell, even the cops and the Heroes Guild stepped carefully in this part of town.

And that was the man Erich now had to go and meet.

Call him naïve, but for a short time he had genuinely believed he could finish the suit and get paid without ever having to meet the man in person.

That naïve hope had held true for just over a week. Right up until Gravity mentioned offhandedly at the breakfast table that there was a party being thrown at the man's estate, and the pair of them
were expected to be there.

He had complained. Vehemently. But Gravity had refused to

budge, and now they were sitting in a queue of cars, slowly trundling their way up the path to the supervillain's mansion.

And the dozens of armed goons who occupied the estate were not the subtle in the way they eyed the guests on their approach. Most had their weapons concealed, but more than a few had more exotic armaments on clear display.

"Is that a plasma rifle?" Erich asked dubiously, as their car inched ever closer to the entrance.

"Probably." Gravity shrugged, none of her usual teasing banter to be heard. Something in her voice caught his attention, and he looked over to see that the usually confident woman's vibrant brown skin had taken on a distinctly pale pallor.

She was nervous.

Erich swallowed as he sank into his seat. His escort being nervous did not bode well. It did not bode well at all. Fortunately for his nerves, he didn't have too long to stew on that discovery. In another minute they were at the front doors of the mansion, and a thuggish looking young man walked over to their car.

"Valet." He grunted to Gravity as they stepped out, deftly catching her key's as she tossed them to him. "Enjoy your evening."

I doubt it. Erich thought as he watched the car - and his only means of escape - pull away.

"Ah, Olivia my girl. I see you've arrived, and you brought our latest employee with you." There was no mistaking who the person who strode up to them was. Hard-Light was exactly as Erich had
envisioned him. A brutal looking man who even at his own party was clad in his iconic skull-themed costume.

Of course, Erich was not so intimidated by the man's presence that he missed out on Gravity's real name. Though some of the fun was taking out of the discovery by the way the woman in

23

question looked just as downcast as he felt as she turned to regard the man who could kill them both with a glance.

"Hello Dad." She sighed. "I brought him just like you asked."

Now that was a bombshell Erich figured he could be forgiven for not seeing coming. Of course, he wasn't so uncouth as to gape, and he liked to think he kept any visible displays of surprise muted to just a slight widening of the eyes. Although that might have just been optimistic thinking on his part.

"Good evening sir, I just wanted to thank you for inviting me to this event." He said, recovering quickly and wondering if he should go in for a handshake, before deciding against it.

Somehow it just seemed too forward. Like an ant trying to shake hands with an elephant.

"No problem at all, kid. I couldn't very well have you building that dynamo of a suit for me without meeting you in person at some point." The man grinned as he thrust his arm toward the doorway behind him. "But we can save all that boring talk for later. It's an important occasion, and my guys and gals need to blow off some steam. I'm sure you feel the same after being cooped up in that shop of yours for the last two weeks."

Definitely, Erich thought. *Just not here. Now. Or anywhere near you.*

The heavy stench of sweat and sex billowing out from the mansion's entrance, like sulfur wafting from the gates of hell, only served to reinforce his plan to leave as soon as humanly possible.

He had zero desire to spend an evening surrounded by mindless fornication, drinking, and drug use. Not because those things weren't fun. They definitely were. But because he was almost entirely sure he would do or say something that would get him in trouble.

Still, he wasn't dumb enough to say any of that aloud. "I'm looking forward to it, sir."

Assuming that to be the end of their interaction, Erich was about to step forward toward the party, when Hard-Light's arm slammed into his chest with enough force to draw a surprised grunt from the young man.

"Just before I let you go, I want you to know something, kid." The villain said, "It's been a rough year for me and my crew. First, that bitch Grey Hood took out my boy Death-Shriek, and now the Brotherhood's causing trouble on my turf. That little toy of yours is going fix all that by giving us a new heavy hitter. So, I expect you and my daughter to be out there all night telling everyone about what the pair of you have been working on."

This time when Erich nodded, he was far more genuine about it.

Hard-Light stared for a few more heart stopping moments before stepping back as if nothing had happened, "Enjoy the party, kid. Don't forget what I said."

And with that parting shot, the man was gone.

Slowly, Erich released a breath he hadn't realized he'd been holding, and behind him he heard Gravity do the same.

"Yeah and fuck you too Dad." She muttered under her breath. "I'm
doing great by the way. Having a real ball. Nice chatting with you."

Erich wisely kept his own frustrations silent. It was unlikely the man would hear them at that distance, but he figured it was better to be safe than sorry.

"So, you never mentioned that Hard-Light was your dad." He tried not to sound accusatory as he said it, but he was pretty sure he failed miserably. He was a shit liar; though not for lack of trying.

25

"It never came up." Gravity shrugged, as she stepped into the mansion.

The place was about what Erich had expected. Once upon a time the ballroom they occupied might have had some level of class to it, but Hard-Light's occupation of the estate had long since done away with that. The party goers and décor scattered around the place would have looked more at home in a strip club than a multi-million dollar mansion.

While there wasn't quite an orgy taking place on the main dance floor, there were definitely a number of couples and threesomes scattered around the room.

"That's not an answer." Erich said, averting his gaze from a young woman and her paramour.

Paramours, he corrected as another man joined the festivities.

"What can I say, Erich?" She said, striding off to whatever new destination she had in mind. "Maybe I enjoyed being able to talk with someone who wasn't scared shitless of my dad?"

Erich watched her go and could only think of her parting words as … kind of sad.

She enjoyed spending time with him? The thought boggled the mind. He had it on very good authority that he was an ass. And not the endearing kind either. The kind that grew on you over time. No, he was just a regular one.

If he wasn't, he wouldn't have been quite so terrified of partaking of the bounty of diversions available.

Just got to find a quiet spot and lay low for a while, he thought. 'Olivia' can tell people about the suit, and I can survive the rest of the evening trouble free-

"Erich!" Someone called as they barreled into him, nearly sending them both sprawling to the floor.

"Sarah!?" He asked, very conscious of the fact he had just nearly cold clocked the boss's other daughter in a perceived act of self-defense.

"Yep." The blonde said impishly, her slim figure pressed into his. "I'm so glad you made it. It's so nice to be able to see you outside of that stuffy little shop of yours."

"Yeah, Hard-Light invited me." He said, searching for something, anything, that might allow him to escape.

"Hmmm," The blonde woman nodded happily as she started dragging him toward the bar, "Daddy's commanding like that."

Erich nodded vaguely at the woman's words as the bartender came over to take their orders. As he ordered, he could feel his mind whirring away inside his head.

He was a cynical guy, and because of that he couldn't help but feel that Sarah's overt attraction to him was unnatural. Sure, he was an attractive enough guy, he supposed, but he was no great catch.
Especially not for a supervillain's daughter.

So he did some research. Which was a fancy way of saying he asked the drug dealer who hung out in the alley beside his store about her. Terry was connected like that.

What the guy had told him – after being bribed with a twenty – was about what he had expected.

Sarah destroyed men. She had a reputation for it.

The bubbly blonde had a list of former conquests as long as Erich's arm. She chose men, seemingly at random, and charmed, seduced or forced, her way into their lives, and then destroyed them. With influence, with rumors, or once, with her own powers.

It said a lot about Erich, that that made a lot more sense to him than the Meta-human simply being attracted to him as a person. So as the hours went on, he sat and nodded, without making any promises or accepting any advances. It was nerve racking, but he thought he was doing a reasonably good job.

"Can we skip this bit?" He blurted out.

"I... what?" Sarah said, stopping midstream.

"The bit where you worm your way into my good graces." He murmured, "If you want to get your jollies off on destroying me, you really don't need to bother with all the subterfuge."

To her credit, the girl's confusion was very believable, "Erich, honey, you're not making any sense."

"That. The whole 'honey' thing." He said, "You really don't have to bother."

"You don't like me flirting with you?" She asked incredulously. "Is this because of the thing back at your shop? That was just business, lover. No need to let it sour things. Besides, you're working for Daddy now."

Yep he was well aware of the fact that he was working for her father. That was the only reason he had finally managed to drum up the courage to speak.

"No, it has nothing to do with that." Erich said, taking a sip of his drink. "I don't like you flirting with me because it's a prelude to you wrecking my life as part of some twisted little game you've got going on."

"You ... you can't talk to me like that." Sarah said as she finally recovered from her shock, the barest crackle of static electricity audible in the air.

As he shrugged, he wondered why she didn't have a Cape name. Her old man and her, assumedly, half-sister did. Maybe he just hadn't heard it yet?

"Looks like I can." He said. Although, for how much longer, remained to be seen. "But by all means, fry me for my audacity... or leave me be."

He was reasonably sure she wouldn't kill him. Hard-Light wanted that suit. That was the method to his madness. He figured it was better to see off Sarah now, while he was still reasonably 'indispensable', rather than wait for whatever scheme she was cooking up to come to fruition.

Admittedly, not the best plan in the world, but he was quite drunk when he started putting it together, five minutes or so ago.

Inebriation wasn't the worst thing in the world though. He would
like to say it was his steely resolve that kept him calm as electricity arced between the woman's fingertips, but if he was honest, it was probably the alcohol.

It was definitely the alcohol that had given him the courage to speak up in the first place.

"Oh, I think I'll do one better than that." The Sarah hissed, fire in her eyes.

He raised an eyebrow, "Oh really, what-"

His question was cut off by the sensation of a mild electric shock to the stomach. Instinctively, he leaned over, and as he did, he felt two soft lips press against his own.

...What?

His eyes were wide open, and so he found himself staring into Sarah's own as their lips locked together. For just a brief moment, he stared into those bright blue eyes. They were very attractive, even on a psychopath. Of course, then they had to remind him of that fact by taking on a distinctively vindictive twist.

Sarah slapped him.

Hard.

In fact, it was so hard that the sound carried over the music and conversation all around them, drawing eyes from all over the party.

Even from the Ménage à trois he had spotted on the way in.

"Bastard!" Sarah shouted, very authentic looking tears forming in her eyes as she stormed off.

Erich watched her go, absently holding his throbbing cheek.

What the fuck was that? He thought.

To his credit, it only took him a few seconds to notice the many eyes on him. The many unkind and angry looking eyes.

Ah, of course, He thought, heart sinking into his stomach. *It looks like I just forced a kiss on the boss's daughter.*

At the man's party.

Surrounded by witnesses.

Shit.

CHAPTER 3

"He's going to kill me." Erich muttered as he threaded a coolant line through the suit.

Hell, he considered it a minor miracle that he had even gotten out of the party alive. It was only the timely arrival of Gravity, and her physically taking him by the arm, that had gotten him out the door and back to the car.

"Hard-Light's not going to kill you." Gravity said without looking up from her work. "He wants the suit too much for that."

"*She's* going to kill me then." He said, very tactfully not pointing out that Gravity never referred to the man as her father. Always as Hard-Light.

His own family situation was complicated enough that he couldn't exactly go around pointing fingers at others.

"That's... unlikely." Gravity murmured, "Sarah might be a temperamental bitch, but she knows not to cross her 'Daddy'."

"Great. So the only thing standing between me and a very messy death is one unstable woman's daddy issues." He said.

Gravity was less than sympathetic, "What can I say, Erich? You play stupid games, you win stupid prizes. Was it that hard to just sit there quietly for a few hours?"

He thought about arguing, explaining the subtle genius of his plan, but ultimately deflated. After all, the results spoke for themselves. He'd underestimated Sarah, and now he was paying the price.

"How are thing's coming with those laser cannons?" He sighed. That was the second topic his complaints had revolved around that evening. He'd specified force blasters in the parts list. Sure, laser weapons were a step up from conventional guns, but they still weren't as powerful or flexible as force blasters. And they didn't hold a candle to the destructive power of plasma weaponry.

Not that he was dumb enough to work with plasma. In any capacity.

"I've nearly extracted them from their coolant jackets." She said as she rubbed an oily smear from her cheek. "Though I still don't see why you couldn't have just left them as they were."

Erich snorted at the very idea.

He wouldn't have used those jackets to cool his beer, let alone high-tech weaponry. Hard-Light was one scary motherfucker, but he knew jack-shit about sustainable design principles. If Erich had installed those cannons as they were when he received them, he would have put two to one odds on them melting the suit's arms within five minutes of its first real firefight.

"Well it's nearly done now, so you don't need to keep complaining about it." He said, "Besides, those cannons will be easier to install into the suit once I've put *my* cooling jackets on them."

His preening was cut short though, as the coolant line he was working on started to kink again. He swore.

At the very least his coolant jackets would be easier to install than *this* pig of a system. He had tried for nearly two hours to get it threaded into the suit conventionally, before giving up and simply pulling off the suit's armor plating so he could get easier access to its innards.

As a result, the suit was currently a little bare. Just looking at it, he couldn't help but see some kind of demented steampunk

skeleton
standing ready to receive an enema from the world's coldest
hosepipe. Though he wisely kept that observation to himself.
He doubted Gravity would appreciate his artistic interpret-
ation of current events.

A loud bang echoed through the shop, causing him to jolt his
head against the suit's frame. Cursing - more in surprise than
pain - he looked up to see what idiot was making such a ruckus.

Which was why he got a perfect view of the shotgun wielding
skinhead who burst through the shop's side entrance, barrel
smoking from where he had shot out the lock.

The two men's eyes met for one heart stopping moment, before
the skinhead was thrown backward. Erich heard a surprised
shriek as the invader was bodily tossed back outside, but it was
quickly cut off by the sound of the door slamming home once
more.

He was like a kite caught in a sudden updraft, he thought numbly.

The repair shop owner simply sat in stunned incomprehension
for a moment, before a powerful grip forcibly dragged him behind a nearby worktable.

"Get down you idiot!" Gravity shouted, drawing her pistol with
one hand, while her other flared with strange green energy.

Ah, so that's what threw him, Erich realized. *Gravity's a Meta.*

He had been wondering, what with her relation to Hard-Light.
Though one's parent being a Meta wasn't a guarantee of developing powers, but it was still far more likely than-

"Snap out of it." Gravity hissed, shoving him in the chest, "Do
you have a gun?"

A gun? He still had a few of the laser pistols he had been working
on for ... No. He didn't. Gravity had taken them with her on the

night of the party. They'd probably already been distributed to Hard-Light's goons.

"No."

"Ok, I want you-" Gravity started, before turning to him with wide eyes, "Wait, you don't have a gun!?"

He shook his head, numbly noting the sound of banging coming from the doorway, and the way that the energy swirling around Gravity's hand seemed to flair in time with each thump.

How interesting.

"How don't you have a gun!? You live and work in *this* neighborhood. Hell, you build guns!"

"Not before a fortnight ago." He pointed out, a little indignation rising to the fore. "And the crooks around here are too terrified of Hard-Light to cause trouble."

Honestly, it was one of the safer parts of the city. That had been part of the reason he set up shop here. Well, that and the fact that it was one of the only places he could afford.

Gravity looked like she wanted to slap him. "Well then, seeing as *you* are apparently *utterly defenseless*, stay behind cover and try not to get shot."

He could do that. In fact, he was reasonably sure he could make it to the staff bathroom and squeeze out the tiny window in there. You couldn't find much better cover than putting a city block between you and a firefight, could you? And besides, Gravity seemed to have everything well in hand here.
As if to mock him for his thoughts, that was the moment that whatever power she had gave way, and the door exploded inward.

"Shit." The woman swore, giving voice to Erich's own thoughts, as the skinhead from before barreled back inside; his nose bleeding and clothes disheveled.

Not that his rage did him much good when Gravity casually shot him in the chest.

As she did, Erich was suddenly reminded of a funny fact about lasers, or rather, masers. People tended to assume that they created a nice and small, cauterized hole.

A perfect cut, as it were.

That wasn't really the case at all. At least not with anti-personnel lasers. They were designed to move energy from point A to point B, as fast as humanly possible.

Specifically heat energy.

This sudden transference of energy has a pretty explosive effect on water – of which the human body comprises eighty percent. Any hit by the beam instantly turns to vapor.

The name for this phenomena was 'explosive vaporization'.

An effect Erich got to see firsthand as the beam struck the skinhead full in the chest.

If he were later forced to recount the experience, he would struggle to say which was worse. The sight of the damage wrought by the shot, or the vaguely damp pop that accompanied it. Needless to say, he looked away as the skinhead's steaming carcass fell to the floor, mercifully dead before he even hit the ground.

A second figure dashed into the room. Another skinhead who's eyes went wide as they took in the corpse of his compatriot. To his credit, he reacted quickly, spinning round to bring his pistol up even as he bellowed with rage.

Gravity already had him in her sights though. She shot him with the same cool confidence with which she had dispatched his friend.

J. R. Grey

Only this time there was no damp pop.

"Meta-Human." Erich whispered, dread filling him, as the figure took the shot full to his chest and kept coming; a slight blemish the only thing to show that he had even been hit at all.

Both Erich and Gravity stared in mute astonishment, before the thug turned to hose down Gravity's hiding spot with bullets. The woman gave a surprisingly girly yelp as she ducked down behind the worktable, narrowly avoiding the shots that winged over her toward the-

The suit! Erich thought. *The moron is going to damage the suit!*

Before he could even think, he was leaping out from his hiding spot. Ignoring Gravity's surprised yell, he grabbed a nearby chunk of discarded armor, holding it in front of him like a shield as he jogged backward.

"Quit firing, you goddamn philistine!" He cursed the man, wincing as stray rounds pinged off the metal in his hands. "Do you have any idea what your messing with here?"

His precious suit was not about to be sullied by the hands of this... this... *thug!*

Only, as he waited with bated breath for more shots to come, nothing happened.
Cautiously peeking out from behind his make-shift shield, he saw Gravity had not wasted his entirely unintentional distraction.

Both of her hands were flaring bright green as she pointed toward the Bruiser class Meta-human. The skinhead was struggling and straining, but he was firmly pinned in place by the force of Gravity's power. He was still standing, if only barely, but it was clearly taxing for him to remain that way as his arms remained slumped against his sides by the downward force being projected onto him.

36

"I'm gonna rip your fucking head off you whore!" The guy roared as his limbs trembled with the exertion of holding himself up. Even from a distance, Erich could see the veins popping up on the guy's crimson face.

"Do something, Erich." Gravity said, still calm, but with an audible strain to her voice as she held both arms out.

"...What?" Erich asked, slowly lowering his makeshift shield.

"Do something!" The woman roared, the light in her hands flickering.

Right. Do something, Erich thought as he looked around for something, anything. Welding torch? Nope. Spanner? Nope. Shotgun. Nope. Suit? Hell no. Cooling Jacket. Nope. Las- Yes, that might do.

"Hold him still." Erich called out as he dashed across the room.

"What do you think I'm doing?" Gravity hissed.

Their temporary prisoner screamed. "You fucks killed Gregor. When I get out of this, I'm going to shove *your* head up his *ass!*"

"Charming." Erich muttered as he started ripping out wires and realigning them with his bare hands.

"Quickly, Erich." Gravity called, "I don't know how long I can hold him."

Because I was totally taking it easy before you told me that. He thought as he franticly jammed a power cable into a slot. *The thought of your severed head compromising my rectum's structural integrity was incentive enough, thanks.*

"Just another second." He called out as he started to turn the device he was holding toward its target, wincing as it audibly shrieked as it dragged along the metal worksurface.

Their prisoner was having none of it, and as the light in Gravity's

J. R. Grey

hands started to die his struggles became more pronounced. "Do you fucks have any idea who the fuck I am? Do you know who you're fucking... with... what the fuck is that?"

"Laser cannon." Erich said simply as he jammed two wires together.

The thug's scream of agony filled the shop as a constant beam of searing red light hit him in the chest. The sheer intensity of the laser's beam had Erich squinting as heat rolled off the cannon in front of him. Even his hands were beginning to sting where he was holding the cannon as the metal of the device started to heat up.

Because of course we'd already removed the coolant jackets.

For just a few seconds Erich feared the powerful weapon wouldn't be enough; that the guy was a rank four Bruiser, or higher, and that the beam was just a painful inconvenience.

He needn't have worried.

The smell was the first thing to tip him off. Not entirely indistinct
from pork, it filled the room just as the skinhead's animal screams of agony started to trail off into silence as oily smoke wafted off him.

Still, Erich didn't cut the flow of power to the laser. Not until its frame started to melt through the bench it was sitting on, and he could physically no longer hold it in place. Although by that point, their opponent was little more than a charred husk. Barely even identifiable as a human being anymore.

When he finally did cut the power he slumped back, ignoring the sound of bubbling metal as the thoroughly ruined weapon sank into the bench.

"Erich?"

Honestly, Erich was amazed no one had come to investigate the screams. As he had said before, Hard-Light ran a pretty tight ship. Screams and gunfire were pretty rare sounds in this neighborhood.

"Erich?"

Then again, why would they? It wasn't like they had anything to gain by coming to see what the ruckus was. No community spirit in this part of town. Not even a decent degree of morbid curiosity. Better to leave it to Hard-Light's goons, the cops or a hero to resolve. Though, did the Guild even come out-

"Erich!"

"Huh?" He gasped, taking his first proper breath in the last few minutes. The tightness in his chest receded as fresh oxygen flowed into his system.

"That's it." Gravity patted him gently on the back. "Just breathe."

What do you think I'm doing, he tried to snark back, but all that came out was a heaving cough.

"Come on, let's get out of here." The woman said, gently guiding him by the arm. "Some fresh air will help."

Momentarily he considered the possibility of their being other attackers outside, but after a moment's thought, found he didn't care.

He just wanted to get away from the smell.

The act of walking seemed a lot harder than it should have been though. His legs felt like jelly, and he had to put real thought into putting one leg in front of the other as he made sure to step around the corpse of their first attacker.

Am I in shock? He thought as the pair of them stepped out into

the cool evening air. *I'm making weapons for a supervillain, and I'm going to pieces over finally using one myself.*

Some badass weapons manufacturer he was.

"You're doing fine, Erich." Gravity murmured, rubbing his back, "It's rough on everyone the first time."

"That's what she said." He coughed.

"Really?" She said with a wry twist of her lip, "That's what you're going with?"

He shrugged as he backed into a wall and slid onto the ground, luxuriating in the cool sensation of the brickwork on his back.

"Whatever." She said, as she pulled out a phone. "You going to be ok while I call up Hard-Light?"
"Just peachy." He shrugged as he stared up at the night sky, breathing in the curious malaise of garbage and exhaust fumes that made up city air. It had rained recently, and dampness was soaking into his pants and shirt, but he found he didn't care. He sat like that while Gravity walked away, and he was still sat there when she returned.

"Right, some of his guys should be on their way. They'll take care of the cleanup."

Of the bodies. Of which he was contributor.

"Do we need to worry about the cops?" He asked, more to make noise than because he was actually interested in the answer.

The last thing he needed was someone running a background check on him. That could unearth all manner of... uncomfortable truths.

"In this neighborhood? No. They know the rules." Gravity said, "A hero might be more tricky, but I sincerely doubt we'll catch any of those around here. Not enough rich folks to impress."

He nodded.

"Seriously though." The woman huffed, "The fucking Brotherhood? And a Meta? Hard-Light's gonna be pissed. Someone from last night's party must have talked. Still, didn't think those racist assholes would be dumb enough to act on it."

He shrugged, not really listening. The dynamics of the local criminal element weren't really what he wanted to think about right now. Which was why he was taken completely off guard when he felt a strange force acting on him, lifting him to his feet.

"Come on," Gravity said, tugging him by the arm as the residual light from her ability faded. "Let's get out of here."
Startled, he followed along as the woman dragged him toward her car. "Where are we going?"

"A bar."

His eyes goggled even as he slipped into the vehicle, "What about the bodies? Shouldn't we be watching the crime scene?"

"Hard-Light's guys will be here any minute. I figure the place will be fine if left unattended for a few minutes." Gravity's white teeth shone brightly in the darkness when set against her chocolate skin. Captivated by the sight, he nearly jumped out of his seat as her car came to life with a throaty roar.

He definitely felt his heart skip a beat when he was thrown back into his seat as the car flew out of its parking space and onto the street.

"The way I see it, you need a drink and a woman." She said.

Even with his mind muddled with the events of the last few hours, he still felt his face flush at the frank statement.

The woman raised an eyebrow teasingly. "You should try it, kid. Sex after a shootout is the best. Nothing takes the edge off better."

J. R. Grey

Erich resisted the urge to point out that she was only a year or two older than him. "Well, if you're offering…"

Gravity laughed, not taking her eyes off the road as they sped through the night. "Nice try kid, but I'm an old-fashioned kind of gal. You'll need to do better than a shootout with Neo-Nazis for a first date if you want to try your hand at romancing me."

"I'll keep that in mind."

She turned to grin at him, "Though you do get some props for saving my ass with the distraction, and that bit with the cannon."

He had to turn away from the woman's dazzling smile. "I was just saving my own bacon and protecting the suit. Nothing more."

Gravity turned back to the road, smile still firmly in place. "As you say, Erich. As you say."

CHAPTER 4

"Gravity, you better open this door, or so help me god..." Ignoring the pounding of his headache, Erich continued banging on the door to the apartment above his shop.

Specifically, *his* apartment. One that he was currently locked out of.

Still, even with his enthusiastic pummeling of the entrance, it took Gravity a full five minutes before she cracked open the door to his home. Naked, and looking none too pleased to have been woken up.

"What?"

"You left me on a bench in the park." He growled, refusing to be distracted by her nakedness - lovely as it was. "Someone stole my wallet, keys and phone, a police officer accused me of being a vagrant, and I had to catch a bus back here."

The woman shrugged. "I didn't want you throwing up in my car."

"So you left me on a park bench!?"

"It's a nice car." She defended. "Besides, your stuff is fine. I took your keys, phone and wallet off you before I left. I even left you your bus pass."

She almost sounded like she wanted to be thanked for that last detail. Unfortunately for her, Erich was not feeling particularly thankful. Perhaps it was the hangover. Perhaps it was the result of the morning shower that had woken him up. Perhaps it was being accused of vagrancy. Who knew?

"Listen you..." He started to say, only to cut himself off as he noticed something.

A love-bite. Actually, a few love-bites. Trailing along the woman's collarbone. Fresh ones.

Rising horror dawned in him, "You didn't."

She grinned.

"I'm going to have to throw out that couch." He complained.

Don't be a baby." She said, before grinning, "it's not the couch you should worry about."

"My bed!?" He moaned in horror, "You slept in my bed. With some random jerkoff from the bar. While *I* was sleeping on a park bench."

He hadn't even slept with anyone in his bed!

"There wasn't a lot of sleeping going on." She winked, "besides it was a woman."

"It's not the gender I care about." He hissed, "It's the fact that you *sullied* my bed."

Couldn't they have used a hotel? He had no idea what kind of pay Gravity received from her criminal exploits, but he was pretty sure it was enough to afford a cheap motel.

"Christ, you're like a kid worrying about cooties." The woman muttered.

Erich ignored her, taking a deep calming breath before reaching inside to grab his keys off the key-rack.

"I'm going downstairs to work on the suit. In two hours, I expect your partner for the evening to be gone, my sheets to be on their *second* wash cycle, and you to be ready to work."

Gravity shrugged, starting to turn away before looking back, "You could come in and join us if you want? Consider it my apology for the bench thing, and a reward for your heroism last night."

Erich froze halfway through stomping back down the hall. His heart thudding in his chest as blood roared in his ears. And other places.

He was tempted. Make no mistake.

It *had* been a while.

His pride warred against the pragmatic allure of a sexy three-some. How many times was an opportunity like this going to come up again?

"Just wash my sheets." He huffed, before continuing his trek downstairs.

"Your loss." Gravity shrugged, nudging the door shut as she retreated back into the apartment.

ΔΔΔ

Erich was still cursing himself and his stubborn pride when he stepped into the shop.

In fact, he was so caught up in his anger and regret it took him a few seconds to note that he had just walked through a doorway that had been battered down last night. Spinning in place, he saw that the door looked good as new.

"Fresh hinges. Fresh lock." He muttered.

Looking around the shop, he found that everywhere else was the same. The bodies were gone. The damage was gone. Hell, even the smell was gone. Replaced by a lemony fresh tint that seemed subtly out of place in a machine shop.

If it weren't for the half melted remains of the laser cannon that was still stuck to one of his workbenches, he might have been tempted to write off the events of last night as a dream.

Whoever Hard-Light's clean-up crew were, they were very good at their jobs. Though it seemed even they had been stumped by the modern art exhibition that used to be the cannon and work-bench. Hopefully they were going to come back at a later date to deal with that.

Sighing and dismissing the thought from his mind, Erich reached over to boot up a nearby omni-pad, scrolling through its menus until he reached the diagnostic app.

To his relief, the suit was entirely intact. His impromptu hero-ics had managed to keep the machine from any real damage.

"Good. Very good." He grinned.

To be honest, he was surprised, and mildly disappointed in him-self, that he had waited until morning to check it over.

Apparently, murdering a man threw me off my game more than I thought.

The reminder of what he had done the night before made his stomach to roil in a manner entirely distinct from hangover nausea. Cursing and seeking to distract himself, he got stuck into the installment of the suit's coolant system.

Though he did find himself stopping on two separate occasions to
ensure that the door was still locked.

Nearly two hours later, he was sweaty and tired, but bathed in the sweet satisfaction of a job well done. The suit's coolant sys-tem was in place, and for all intents and purposes seemed to be working as intended.

Though he wouldn't really know for sure until he put it through its paces.

Which I'll need Gravity for. Whenever she deigns to grace us with her presence.

As if on cue, he heard the familiar sound of footsteps behind him. His muscles tensed slightly at the noise, before he chided himself for jumping at shadows. He wasn't about to let the incident from last night turn him into a paranoid wreck. Or at least, more of a paranoid wreck.

"About damn time you got here, Gravity." He grunted with deliberate calm, "If you're quite done with your conquest of the evening, I need you to contact Hard-Light and ask him if he wants me to install the remaining laser cannon. We can do it; but having just one will make the suit's oversized cooling system kind of redundant."

Which he was loathe to let happen. Nothing frustrated him more than leaving a job half done.

"As gratifying as it is to learn my girl's got a healthy sex life, that's not why I'm here." Hard-Light's deep baritone caused him to jump, slamming his head into the frame of the suit for the second time in as many days.

"Fucking Christ!" He cursed, clutching at his throbbing skull, before turning to face the supervillain, "I mean... It's good to see you, sir."
The man ignored his words, stepping past him to look at the suit. As he did, he dropped a bag full of *something* on the ground.

Erich was forced to stand in awkward silence, head stinging, as he wondered if he should start begging or get ready to run. Gravity had said Diego wouldn't kill him for what transpired at the party, but now the man was standing in front of him, Erich wasn't feeling quite so sure.

"You can quit pissing your pants over there." The man said after nearly a minute of heart-stopping silence. "I'm not about to fly off the handle over my other girl's little stunt. I'm not quite as blind to her games as people seem to think I am."

Erich knew he should have felt relieved at that news. But he didn't. The feeling of danger that had been present ever since the man had stepped into the room had not dissipated with his words.

"Though Erich, with what I've learned about your history." The man said, finally turning to regard the stunned repairman, "you might be wise to be nervous. Or should I call you, Jason? Fake identities can be such a bitch to keep track of, right?"

Erich thought his heart would explode in his chest. For just a second, he considered trying to run; eyes darting to the open door as he gauged his chances.

The sound Hard-Light's energy blade humming to life strangled that idea in the crib though.

"Don't run." The man growled. "Talk. Who knows, if I like what I hear you might even walk out of here in one piece."

Erich nodded numbly, feeling the fight go out of him as he slumped against a desk.

"If you know who I am - or was - you know who my sister is, right?" He said without preamble.

The supervillain nodded slowly.

"And my mother, father and grandfather?" He continued.

Again, the supervillain gave a slow nod.

"Right, well, not to knock around the bush, but I'm a genius." Erich said, "I can do more with Meta-tech than most Artificers can even dream. The fact that you hired me to work on that suit should be proof enough of that." He said gesturing to the silent frame.

"It's very impressive, kid." Hard-Light said, "But I'm not hearing a reason not to take one of your limbs off for trying to deceive me and my crew."

"Not intentionally!" Erich said, "I'm not like ... some kind of ... undercover agent or something."

The villain shrugged, "That remains to be seen; though the fact that it was so pitifully easy for me to see through your fake documents, says that might not be total bullshit."

The man looked momentarily contemplative, "The Guild would have done a much better job of creating a fake identity. That, and the fact that you helped my little girl last night, are the only reasons we are having this conversation."

Erich nodded hastily, "Right. So I'm a genius. Top of my classes. In everything. Forever. Prodigious talent with Meta-tech ... And it means sweet fuck all to anyone."

Hard-Light quirked an eyebrow.

"I'm serious. All my life I've been in my sister's shadow. In everything. Always." Erich shrugged, "I didn't particularly mind. Not even as a kid. It was what it was, and I never cared much for fame or being popular."

"I'm not here to hear about your 'awful' childhood, kid. I want to know why the supposedly dead brother of the Blur is in *my* organization, wearing a fake name." Hard-Light huffed.

"Right, right." Erich said hurriedly. "Long story short. I couldn't find a job. Anywhere. No one wanted me. Too much of a security risk, see. Too many guys like you - no offense - who would use me to get at my sister."

Erich took a deep breath to calm himself, "Well, as it turns out, they were right. One day, out of nowhere, the café I'm in explodes. Literally explodes. Bodies everywhere. Very messy."

He could feel a cold sweat forming on his neck as he remembered it: the heat, the flames … the smell of burning flesh.

"I get out by the skin of my teeth. A bit of tech I was tinkering with protected me. Totaled the device in the process but saved my hide." Erich grinned weakly, ignoring the queasy sensation in his stomach as he remembered just how close he'd been to dying. Pure luck had been what saved him.

"Everyone thinks I'm dead. Villains are coming out of the wood work left and right, all claiming to be the ones responsible."

To date, he still had no clue which of the pricks was actually responsible. He didn't really care either. He wasn't Jason anymore. He was Erich.

"Faster, kid." Hard-Light said, bringing up his energy blade with a deadly hum.
"I saw an opportunity!" Erich shouted, "A chance to escape from my sister and my family's legacy. I took it. Easy enough to do. I knew a few people. People I could pay off to create an ID!"

Hard-Light still looked dubious. "So you, a genius, came to this shithole of a city and set up a repair shop?"

Erich shrugged nervously, "Makes more sense than you think. Forging an ID for a new identity is one thing, recreating all my qualifications is entirely another. No one in my preferred fields would hire me without them. Easier to set up shop. Better with tech than people."

Hard-Light grunted noncommittally, Erich could see in his eyes that he was thinking about it though.

Not that it matters, Erich thought cynically. *This life is over.*

Even if the thug didn't kill him, he would try and use him as a tool to get at his sister. As usual. He would be dragged back to being Jason once again. Probably be slapped with some criminal sentence for faking his death. The headlines would be all over it. A chance to smear a leading hero's perfect image.

In the end that was all his life amounted to: a weak spot in his sister's.

"Alright." Hard-Light shrugged.

"Alright, what?" Erich laughed bitterly.

"Alright, I believe you." The supervillain said, pointing to the bag he had brought in with him, "I've left the new weapons for the suit in there. Force blaster this time."

Erich barely heard him. Hell, he could scarcely believe his ears. "What? You're not going to … I don't know? Take me hostage?"

Hard-Light looked at him like he was slow, "Do I look like I want to tangle with the Blur? She's so out of my league it's not even funny. No, it's better for me if everyone continues to believe you and your mechanical skills are dead."

Erich had to concede that the man had a point. Blur would wipe the floor with him. It wouldn't even be a fight.

Hard-Light continued, "As *interesting* as your origins are, they don't change *my* problems. The Brotherhood's getting to be more of a pain in my ass by the day. This latest attack is just the latest in a long line. I need that suit, and to get it, I need you and your scrawny ass to keep working on it."

Erich couldn't believe it was that simple.

… But he wanted to.

"Sure." He said numbly, not quite able to believe what was happening.

"Good, get to it." He said, already walking back toward the doors. "Don't make me regret this, kid."

"I won't." He called back.

As the doors slammed behind the supervillain, Erich slumped even further against the desk

"What the fuck?" He breathed leaning back against the metal, before wincing as a stab of pain went through his head where he'd banged it on the suit.

"Motherfucker," He cursed, shooting up, "Fuck, I can't be bothered
thinking about this shit. I need some Tylenol."

He winced as his sudden movement gave him a whiff of himself, "And a shower."

Who knew? Maybe the world would start making sense again afterward.

Though he sincerely doubted it.

△△△

Erich still didn't quite believe Hard-Light words, even two days after the man's visit. Sure, the guy hadn't told anyone else Erich's origins as far as he was aware, but he was still pretty sure the villain had some long-term scheme for him in mind.

Even if Erich had no idea what it was.

At the end of the day, he decided not to think about it. It wasn't like there was anything he could about it anyway. He had zero faith in his ability to evade the supervillain if he tried to go to ground again.

He was an engineer at heart. He built things. He fixed things. Fake names and living on the run was so far beyond him it wasn't even funny. The fact that it had taken Hard-Light all of two weeks to find out his real name was proof of that.

Was he avoiding the situation? Probably.

He already had enough problems as it was; nightmares about the guy he had killed, and a general inability to sleep because of them ranking least among them.

As a result, he was feeling fairly groggy when he stumbled out of bed that morning, roused by the sounds of someone pounding on
the door.

He got ready to yell out to Gravity to answer it, only to remember that she wasn't there. Some criminal thing that would apparently keep her out for the day.

Under different circumstances he might have been worried about another Brotherhood attack, but Hard-Light had taken to posting a few goons around the shop at all hours of the day after their little chat.

To date, Erich still wasn't quite sure whether they were protecting the suit or watching him. Another thing he tried not to think about too hard.

Cursing his poor luck, he staggered toward the door, getting ready to cuss out whoever was so rude as to pound on his door first thing in the ... he checked his phone.

Afternoon.

Fuck, he needed to get over this guilt bullshit.

He ripped open the door with an angry sneer, "What!?"

To find the surprised face of Sarah Williams staring back at him, one delicate hand still raised to knock.

"Ah, hi?" She said, recovering quickly.

Erich simply stared in open mouthed stupefaction.

"You going to invite me in?" The attractive blonde criminal said. "We need to talk, and this hallway isn't really the place-"

Erich slammed the door, running to find *something* to defend himself with, even as an indignant shout echoed from the hall.

CHAPTER 5

The knocking did not abate.

"Go away!"

"Not until you talk to me you jackass." Sarah's voice was muffled by the door, but her irritation was clear.

"Well you're going to be there a long time." Erich grunted as he cocked his new pistol. An entirely conventional model, but it was all he could get his hands on at short notice. Still, it would be plenty effective against Sarah.

"Not if I break this goddamn door down."

Shit. She would do it too.

Fuck it. Let's get this over with.

"What?" He asked as he cracked the door open a few inches, keeping his pistol just out of sight.

Sarah still looked furious, but she swallowed it down after a few moments. "I need to talk to you ... I need to ... apologize."

Erich couldn't believe his ears, "You? Apologize?"

"Yes." She sighed. "Now are you going to let me in?"

He really didn't want to, but he was pretty sure that Sarah wouldn't budge on the matter. Grudgingly he opened the door.

The blonde scoffed at the gun in his hand, but stepped inside nonetheless. "About time."

"You were much more charming when you were trying to kill

me." He deadpanned.

"And you were much more charming when you were terrified of me. And I wasn't trying to kill you." She scowled, before hesitating, "...Well, at least not until the very end."

Erich didn't believe a word of it. Which must have shown on his face.

"I wasn't!" The woman flushed. "Not until you insulted me at least."

Erich shook his head, "Sure. Now why are you here?"

"Daddy wants me to bury the hatchet." Sarah sniffed, "He doesn't want his right hand and his lead mechanic at each other's throats. Not if we're going to be working together."

Erich nearly choked on the glass of water he'd just grabbed. "Lead mechanic?"

The woman shrugged, "He must have been happy with what you were doing with that suit. He announced it as soon as he got back the mansion."

Great. Erich thought. He'd just been unceremoniously moved into the supervillain's permanent employ. *So much for a quick repair job.*

"Right. Well, message received. Apology accepted. You can go now." He sighed, slumping into a chair.

The Meta-human practically growled, "Do you have to be so aggravating?"

"You tried to have me murdered." Erich said, nearly gesturing with his gun before thinking better of it. Being armed in her presence
was one thing. Actually aiming a weapon at the boss's daughter was another.

"You insinuated I was some kind … succubus!"

"Well you are, aren't you? You string along men and them break them! It's some kind of twisted game for you." He pointed out.

The blonde actually started to flush red, "I do not! Where did you even get such a ridiculous idea?"

He almost said 'Terry' before thinking better of it. Mentioning that his primary source of information was the heroin dealer who hung out outside his shop probably wasn't the smartest move.

Actually, using the man as a source of information suddenly didn't seem so smart either.

"Hard-Light mentioned it to me the other day." He remembered triumphantly, "He said he's not 'entirely ignorant of your little games'."

Which certainly suggested to him that Terry's info hadn't been complete bullshit.

Though his confidence in that belief was left a little shaken when Sarah looked at him like he was an idiot.

"I'm Daddy's right-hand girl. It's my job to keep an eye on his underlings. That means I have to get close to people. And some-times I have to *deal* with them if they're getting out of line." She shrugged, "If I'm a little flirty - and get rid of a few I don't like as I do it - what of it?"

Ah, that made sense. In fucked up kind of way, to be sure, but sense nonetheless.
Not that he was about to admit that. "Sounds a lot like a succu-bus to me…"

"Shut up." She hissed, "God, I can't believe I was ever attracted to you."

Erich couldn't believe it either.

Literally couldn't.

In fact, he still wasn't entirely sure that this whole 'apology' wasn't an act to lure him into a false sense of security.

Still, if what she said was true - and that was big if - they were going to be working together in the future. It would probably be for the best if they at least superficially buried the hatchet. That, and if Hard-Light was the one to instruct her to come here, he didn't want to be the obstacle to the man's desires.

Though he would be confirming that that was the case for himself later. He wasn't an idiot.

Usually.

"Right, I'm sorry as well." He lied, running a hand through his hair, "I shouldn't have said what I did."

"I accept," Sarah said, with what was probably an equally fake smile spreading across her face.

Deed done, the pair stood in silence for a few moments.

"Now what?" Erich asked when it became clear that she wasn't going to leave.

"Now you show me the suit, lover." Sarah grinned, "If I'm to act as my father's right hand, I need to know what capabilities his new heavy hitter will have. It will also aid me in picking out a pilot for it when it's complete."

Erich ignored the fact that the woman had returned to the pet names. Instead he was focused on the complicated sensation that arose in his stomach at the thought of giving away the suit. Sure, he had zero desire to pilot it himself, but he wasn't entirely comfortable with someone else having it either.

Especially not some barely literate thug. He grimaced. *Is this what if feels like for a father when his daughter is getting married?*

If it was, he wasn't a fan. Good thing he never planned to have kids.

"Right." He said, pulling his mind away from the ridiculous direction it had turned, "I'll take you down and show you around."

"I'm sure it will be enlightening." Sarah smiled thinly, no doubt noting that he had slid his gun into his pants rather than put it down. "Though you might want to get dressed and showered first, honey. You smell like a skunk that slept in a brewery."

Erich glanced down at the crumbled clothes that he had been wearing when he collapsed to bed last night.

"Right," he muttered, heading back towards his room.

ΔΔΔ

"Sugar, who cares if the chest is better shielded?" Sarah grumbled wiping a stray hair from her soot stained face as she looked up from her Omni-Pad. "You're leaving the shoulders almost completely unprotected."

Equally filthy, Erich scowled as he fiddled with the suit's shield emitters. "The shoulders don't need shields because the pauldrons are the most heavily armored part of the suit."

The woman huffed, "Yes, if you ignore the fact the *joints* are exposed every time the arms reach above its head."

Ignoring her complaints – much as he had all morning - Erich slid down off the suit. "Alright, turn it on."

The blonde rolled her eyes, but did as he asked.

With a low hum, yellow barriers made of solid light flared to life around the suit, creating a second layer of armor that floated just a few inches above the first.

Heart swelling at the sight, Erich's eyes flicked down to his own omni-pad.

"Power drain is negligible." Sarah murmured, giving voice to his own thoughts. "Heat generation is within acceptable parameters."

Erich was impressed. The shields were beyond just being efficient. They were downright supernatural. Say what you would about the rest of Hard-Light's designs, but when it came to tech dealing with his namesake, the man was an unparalleled Artificer.

"Alright, now shift emitters two and four a few inches to the right and left respectively." Sarah murmured, jarring him from his moment of triumph.

"What?"

The woman scoffed. "Just do it."

Erich thought about arguing just for the sake of it, but reigned in the desire at the last second. Remembering that he was supposed to be playing nice, he did as she asked, his fingers dancing across the pad's controls.

He could always change it back later.

Before his eyes, the solid light barriers started to twist around the suit. Sliding into a new configuration as the projectors on the armor's surface shifted position.

"There, isn't that much better?" Sarah smirked when the barriers finally stopped at their new destinations.

Erich hated to admit it, but it was.

The chest had a little less coverage than before, but the double overlay from before was still mostly intact. More importantly, the shoulder's joints were now almost entirely covered by the floating panels of solid light.

"You're good at this." He admitted grudgingly.

To his surprise, Sarah blushed a little, before hastily covering it up with a disdainful sniff, "When your dad's an Artificer, you pick up a few things. Even if it's only to keep him from blowing himself and the house up."

That made a surprising amount of sense. It also explained Gravity's surprising degree of competence and familiarity with Meta-tech. The pair of half-sisters had probably spent nearly as much time around Meta-tech as he had growing up.

Though they both obviously lack my prodigious intellect, he observed.

"Speaking of which," The woman said, a hint of eagerness entering

her voice. "I still say that you should skip over force blasters entirely. Switch up to plasma and we can really turn this suit into something to be feared."

Erich ignored the insinuation that his masterpiece wasn't already something to be feared.

"Yes, it would be." He acknowledged, "If only because it would be as much of a threat to its pilot and allies as any hypothetical enemy. The reason no one fucks around with plasma is because magnetic containment systems have a tendency to fail when some Meta decides to throw the suit containing them through a few buildings."

And that wasn't even getting into how cost prohibitive a plasma-based weapons systems could get; not just in manhours but maintenance costs, and initial set up.

Even madmen like the Master steered well clear of the stuff for that reason.

Sarah rolled her eyes, clearly about to continue, but she was mercifully cut off by the sound of Erich's omni-phone going off.

Relieved at the interruption, Erich quickly glanced at the number before answering the call.

"Hello Olivia."

"I told you not to call me that." The woman said from the other side of the phone, "I'm calling because I just got finished with the thing I told you about, and I was about to head down to the bar. Figured I would take pity on you and invite you along. Who knows, you might even manage to get laid this time."

Erich sighed at the casual mention of his nonexistent sex life. The woman was obsessed.
Still, he did want to go. Sleeping was becoming something of a problem lately without a nightcap of one form or another. The usual rigmarole of a guilty conscience, he assumed. Getting knockout drunk of an evening was rapidly becoming his go to solution.

"I'll be there so long as you swing by the shop to pick me up."

"I can do that."

"Oh honey," Sarah sing-songed from across the room, "Don't you think it's a little cold to make plans with my half-sister while you've got me here with you? Even after we promised to make up?"

Erich wondered how she knew he was talking to Gravity. Then he realized that it was a pretty easy guess to make. It wasn't like he knew anyone else in this city. Which would be kind of sad if he didn't find people an irritating inconvenience at best.

And he didn't see how making plans with Gravity was snubbing Sarah.

"Who's that?" Gravity teased through the phone, "Have you got a woman over? Damn kid, I've only been gone a day and you've managed to snag someone. Maybe you don't even need my help to end that dry spell?"

Erich scoffed, "Hardly. It's your sister."

"Half sister

"Half-sister then." He sighed, not really caring about whatever beef they had with each other. "She came over this morning to 'bury the hatchet'."

"And you believed her?"
No. But he wasn't about to say that aloud.

"Sure. Why not." He monotoned. "She's spent that last few hours helping me with the suit."

"Whatever, I'll be there in half an hour. Try and wear something nice." He could practically hear the scowl in her voice as she hung up.

Sliding his phone back into his pocket, Erich turned to Sarah. Who was still watching him with an emotion he couldn't quite place.

"Well, I'm sure you can work out what that was about." He murmured, "Thanks for your help today, but I imagine you'll be wanting to report back to Hard-Light."

"Actually," the blonde said, momentarily hesitating, "I think I'll join you and my... half-sibling for drinks."

What?

No seriously.

What?

△△△

"I can't believe you brought her."

Erich stifled a sigh of relief that Gravity had finally broken the silence. The car ride over had been stiflingly awkward because of it. The tension between the two half-siblings had been tangible.

Even to him.

"I didn't bring anyone." He said as he took a sip of his drink, "She chose to join us."

And he wasn't about to tangle with the lightning flinging Meta a second time. If Gravity had a problem with her sister's presence, she should have been the one to argue it.

"What's the matter Olivia? Afraid of losing your new toy." The woman in question gave a catlike grin from across the table.

Erich quirked his eyebrow at being referred to as a toy - and Olivia's - but kept his peace as he sat back and sipped his drink.

"Don't call me that, *Sarah*" Gravity growled, "And no, he's not my toy. He's an assignment. One that your precious *Daddy* saddled me with."

Wow, if Erich were a more sensitive soul that might have hurt.

"He's your father too Olivia." The blonde smirked.

Gravity just scoffed, taking a hearty swig of her own drink.

"Besides," Sarah continued, "I think we both know that our dear old Erich is more than just an 'assignment'."

I am?

"We don't all want to play your stupid power games, Sarah"

Gravity scowled over the rim of her glass.

Power-what-now?

"So you say, but your actions say otherwise." Sarah smiled, sliding around the table to lean up against a suddenly very still Erich. "You're still sticking around long after your services are no longer required. Daddy's got a couple of our employees watching over our

newest asset at all hours. He's assigned *me* as his new liaison. Do we really need the organization's second heaviest hitter watching over him as well?"

Erich didn't miss the trace of bitterness in the blonde's voice when she mentioned Gravity's power.

Was she jealous? Why? Lightning powers kicked ass.

Still, he wasn't so distracted by the question, or the soft femininity pressed up against him, that he wasn't fingering his pistol under the table.

Boss's daughter or not, if he felt the slightest spark touch his skin, she was getting a round through the kneecap. He figured he could explain it away as jitters if pressed on it. It was pretty much the truth anyway.

"Hard-Light's goons wouldn't last five seconds if anyone seriously tried to get at him." Gravity said with a flippant wave of her hand. "The Meta from the other night would have torn them to pieces without even breaking a sweat."

What a lovely image.

Sarah shrugged, which did wonderful things to her décolletage – which, now that he thought about it, was probably the point.

"Perhaps, but that's never mattered to you before. In fact, I can't recall you ever taking an active interest in the actions of the organization. Dear old Daddy usually has to twist your arm to get you to do the bare minimum."

Right it had been fun at first, but Erich was getting sick of all this double speak. Informative as it might have been.

"Alright I've had enough of this shit." He sighed, "Sarah, you seem to think Gravity wants something from me? Well, I can tell you right now that's total bull-"

The door exploded.

The noise was so shocking Erich nearly plugged one into Sarah out of sheer surprise.

"Down!" Gravity yelled, flipping over the table and dragging him behind it. Idly he noticed that Sarah was totally ignored by her sibling. Fortunately for her, she was no slower in diving behind their makeshift cover, even without her sister's help.

"Again!?" Erich whined, as bullets sprayed through the windows, occasionally finding purchase in bar patrons who weren't quick enough to hit the deck.

"Apparently." Sarah said, as she unholstered and primed her laser pistol with practiced ease.

"We're just that lucky, kid." Gravity grinned from her position crouched next to him.

If he were in different circumstances, he might have wondered at the chances of two shootouts involving him occurring within a week of each other, but at the time his primary concern was whether the table he was crouched behind was bulletproof.

His gut instinct said no. Not even close.

Well, at least he had a gun this time. Even if it was a diddy little *normal* pistol, it would still be more than enough to put a regular person down if it hit.

After a few more seconds of heart stopping carnage, the shooting
finally stopped. An eerie silence settled in, broken only by the sobbing of wounded and shocked bar patrons.

Then *something* stomped into the entryway of the bar.

That has to be the ugliest set of power armor I have ever seen, Erich thought as he risked a quick glance. *Why the last time I saw something that shoddy – Oh.*

Oh shit.

"Where's the fucker who stole my suit?" A familiar voice called out from within the metal monstrosity, "The Crusher has returned to take back what is rightfully his!"

Erich sank back behind the table with a heavy sigh.

Of fucking course. He thought as he eyed his tiny peashooter.

I am one with the table. The table is one with me. I am one with the table. The table is one with-

A round winged through the table, narrowly missing Erich's head as he clutched his pistol. He promptly dropped even lower, doing his best to imitate a worm burrowing into the earth.

"You know, after our last little scuffle, I was kind of expecting something a bit more impressive." Gravity drawled as she casually plinked away with her laser pistol. "Are you going to get up and shoot any time soon?"

Erich looked at her like she was stupid. "Would it achieve anything other than me wasting ammo?"

If her upgraded laser pistol wasn't getting through the Crusher's shields, his pistol didn't stand much of a chance.
"Might distract him from me for a few seconds." She shrugged.

Hard pass. He was hunkering down and letting the career criminals do the fighting. A decision that was only reinforced by the sight of Sarah diving to the side as a spray of machine gun fire pelted the pillar she had been hidden behind.

Nope. Not a chance. He had a perfectly good justification to stay down and he was using it. The only possible reason he might have to get up and get involved were if-

"Oh look, he's brought a few of your old friends, Gravity." Sarah snickered from her position on the floor, just as a new voice chimed in.

"Kill that nigger bitch!"

Ah, The Crusher had brought the Brotherhood with him. Because of course the Neo-Nazis would hire a near worthless Artificer with an undisclosed addiction.

Just so long as he was white it was all gravy.

Unfortunately, he'd just lost his only justification to stay out of the fight, because the two skinheads – a man and a woman – definitely weren't wearing bullet resistant armor.

They weren't wearing much at all if he were honest.

Now he was going to have to start getting involved in this little shootout.

Unless...

"Sarah?"

"Yes, honey?" Sarah answered, somehow still managing to sound sensual while crawling across a rubble strewn floor in the middle of a firefight.

Not that he really noticed. He had other concerns. Like avoiding said firefight. "What color are the suit's shields?"

"What?" The woman asked incredulously as she exchanged fire with a skinhead who was trying to advance on her.

"The shields. When you shoot them what color do they flare? And what shape?" Erich repeated as Gravity's power lifted another thug into the air, prompting Erich to reluctantly aim a few shots in the man's direction.

None hit, as he had half expected, and the thug fell back to the floor with a loud thud. Shot or not, that had to have taken the wind out of him.

"It's blue," Gravity growled, aiming a stink eye his way for blowing their opportunity to take one of their assailants out of the fight. "And looks like a bubble."

Right.

Shit.

"Cover me."

"What?" Gravity started to say, before Erich burst from cover and sprinted for the bar with all the speed his two legs could give him.

He would like to think it was sheer surprise at his sheer testicular fortitude that kept the two still upright gunners from shooting at him for the first meter of his dash, but after a millisecond of surprise, he felt the telltale whips of hot lead flying past him. A few milliseconds of surprise was all he had needed though. Throwing caution to the wind, he dived over the bar with all the grace of a beached whale, sending discarded drinks scattering to the floor with a crash as he did so.

"Hi." He grunted with a tinge of hysteria to the bartender he'd landed almost on top of. "Could I get a drink? Something with a high alcohol content? Real tractor fuel stuff."

The woman looked at him like he was mad – which, covered in discarded drinks and shattered bits of glass, he might well have been – but after a moment's hesitation reached out to grab a nearby bottle of spirits.

"Thanks." Erich said as he tore a chunk of fabric from his shirt and stuffed it into the neck of the bottle, flinching only slightly as bullets continued to thud into the bar they were hiding behind.

Then he... hesitated, a sinking feeling forming in his gut.

"You don't happen to have a lighter do you?" He asked, hoping desperately that he hadn't just risked his life for nothing.

Fortunately for his continued sanity, she did.

Hefting his impromptu Molotov in hand, he recalled where his target was relative to his new position.

Then he lobbed it through the air, making sure to not let even a single hair on his head rise above the safety of the bar.

There was a reason he had installed Hard Light panels onto his own suit rather than the typical 'bubble shield' most people favored; bubble shields only intercepted objects traveling above certain speeds, or energy exceeding certain levels.

Of which a lazily lobbed Molotov cocktail possessed neither.

He wasn't entirely sure he heard the impromptu incendiary device explode against the armored plates of the Crusher's suit. He knew he definitely didn't see it.

He definitely heard the screaming that started immediately after though.

"Oh god." He cursed, pulling his shirt up as an impromptu face mask. "The smell."

He hated that smell so goddamn much.

The rest of the firefight passed as he expected. A few more shots rang out, screams tapered off, and the sound of scampering feet could be heard, before the shop finally went silent.

"Erich honey, you still alive?" Sarah called out, sounding as exhausted as he felt.

Still bizarrely seductive about it though.

"For a given definition of alive." Erich answered as he clambered back up to his feet, brushing bits of glass and beer off him as he did.

"Well you did a pretty decent job of taking out the mook with the mech." Gravity grinned, gesturing to the smoking remains of the Crusher's suit. He could see a few laser holes drilled into the suit's carapace, which suggested that his Molotov wasn't quite enough to finish it off.

It certainly provided an ample distraction though. He thought. *Probably shorted out the shields too.*

Which was exactly what he had been hoping for. Even if he hadn't
particularly *wanted* it.

Do I count that as me as killing him? He wondered, pondering over the shape his nightmares would be taking in the coming days. *Does it matter?*

"Do we need to run or something?" He asked, drawing himself from his melancholy thoughts.

The cops hadn't shown up to his last shootout, but that had been at a secluded shop, deep in Hard-Light's territory. The area they were in now wasn't exactly affluent, but the residents could reasonably expect the cops to show up if they called them. As evidenced by the fact that most of the bar's patrons were still cowering on the floor, waiting for someone to come and save them.

"Probably a good idea." Sarah answered, "I'll call Daddy from the car. He probably already knows, but it never hurts to let him

71

know myself."

Nodding, Erich started to turn towards the doors, only to freeze in place as the distinctive wail of cop cars echoed from outside.

Looking to Gravity for advice on what to do, his heart sank as she scowled and dropped her gun on the floor.

"Shit." He said, doing the same.

△△△

"So... you have no idea why these individuals attacked the bar where you and compatriots – who *are* suspected criminals – were staying? You also don't know where the weapon we found on you came from? And finally, you claim you had nothing to do with the deaths that occurred, despite their being at least seven individuals who have testified otherwise?"

"Yes?" Erich nodded uncertainly, trying not to squint at the bright light blazing into his eyes.

The detective in front of him sighed, slowly running a hand through her brown hair. "You do realize, even if the courts rule that *everything* you did in that bar was an act of self-defense, you're still facing one count of illegal possession of a firearm? Which carries a mandatory minimum sentence of three to five years. And that's before we even get into the directed energy weapons your friends were carrying, or any involuntary manslaughter charges that might be levied."

The tired looking Latina woman looked him dead in the eye, "Now for the last time, do you want to tell me what happened at that bar tonight?"

"...No?"

A loud bang caught Erich off guard, making him flinch as the woman's partner slammed his hands into the table.

"Quit jerking us around you little shit!" The man roared, "We know you were there with Diego William's daughters. Which means we know you're guilty of *something*. The only question is what, and how many years we get to slap you with. And that slimy son of a bitch isn't going to be there to help you."

Erich respectfully disagreed. There was a very good reason that Diego William's wasn't behind bars, even with all the criminal acts attributed to his name.

As if to answer his thoughts, the door to the interrogation room opened, admitting a police officer in a fancy looking uniform. "Please uncuff the witness, detectives. He's free to go."

"What!?" The woman protested, "But sir, we-"

"That was an order detective." The captain grunted sharply before stepping back outside.

Erich struggled to keep the smirk off his face as one of the ashen faced police officers walked over to uncuff him. As he moved to stand up, the 'good cop' of the duo leaned over him.

"Don't think your friend Hard-Light's always gonna be there to save you. One day there's going to be a reckoning in this city. And you and all the rest of your gutter trash friends are going to be washed away."

Erich resisted the urge to laugh as he was led outside. It was just so melodramatic. Idly, he wondered if his mother or sister had ever said anything similar. He could totally see it happening.

Not that what the female detective said would ever come to pass.

Once upon a time, the power of the judicial system might have worked to put men like him away. Nowadays it had so many loopholes and corrupt officials working it, that it was little more than a whipped dog, quick to do the bidding of anyone with enough power or money to pressure it.

Head held high, he was still feeling smug when he stepped out of the police station's double doors and onto the street.

That sensation disappeared immediately when he saw Hard-Light was waiting for him on the sidewalk, a bevy of his goons around him, and a very nervous looking Gravity and Sarah beside him.

△△△

"Do you have any idea what your little escapades have cost me?" The man growled as he sat on the edge of his desk, looming over all three of them. "The favors I had to call in?"

Erich wisely kept his mouth shut, shifting on what had to be the world's most uncomfortable chair.

"Daddy, it's not our fault..." Sarah started to say, only to be cut off by a glare that could melt steel beams. Figuratively. Hard-Light was a pure Artificer as far as Erich was aware.

"Not your fault?" He repeated, "Even though the lot of you were dumb enough to leave the shop - and the protection I posted around it - to go waltzing around the city? Did none of you think that *just maybe* the people who are after you might have seen an opportunity there?"

Ah... No.

The thought that the Brotherhood would still be out to get him hadn't even crossed Erich's mind. In his head he had already partitioned the whole Brotherhood thing into a 'past event', with no bearing on his future.

Glancing around, he could see similar thoughts were crossing Sarah's mind, but to his surprise, Gravity looked more defiant than confused.

"I didn't think they would risk it that close to the Hero Guild's branch headquarters." She groused.

That bitch! He thought. *She knew it was a possibility and invited me anyway!?*

"Didn't think they would risk it? In case you haven't noticed, dear daughter of mine, they're gearing up for a war. My sources tell me they're scooping up every low life Meta they can possibly get their

hands on. A little thing like city limits aren't going to stop them."

Well, that explained how the dearly departed Crusher came into their employ.

"Whatever." The man grunted, "Get out of here. I don't want to see any of you until the assault tomorrow."

"Assault?" Erich chimed in, almost instantly regretting it as one bloodshot eye rolled towards him.

"Yes. Assault." The man said, "The Brotherhood's been hitting us for weeks, so we have to hit them back or risk looking weak. One of my boys' has found one of their warehouses. Probably used as a drug lab or some shit like that. We're going to go in there and kill everyone one of those Nazi fucks we can find."

Right. Of course. Supervillain stuff.

"And why do you need me there?" He asked sheepishly.

"I want the suit." The man growled, "This is our chance to finally show our guys and gals that we have a new heavy hitter in our lineup."

Erich was horrified, but to his immense relief, Sarah was the one to point out the obvious problem with that plan. "It's not finished yet, Daddy."

Not entirely true. The shields were in, and the force blasters were working fine. There was still a minor issue with the HUD, but that was the work of an hour or two. Heck, it could probably be fixed using a hot patch from off the web.

Not that Erich would ever lower himself to using one.

"I don't care. It's as ready as it needs to be." The Artificer grunted.

"But Daddy, we don't have our pilot picked out yet." She said, "And even if we did, it will take us at least a week to calibrate the suit to them."

"Is that so?" The man asked, not taking his eyes off Erich. Reluctantly, the young man nodded in assent.

"Well then. The solution is simple." The man grinned.

It was?

"Our lead mechanic can pilot the suit." The supervillain laughed, "I've seen the video of him walking around in it, so I know the suit is already calibrated for him."

Gravity actually had the temerity to scowl in the man's presence, "That's bullshit. It's a completely unnecessary risk of one of the organization's valuable resources. And Erich can't aim for shit."

The villain's energy blade hummed to life with a threatening thrum, cutting off all his daughter's protests instantly.

"He's going in the suit. I expect to see him, and it, at this house tomorrow evening so we can go over the plan." He scowled, "Now everyone get the fuck out of my office."

The three of them couldn't get out of there fast enough. Only once they were well clear did Gravity choose to speak.

"Christ, I'd rather go through another firefight than deal with the old man when he's like that."

Sarah looked like she wanted to complain, but she was just as pale and shaken as the rest of them. "Daddy can be… intense. He wasn't
wrong though. The Brotherhood's running rampant, and the Red Squares are doing nothing to rein them in."

The blonde shrugged uneasily, "We need to score a win, and Erich's suit will be our means of achieving it."

Erich was reasonably sure they would survive another week without his suit doing *anything*. They'd survived this long, after all.

Hard-Light wasn't having him pilot the suit because they needed it now. He was doing it because he was pissed and he wanted to take it out on someone.

Which fit right in with being a supervillain, honestly.

"I… I need to go run some diagnostics on the suit." He said woodenly.

The two sisters stopped glaring at each other, turning to him with an eerie synchronization.

"I'll help."

"I'll come."

The two snapped back to each other, glares only redoubling.

Erich watched on with mild exasperation before walking away. He had doubted it before, but now he was coming around to Sarah's way of thinking. Gravity did want something from him. She was just more subtle about it than Sarah.

"Going to be a long night." He muttered.

CHAPTER 6

Erich woke to pain. Which wasn't all that unusual. Muscle soreness. Hangovers. A fleeting sense of wrongness about the direction his life was taking. All were pretty typical sensations.

No. What was unusual about this particular pain was that it came about as a result of an elbow that was firmly jammed into his kidneys.

"God no." Erich muttered, staring at his slowly waking bedmate.

"God yes, lover," Sarah murmured as she leisurely stretched. Not unlike a cat rising from a nap.

"We didn't sleep together." He deadpanned, roughly shoving away the limb jammed into his side. "Well, we slept together. But at no point did we bump uglies... or get our uglies involved in any way."

"You missed your calling in life, honey. You should have been a poet." Sarah said, rising from the bed.

Even though she was still fully clothed, her hair was a mess, and she had a streak of oil across her brow, Erich had to admit that she looked ravishing in the morning light. Or mid-afternoon light, he corrected after a quick glance at the clock.

"Care to join me in the shower?" She teased.

He didn't dignify the question with a response, rising from the bed and striding from the room with almost indecent haste; ignoring the delicate chuckles that followed him out.

He needed coffee. And a shower. One he could have now. The other would likely take a while. Time spent living with Gravity had

taught him that much. He doubted Sarah would be any different.

Striding into the kitchen, he could see Gravity sprawled out on the couch. Fully clothed and just as filthy as he and Sarah were, she was the picture of feminine grace as she snored loudly.

Sighing, he set about making two cups of coffee.

"Wugh!?" The woman slurred, when a few minutes later, the warm beverage slammed down onto the coffee table next to her.

"Coffee. Drink." Erich instructed as he slumped into his own chair. "Last night's retrofits were good, but I want to make sure that everything is running *perfectly* before I'm forced into that metal hulk."

It actually hurt him to say that, but his feelings were what they were. The knowledge that *he* was going to be the one riding the suit into battle had cooled his feelings towards it considerably.

"Really?" Gravity slurred blearily, reaching for the cup, "And what makes you think I want to spend another moment in that cave of yours, after spending damn near all night there?"

Erich quirked his eyebrow but said nothing. Even if he didn't know exactly what the young woman wanted from him, now that he knew Gravity wanted *something*, he could leverage it to his advantage.

"Fine." The woman groused after a few moments of silence, "But that bitch better not be there."

If Sarah was there, she was there. Erich doubted she would be though.

J. R. Grey

As Hard-Light's right-hand woman she would probably be back at
the mansion organizing the 'troops' for the attack. Despite Gravity's apparent relative power, it had grown clear to him that she didn't have nearly as much responsibility within Hard-Light's organization.

He figured there was a story there, but the only part of it that he cared about was the fact that she would be free to help him with the suit.

It was nearly half an hour later when Sarah finally emerged from his apartment's tiny bathroom.

"Tada, children," She sing-songed, "Your goddess is here!"

"Tch," Gravity hissed, "you couldn't just have showered back at the mansion?"

Erich might have said something similar, but he found himself rather distracted by the sight before him; Sarah clad in just a towel, skin glowing and fresh out of the shower was something of a sight to behold.

"Please," Sarah scoffed at her irritated sibling, "Some of us actually care about our appearance. I couldn't go out in public looking like this."

"You don't even have a change of clothes."

"No, but you do." Sarah pointed out.

Gravity looked ready to explode, but the blonde simply smiled and pointed behind her "Oh look, you better grab that shower before Erich gets to it first."

Erich had been planning to do exactly that, figuring the brewing argument between the two sisters would serve as a great distraction for him to sneak in next.

That plan promptly went to hell as soon as Gravity glanced at him.

"You better not touch my clothes!" The woman called as she sprinted into the bathroom.

Erich watched her go, hopes of getting clean anytime soon dashed before they even began.

He sighed, directing a resigned glare in the blonde's direction. "You're the worst."

The woman shrugged, a mischievous smile stealing over her features.

"I try."

ΔΔΔ

"No, listen you idiot." Erich said, "I don't care if you wear the armor. In fact, I firmly believe the genetic potential of humanity would experience a net increase if someone were to make your insides turn into outsides."

He sighed, "But Hard-Light told me to check your kit, so put on the damn vest before I inform him that you care more about showing off your abs than following his instruction."

The thug across from him grabbed the vest, but couldn't resist a final a sneer as he swaggered back towards his little posse.

"And tell your gaggle of girlfriends to get their asses over here too." Erich yelled, "I can still see a bunch of them without vests."

For a second it looked like the band of angry young men were going to ignore him, but Sarah's soprano voice sailed clear across the garage, "Do as he says people. We wouldn't want any of you
suffering nasty accidents, right?"

Despite the cheeriness in her voice, the threat was clear, and the reticent goons hurried over to him with almost unseemly haste.

Idiots, Erich snorted.

Even with Sarah's intervention, getting the rest of the gang-bangers fitted out took longer than it rightfully should. The whole farce only served to reinforce just how much the fancy hard-light barriers implanted into the vests were wasted on them.

At least as far as Erich was concerned.

He didn't even want to think about the fact that his upgraded laser pistols were in the hands of these men and women.

Not for the first time that evening, he found himself cursing Hard-Light's decision to appoint him 'head mechanic'.

"*Only* mechanic would be more accurate," He muttered under his breath as he adjusted the frequency on a radio earpiece, before handing it off to a garishly tattooed young woman.

"All right punks," Hard-Light's voice bellowed out from over near a fleet of white vans, cutting through the noise with casual ease "Get your asses over here so I can tell you the plan."

Erich stormed over, glad to be momentarily free of dealing with the masses.

"This is the warehouse we're looking at," Hard-Light said, gesturing to a crudely drawn map, "It's been built in the typical eighties fashion, so any of you who have been on dock runs know what to expect. Wide open space, one set of big doors, two or three small exterior doors, and a gangway leading to the foreman's office."

Around him Erich could see a few people nod in recognition. Sarah stepped up, "At first, we thought this was some kind of drug den, but some recent intel suggests they really are using it as a warehouse. Mostly for mechanical parts from what we've observed, but that may just be cover for heavier artillery."

Hard-Light stepped forward again, a familiar gleam in his eye, "Which changes things. This no longer a churn and burn operation. It's now a smash and grab. Kill everyone inside, and then pile everything that you can back into the vans before the feds show up."

Typical Artificer. Erich thought. *Avarice, Hard-Light is thy name.*

Sarah nodded, "Which means that the vans will be full, and thus won't be able to extract you afterward. So, if I were you, I would use these few minutes before the operation starts to plan out your escape route; because most of you are going to be getting home on foot."

A muted grumble passed through the room, but it was instantly silence by a glare from Hard-Light.

"We going for ransoms?" A voice called out after a few awkward moments.

"No prisoners." Sarah shook her head, a stony mask falling over her face. "Brotherhood never pays, and it's too much of a pain in the ass to hold onto them."

Erich tried not to wince at the number of eager chuckles ran through the crowd. To his surprise, and relief, Sarah looked almost as uncomfortable as him; though she was clearly trying to hide it.

After a few moments of restless shuffling, Erich willed himself to relax. What had he been expecting anyway? He knew what kind of
people he was surrounding himself with when he signed up.

Now if only my subconscious could learn to accept that. He thought glumly, trying to stifle the uncomfortable rumblings of his gut.

J. R. Grey

"What's happening with the suit?" A feminine voice called out, the crowd turning almost as one to regard where his beauty sat hunched over in the van that had brought it to the mansion.

In the low light of the garage, it looked pretty impressive. The paint was chipped, and some parts still had flecks of rust attached, but overall it gave off the impression of a simple, powerful, machine.

It was designed to break things and avoid being broken in return; every part of its design reflected that fact.

Hard-Light stepped forward again, a malicious smile lighting up his features, "Our newest associate will be piloting it."

Erich had to resist the urge to shuffle once more as all eyes fell on him.

Instead he did his best to stand with his head held high. He knew that if he showed even a hint of weakness, a crowd like this would eat him alive.

"As the one who built it, he's got the most experience with it." Hard-Light leaned in, as if to tell a secret, "And considering he's already bagged two Meta's *without* the thing, I shudder to think what he might do *with* it."

Huh, I suppose I have, haven't I? How funny was that.

"Alright, you lot, start mounting up." Hard-Light said, "The Brotherhood's got a barrel of kickass headed their way, and we're gonna be the ones to deliver it."
Erich resisted the urge to sigh in relief as everyone started to walk away, ignoring attempts by people to draw him into conversation.

There was nothing here he wanted to hear.

He had a suit to clamber into. God help him.

"You doing ok?" Gravity asked, appearing out of nowhere.

"That a real question?" Erich responded, about to ask her where she'd been all evening. She'd all but disappeared the moment they arrived at the mansion.

It was only as he turned to look at her that he found out why.

"Nice costume." He snarked.

Utterly unruffled, the woman grinned as she did a little pirouette. "You think so?"

Erich shrugged, "The helmet looks decent enough. Might stop a bullet." Which was more than he could say for the rest of her uniform.

Though he had to admit that it did flatter her figure. The black and yellow did work very nicely with her chocolate colored skin. And the sleeveless nature of it did a lot to show off her nicely toned arms. Though he personally would have chosen something that might block bullets instead.

"What's with the cat ears?" He asked.

She smiled, lifting it up next to her head, "They're cute, and it's where the sensors are held."

That caught his interest. "Sensors?"
The villainess shrugged, "Sensors. Comms. Batteries. The total package."

Hmmm, maybe she would let me a take a look at it later? Who knows, I might even be able to make some improvements.

"Focus." Gravity jostled him. "We're about to go into a fight. You can think about my helmet later."

Erich scowled, but had to admit that she had a point. Swallowing his rising dread, he clambered into the van, ignoring the groaning of its suspension as he did.

Taking a steadying breath, he pressed the suit's ignition key against the scanner positioned just under the armpit; the chest piece opening with a hiss to expose the padded interior. Sparing a final glance backward at the rest of Hard-Light's crew clambering into their own vehicles, he sighed in resignation before climbing inside.

Which, despite his best efforts, had never quite become comfortable after the total mess Crusher had made of the initial design.

Parts jabbed into strange places. Some spots were oddly warm. Hell, he had a coolant line running right between his legs.

Still, he couldn't deny the tiny tingle of excitement he could feel as the helmet closed back down around him. The shudder of electricity that ran up his spine as he felt the entire suit hum to life. The slight skip of his heart as synth-muscle stretched and strained as it started to warm up.

There was nothing quite like it; the feeling of power and invincibility that came from wearing half a ton of high-tech power armor.

"Mechromancer Online." Gravity's voice announced with entirely
uncharacteristic solemnness.

When did she even get time to record that!? He cursed as the video feeds booted to life.

"Gravity," Erich hissed, "Did you change my suit's audio prompts?"

The woman didn't even try to hid her grin as she slid her helmet over her head.

"Do you like it?" She asked, as she slammed the van's rear doors closed and collapsed onto a bench.

Yes. Yes, he did. A hell of a lot more than the computer-generated voice he had been using before.

Would he ever admit that?

No.

"The *Mechromancer*? Really?" He asked, latching onto the one thing he could think to complain about.

Even with her helmet clasped over her face, Erich could see her excitement in the way her hands twitched.

"It's your Cape name!" She squealed gleefully, "If you're going to be wearing that badass suit, you need a badass villain name."

Erich couldn't deny, it did sound pretty badass.

Again, not that he would ever admit it.

"It's alright, I guess." He attempted to shrug, only to wince as the suit held him firmly in place.

"Ha," The woman pointed at him, "That's 'Erich talk' for it's totally amazing, but I'm too much of a weeny to admit it."

"A *weeny*? really?" Erich sighed, "What are you twelve?"

The woman shrugged, sending a stab of envy through his shoulders, "I calls them as I sees 'em."

Really?

Suddenly the prospect of an assault on the Brotherhood's warehouse didn't seem so bad. For one thing, it would get him out of this van, and thus, out of this conversation.

"Don't let her take all the credit," Sarah's voice chimed in over the radio, "I helped."

Gravity scoffed, "Please, you didn't even know what a necromancer was."

"No, not until I looked it up." Sarah replied, "but I know enough about Erich to know he wouldn't have appreciated your other suggestions."

Despite himself Erich was curious. "What other suggestions?"

Sarah sounded totally gleeful, while Gravity's body language suddenly looked decidedly less so.

"I'll save you from having to hear the worst of them." Sarah laughed, "Let me tell you now though; the one she originally wanted to go with was *'The Red-ucer'*."

Erich all but shuddered, and even though he couldn't convey even a hint of body language through the suit, Gravity still managed to pick up on it.
"Hey!" She protested, "It was a good name."

No. No, it wasn't.

"Why red though?" He couldn't help but ask.

Reducer was self explanatory, if a bit odd. Red made not a lick of sense to him though.

"Well it's got red on it doesn't it?" Gravity pointed out.

Yes. It did. If only on the bits that Erich still hadn't gotten around to scraping off yet. The Crusher might have wanted to ride around in a big red target sign, but Erich was content to pick something more subdued.

And easier to camouflage.

"Thank you, Sarah." Erich said over the open line, ignoring the look of betrayal from the woman in the van with him. "You picked a great name."

"Not a problem, sugar." The blonde's smug voice came over the radio, "I love nothing more than..." Her voice cut off for a moment.

When she came back, she was utterly serious, "Get ready, we're nearly there."

Erich swallowed nervously, as he nodded.

The impromptu conversation on the way over had almost distracted him from the coming violence. Now that he had been reminded again, his guts were all but twisting themselves into knots.

"You'll be fine, Erich." Gravity said with surprising softness, one hand pressing against the cool metal of his suit. "You've been in two
fights already, and you came out just fine. Better than fine even."

Better than the other guys at least, he thought with grim humor, the reminder setting his heart a little more at ease.

"Thanks, Gravity." He murmured quietly, trying to fight down the flush that threatened to overtake him completely.

If the yellow clad woman heard any indication of it, it didn't show in her actions, as she gave him a quick thumbs up, before reaching out for the latch to the van's doors.

"Ready?"

"As I'll ever be." He joked.

Taking the weak attempt at humor for what it was, Gravity shoved the doors open, letting the cool night air spill into the muggy confines of the van.

"Let's go then."

"Blasters Online. Barriers Online. Targeting System Online." Gravity's computerized voice announced, each positive system announcement acting to calm Eric's troubled thoughts.

"Fuck it." He whispered, clambering out after her.

CHAPTER 7

The first shots were already being fired when Mechromancer's armored boots thumped down onto the concrete.

"They had some guys on the doors," A female voice chimed in on the radio, *"Mooks barely even knew what hit them."*

"Good," Hard-Light's voice chimed in, *"Sarah, Chavez, take some people to secure those side entrances. I don't want any of these fucks escaping."*

From his vantage spot, Erich could see where a group of goons were already searching through the pockets of the dead sentries, the telltale flickers of light barriers marking them as allies. He was halfway toward them before his HUD to lit up with a new targeting solution from a nearby alley.

With deliberate motions, he raised his arm, "Aim assist on."

"Acknowledged." The suit intoned, Erich's arm turning rigid as the suit's pneumatics took over, artificially guiding his palm mounted blaster in the direction his right eye was looking.

With a tiny squeeze of his fingers, he felt energy rocket through the limb as a bolt of force blasted out from his palm. The skin-head, bags of takeaway in the process of being discarded after hearing the gunshots, didn't even see it coming.

Erich had to resist the urge to cringe as a wet crunch rang out.

"Nasty." Gravity murmured, turning away from the stain that now liberally smeared the walls of the alley.

"Bit too much power," He blanched, also turning away from the nauseating sight.

It felt easier though. The taking of a life. His breath had barely twitched as he had pulled the trigger. Was he really getting used to living like this? Or was he just getting better at hiding the guilt? He didn't know. And to his surprise, he found he didn't care anymore.

What was of greater concern to him was tracking ability of his suit. It had done so well!

He hadn't had high hopes for it considering the base code had come from an omni-phone app. One that had the obnoxious ability to superimpose little cartoon hats on people's heads through the camera. A frivolous waste of technology.

He couldn't help but wonder what the original creator of the abominable thing would think if they knew their little toy had been used to form the basis of his weapons system. He couldn't imagine they would be pleased.

"Aim assist off." He said, the thought bringing a smile to his face.

"Acknowledged."

"Nice cannon," Hard-Light said, striding over, "now get that oversized tin-can over here. The fucks locked the doors from the inside."

Erich knew the villain could easily force them open himself, but he also knew better than to suggest that. So instead, he stomped over to the front entrance, as quickly as the heavy footfalls of his suit would allow.

As he expected, the thick metal of the warehouse's massive doors proved no impediment to his suit. Like a hot knife cutting through butter, he drove his fingers into the gap between the doors.
The sound of shrieking metal was music to his ears. In fact, it was intoxicating. The sensation of power that accompanied it.

Bullets started to ping off his barriers from inside as the gap widened, but he paid them no mind.

Besides, as quickly as it started, the rain of fire started to diminish as return fire from his side forced the defenders to duck.

"Are you using me for cover?" He asked, after a quick glance at his rear camera.

"Your fat ass is big enough for it." Gravity shrugged, "and it's not like we have a lot of cover to work with out here."

Erich was just about to respond, when a loud ping drew his attention back to what he was doing.

"Barriers down to ninety percent."

"Shit," he muttered.

The suit's tough, not invincible, idiot. He thought as sporadic gunfire continued to spark off his barriers. *Are you trying to kill yourself?*

"Flashing," He announced over the comms, "close your eyes and cover your ears."

After an agonizing second waiting to ensure everyone had heard him, he spoke up.

"Activate Flash"

"Acknowledged."

The oversized headlamps on the suit's head and chest lit up, just as
the front mounted directional speakers let out a deafening shriek. The effect was not all that dissimilar from an oversized flashbang going off.

The fire from his front cut off almost immediately.

"Advancing." He called out, not caring if anyone heard, as he brought both arms up. "Sixty percent power to blasters, wide sweep mode." He muttered into the suit.

He didn't wait for the acknowledgement before he started firing, aiming in the general direction of the nearest hit box. The wide angle of the firing mode dissipated some of the force of the shot, but it was more than sufficient to send a young man and woman sprawling across the floor, their cover flying with them.

"Barriers down to eighty percent." The voice intoned as sporadic gunfire started to pick away at him once more.

Throwing accuracy to the wind, Erich fired at every target he could see, aiming for cover as much as people as he continued advancing forward, occasionally kicking crates, and people, aside as he moved forward.

And as he had hoped, his allies from outside picked up on his plan, and started firing into the now completely exposed members of the Brotherhood.

"Focused mode, eighty percent power." Erich instructed as he saw someone beginning to turn and run, attempting to disappear towards the crate filled rear of the warehouse.

"Acknowledged."

The man didn't get far, Erich's shot took him square in the back. With a lower power setting, the thug didn't quite explode, but there
was a distinctly wet crack as the force of the shot sent him sliding across the floor.

He didn't get up again, nor did he appear quite structurally sound anymore.

Not that Erich really had time to dwell on it, as he turned to track the next-

"Enough, Erich!"

He hesitated as Gravity's voice rang out over the comms. Just long enough to notice a very important fact.

He had been about to shoot a friendly. Well, relatively friendly. The man in question didn't look very friendly after nearly being the victim of a friendly fire incident.

These guys need uniforms.

Looking around, he could Hard-Light's goons moving up into the warehouse, stepping over the trail of destruction he had left on the way in.

"Still with us, Mechromancer?" Gravity asked.

"Y-yeah," he coughed, belatedly realizing that he needed to breathe, "It all happened so…"

"Fast?" She smiled.

"Yeah."

She gave him a commiserating look, one that was clear even through her helmet. "Meta fights can be like that. Especially when the other side doesn't have one of their own. One side just has so
much power over the other that they bulldoze right through them."

She gestured to the piles of shattered and thrown crates strewn across the entrance area. As she did, Erich found himself deliberately ignoring the dozen or so bodies, not knowing which ones he was directly responsible for and which he wasn't.

The guilt he had been so quick to write away as nothing before came back in full force. Especially when he saw that the flattened nature of one suggested he might have… stepped on him.

The thought made him feel ill, and he had to turn away.

The last thing he wanted was to throw up in his suit. He was already going to have to hose down the feet. Hopefully he could avoid having to do the insides as well.

"If you hadn't been here then this would have been a decent spot for them to hunker down." Gravity continued, ignorant of the morbid nature of his thoughts, "Clear lines of sight. Large open space without cover for us to have to cross. Lots of ammo. They could have kept us at bay until either cops or reinforcements arrived."

Or Sarah and the other mook brought their people in through the side entrances. He supposed.

Still, he got what she was saying.

He and his suit had just walked through their carefully constructed defenses. Shrugging off small arms fire as it were nothing.

Well, not nothing. He noted, glancing at his barrier read out. *Seventy six percent.*

High, but still far too low for his liking.
Sure, the suit could bounce most calibers of small arm off its armored parts, but the delicate joints could be damaged by even a pistol if it struck them at the wrong angle.

And that didn't even take into account explosives, meta-abilities, or someone just plain setting him on fire.

As the dearly departed Crusher discovered the hard way. He thought cynically. *Far from invincible, indeed.*

"Didn't see you use any of your abilities." He noted, as he started to think about possible upgrades to the suit.

"My stuff's not good for big firefights like this. I'm much better at totally locking down just one person," She shrugged, "but I have to have vision on them, and it's pretty obvious when my powers are working."

As she spoke her hands lit up green, as if to emphasize her point, "Anyone could plug a bullet in me while I'm standing there like a moron."

That made sense. Now that he thought about it, it had also been the case in their other fights as well. At the time he hadn't thought much of it, focused as he was on not being murdered, but afterward he had wondered. Never quite got around to asking about it though.

"Even then, I can only use my ability so many times before I exhaust myself. To be honest it's a pretty crap power." She said, starting to trail off, and if Erich weren't in the suit, he might not have picked up what she said next.

"Still better than Sarah's though." She smirked.

What was the deal with Sarah's power? Because now that he thought about it, she hadn't used it in the firefight at the bar either. Was everyone's ability secretly crappy or something?

"Quit standing around you morons. We've got to get all this crap loaded up and shipped out." Hard-Light growled as he strode inside, gesturing to the many machine components that had been scattered about the place during Mechromancer's mad dash.

The goons were quick to move under their boss's supervision, one rushing over to grab a forklift.

"Mechromancer," the villain called, making him wonder when the guy had learned his new Cape name, "Good work breaking through. Saved me having to make the effort, and let me know I didn't waste my money after all."

Erich resisted the indignant response that welled up in him at the idea that he was worth even a cent less than the man had paid.

"Thank you, sir." He said through gritted teeth, glad his speakers served to slightly warp his voice.

"Boss." The man corrected. "You're part of my crew now, that means you call me boss."

As if calling the man 'Sir' wasn't torture enough? "Thank you, boss."

"Good," the older man nodded, "Now start loading those boxes into the vans. That big ass suit will probably be quicker than the forklift."

That really tested Erich's ability to restrain his tongue. Use *his* suit to perform menial labor? Why not just take a dump in the central processor while you were at it?

"Will do, boss." He managed to grind out.

ΔΔΔ

He was on his third box when Sarah and her team showed up.

"Hello, Daddy!" The blonde woman smiled. "You guys stole all the fun. No one even tried to escape from our side."

The villain barely looked up from his inspection of a nearby crate, his voice slightly slurred, "Must have all tried to get out from Chavez's side then. Probably why she's not here yet."

"She isn't?" The bubbly blonde asked. "Have you tried calling her on the radio?"

No. The man had become less and less coherent over the last few minutes. A side effect of his ability and his brain trying to find uses for the mounds of parts they were extracting from the warehouse. To be honest, Erich was impressed the man had even managed to answer his daughter's first question.

Which Sarah was quick to pick up on. Sighing, she reached for her earpiece, "Chavez? What's taking you so long. We need your guys to get over here and start helping load up the vans. Especially if we want to get out of here before anyone else shows up."

It was strange to him, the way she could flip back and forth between sultry, bubbly and commanding. Bubbly annoyed him. Sultry... discomforted him. Commanding though?

Commanding he could respect.

"Chavez?" Sarah repeated after not receiving a response. Cursing, she turned to one of the nearby goons.

"Francis, get over there and tell that jackoff to turn her radio on." The resigned way the woman said it suggested that this wasn't the
first time the woman in question had forgotten to do so. It made him wonder why she was selected to lead a team in the first place.

It was moments like this that reminded him how little he really knew about Hard-Light's organization. His only real point of contact with it was through Sarah and Gravity, and neither sister was prone to talking about the gang.

He really had to stop thinking of them all as just, 'goons'. He had been able to get away with it before because he assumed it been a temporary acquaintance. Now it was liable to get him shot in the back one day.

It was nearly three minutes later when an ashen faced Francis jogged back toward the group. Why the idiot hadn't thought to use his radio, Erich had not a clue.

"We've got a problem." The man stammered, heading toward Hard-Light before realizing the man was off in his own little world, and switching back toward Sarah, "I... I... you're going to want to see this for yourself, ma'am."

Sarah leveled a speculative eye at the young man, before quickly taking charge.

"Mechromancer, Grey and Smith, come with me." The blonde instructed, "Gravity, keep an eye on dad, and send him my way when he snaps out his episode. The rest of you, keep piling stuff into the vans. I want them fully loaded by the time I get back."

The assorted mooks didn't look happy but nodded nonetheless as two of their number peeled off to join us.

"Alright, let's go see what all the fuss is about." Sarah said, electrical sparks flying from her hands. "This better be worth my time, Francis."

ΔΔΔ

"We didn't hear any shooting." Smith said.

"Probably happened when the firefight at the front started." Grey responded, cautiously stepping over one of the bodies, "Clever fuck must have timed it just right."

"I don't think so." Sarah muttered.

Erich had no idea how the three of them were so calm about this. He felt like he was about to soil his suit. Hell, even Francis had the good sense to be terrified. The young man was practically shaking in his boots as he clutched his gun and surveyed the carnage.

The cooling corpses of Chavez's team were strewn all over the empty street just outside the warehouse's side door, and the woman herself had been hung from a street lamp by high-tension cable.

The others hadn't fared any better; they'd been impaled by throwing discs, sliced open at the throat, had their necks snapped, chests caved in...

The list went on.

Whoever did this had been good. Very good. Even to Erich's amateur – and slightly nauseated - eyes, he could see that they'd been picked off one by one. For one thing, the bodies were all facing in different directions. For the other, all the bullet holes were spread out all over the alley.

Well, not at the doorway, but there was an obvious reason for that.

The Brotherhood gang members had clearly attempted to escape and been mercilessly gunned down right at the precipice of
freedom. The bullet hole spacing *there* was tight and controlled, not wild and arbitrary like it was everywhere else.

"Whoever did this, did it after Chavez took out the Brotherhood members who tried to escape." Sarah said, gesturing to the pile of skinhead corpses.

Which meant that they *should* have heard gunfire, Erich surmised. After all, the Brotherhood wouldn't have started to run until it was clear the battle was lost. Fanatics were stubborn like that. The gunfire at the front would have wound down by the time the massacre here started.

"Why did none of them radio for help?" Grey asked the next most obvious question.

"A localized jammer?" Erich put forward, determinedly dragging his eyes away from a corpse that had been pinned to a brick wall - with a throwing knife.

It didn't help that his targeting computer kept trying to highlight the man's face.

Sarah looked skeptical, "That didn't affect our radio, all of a hundred meters away?"

Erich would have shrugged if he could, "A *very* localized jammer."

Sarah shook her head, "No, I'm thinking that this was a Meta ability. Something that canceled sound. It would explain why we didn't hear gunfire, and none of them radioed for help. Would have made picking them off one by one easier too."

"That would make sense," Grey put in, "Doesn't matter if the radio works if there's no sound to transmit."

Erich was still partial to his jammer idea, but he would freely admit that it was because he tended to frame everything through the eyes of technology. Logically, Sarah would be the same, but in reverse. Grey was obviously biased towards the boss's daughter, so her opinion counted for nothing.

"Daddy's not going to be happy about this." Sarah murmured as she fingered her gun.

The fact that eight of his guys got wiped out by one or more Metas, completely silently, from all of a hundred feet away? Yeah, Erich couldn't imagine the guy taking that with solemn dign-

"Erich, you can tell him."

Fuck.

CHAPTER 8

As Erich emerged from the suit, he felt less like a man emerging triumphant from battle, and more like a creature being spawned from the belly of some great metal beast: sweaty, tired and more than a little uncomfortable.

"You need a little help there, uh, Mechromancer?" The way the driver's voice hitched at the end was very telling of his lack of surety on Erich's new moniker.

Erich didn't care. He just wanted the man gone.

"I'll be fine." He murmured, as he clambered back up to his feet. "Get the van out of here so I can shut the roller doors. The last thing I need is for someone in this neighborhood seeing that I've got a super-suit in here."

He knew he should have been more polite, especially after his recent revelation at the warehouse. But the battle, and discovering the slaughter of Chavez's team had drained him entirely of the ability to care.

The driver shrugged and hopped back into the van before reversing back out.

Erich watched him go before limping over to the controls to let the roller doors slide slowly back down again, hitting the concrete floor with a clang. Again, the garage was covered in darkness, and Erich was alone once more.

Gravity had to do something back at the mansion, and Sarah obviously had to take charge of the 'troops'. So, for the first time in a long time, the shop was empty but for himself and his tools.

He didn't know whether he liked that or not. Aggravating as they were, the sisters had grown on him.

Not unlike a rash.

"Shower or hose?" He wondered as he gripped the damp fabric of his shirt.

Blood was no good for the suit, and the feet were liberally coated in it, but on the other hand, he *really* wanted a shower. The suit's cooling system was good, but it wasn't so good that the thing didn't feel like an oven after an hour or two of operation.

"Need to move that coolant line as well." He grumbled into the darkness.

Putting it right between his legs had not been the smartest design decision. The sensation of liquid nitrogen surging through a pipe right next to his perineum had served as a reminder of that fact, each and every time it happened.

Honestly, he would be impressed if could even still have kids after that test run.

Still, despite its problems, the suit had performed... adequately.

He should have felt some elation over that fact, or the fresh batch of cash now sitting in his bank account, but instead he just felt tired. The sensation of bones snapping under his feet kept coming back to him.

In the end though, it was his obsessive need to keep things properly maintained that finally won out.

So, stripped down to his boxers - and armed with a bucket and a sponge - he sat in the dim light of the shop cleaning bits of blood and viscera off the suit's feet.

It was vile and tedious work, but he had learned to expect as much. If she was there, Gravity could have simply levitated the stuff off, but he had to do it the hard way.

That was what his entire life boiled down to in the end; vile and tedious work to achieve the same that results others might attain with arbitrarily assigned gifts. That was why he could out-build and out-think them. He wasn't afraid to get his hands dirty, and really go the extra mile.

He would never half-ass anything. He wasn't like those Metas with their underserved powers! He'd become mighty with his own two hands! He'd-

He dunked his sponge into the now filthy red water of his bucket, turning his mind away from the rant threatening to build up inside him.

Anger would achieve nothing. He couldn't indulge it. Besides, what had he achieved really? Built a suit and killed a few gang-bangers? If his sister put her mind to it, she could wipe out a small army in a morning. He needed more. He needed to go bigger. He needed-

Fresh water He thought, glancing at the blood and detritus clouding his once clean bucket.

ΔΔΔ

"Problem, lover?" A feminine voice asked as he tramped into the kitchen, bucket in hand.

"S-Sarah?" Erich gulped, suddenly very conscious of the fact that he was wearing little more than a pair of boxers - and whatever blood happened to spill on him.
If the woman in question was put off by his attire, or lack thereof, it didn't show in her face as she lounged on the counter top.

"What are you doing here?" He hissed, heart thudding in his chest as he dumped the empty bucket into the sink. "Shouldn't you be, I don't know, organizing?"

The woman shrugged, "Daddy snapped out of his little trance on the way back home. He wasn't best pleased about what went down with Chavez, but he was more concerned with checking out our haul. He's organizing things back at the mansion right now."

Erich nodded, not entirely sure as to why that translated to her showing up at his shop.

"Don't be so cold, honey." The woman drawled when she saw his expression, "I told you, I'm going to be your liaison for the organization going forward. That means we'll be spending a lot more time together."

"Where's Gravity?" Erich asked, very conscious of the fact that in addition to being close to naked, he wasn't armed.

He was reasonably sure that he and Sarah had buried the hatchet, but 'reasonably sure' was not a great deal of comfort when stuck in a confined space with an incredibly dangerous criminal. Nor would he put it past her to have him think that, right before she stuck the blade in.

The first signs of irritation appeared on the blonde's face, but they were quickly smoothed away. "Called away on a little errand. Some pissant little shop has been holding out on us. She got sent to reeducate them."

The Meta-human waved a hand airily, "But enough about her. I'm here to celebrate our new relationship!"
As she spoke she raised a hand, revealing... a blank DVD case.

"What's that?" He asked warily, scrubbing his hands meticulously clean with the aid of some alcoholic hand rub.

A distinctly feline grin took over the woman's face, "Oh, I don't know? Just a fresh batch of Death Dome videos, straight from the West Coast. With commentary by the Face himself."

That... that was incredibly illegal.

Not just the contents of the DVD itself, but the fact that it had come from the West Coast. Even thirty years after the Master's defeat, the US government and the Guild had yet to reclaim the area. Nowadays, it was little more than a lawless warzone for constantly changing warlords.

Then Erich remembered that he was in the process of washing someone's lifeblood from his hands, and a little smuggled contraband didn't seem quite so world changing.

"And you want to... watch it? With me?" He asked uncertainly.

The blonde rolled her eyes, "God, you can be such a dweeb. Yes. Yes, I want to watch it with you." She smiled, "I figured it would be something to bond over."

Erich wasn't too sure why she thought he would want to bond over the shared viewing of a murderous, highly illegal, Meta-human blood-sport - especially after having just finished his own version of the subject - but he was at least socially savvy enough to know that refusing would be awkward, and potentially painful.

For me.

At least he had gotten the suit more or less clean before she showed up. Or had she been waiting for that to happen. He wouldn't put it past her.

"I'll go shower and grab a change of clothes." He said hesitantly.

"Don't take too long." Sarah grinned as she slid off the counter top, "The fight earlier really got my motor going and I would hate to have to finish without you."

Erich hoped she wasn't implying what he thought she was implying, but he knew in his heart of hearts she was.

He grimaced, *Because of course, violence would have to be a turn on for her... Not a succubus my ass.*

He never thought he would say it, but he actually missed Gravity. If only because her acts of exhibitionism could occasionally be fun for him, when he wasn't trying to focus on something.

He sincerely doubted Sarah's apparent sadism would come with the same benefits.

ΔΔΔ

"Do you think anyone would find this odd?" Sarah asked, in a brief lull between bouts of spine-chilling gladiatorial violence.

Two supervillains sitting – and yes, he had accepted that recent events had firmly labeled him one - on a couch watching what was essentially a snuff film in the middle of the night? Right after pulling off a dangerous and draining assault on their competitors.

"A little." He said. "But what does it matter. I couldn't sleep if I wanted to, and you have your 'condition' to think of."

Said condition being the reason that she kept shifting in a manner
that clearly wasn't discomfort. Or at least, the conventional meaning of the word. Nor did Erich miss the way the attractive blonde's hands roamed to and fro over herself as the night wore on, only stopping when she noticed what she was doing.

He had been wrong. Sarah's own kinks *were* just as entertaining as Gravity's in their own special way.

At least more-so than what was happening on screen, which was honestly more than a little grotesque to his sensibilities. Although, he couldn't help but note that there hadn't been all that many deaths. The matches were incredibly dangerous, yes, but most ended when one side took a wound that kept them from continuing. It seemed to be considered poor form for a gladiator to kill their opponent outright.

"You mean the fact that all this violence is getting me off?" The blonde said ruefully, one hand deliberately reaching up to unhook another button from her top, giving a tantalizing glimpse even deeper into her already plunging neck line.

Erich shrugged, "It is what it is."

He wasn't about to judge. He wasn't exactly a picture of great mental health either. He certainly had his own hang-ups. Budding alcoholism least among them. And at least Sarah was on the right career path to indulge *her* hang ups.

Although he still found it a little discomforting how the woman's breath hitched every time one of the combatants on screen took damage. She had practically moaned when one poor cyborg woman lost a limb.

"You really mean that, don't you?" Sarah asked, a strange expression falling over her face, "You really don't care."

He wouldn't say he didn't care. He had his own preferences, he just didn't give them that much weight. He did what he had to do to get by.

"I think I see what Olivia likes about you."

That he didn't care? That he was indifferent? What a strange reason to like someone. He would have thought there were a few people in Hard-Light's crew who had similar dispositions.

"Unfortunately for her, I like you for an entirely different reason, and I'm not afraid to push to get my way."

Erich was about to ask what the hell she was talking about, when a soft pair of lips settled on his own.

$$\triangle\triangle\triangle$$

"You slept with her." Gravity deadpanned from across the kitchen counter.

He nodded sheepishly, one hand idly running up to trace a scratch running all the way down his back. One of many.

Sarah, predictably, was something of a scratcher. And a biter. And a shocker.

...Mostly a shocker.

Gravity had shown up that morning, just as the blonde had left.

"You know she's manipulating you right?" The woman pointed out as she took a sip of her coffee.

Again, Erich nodded, ignoring the stab of pain that ran up his neck from the action. "She mentioned something about me growing in
power and being able to help her."

"Always with the power-plays." She sighed and leaned back in her chair, "She was probably impressed by your suit's showing last night. Wasn't too sure if you were blowing hot air or not. And clearly you weren't, so she made her move."

"Is my support really that much of an advantage?"

Gravity snorted in disgust, "This is the problem with being a shut-in Erich. You know sweet fuck all about what's going on beyond your shop or that suit."

The rebuke stung, but he couldn't deny it was true. He couldn't help it though. He just wanted to build things. Not worry about criminal power dynamics.

"Listen, North Granton has three big factions in it. Of those, the Brotherhood and Red Squares are just branches of larger organizations spread out across the country. Hard-Light's gang is the only one that exists in just this city, and that's because our 'gang' is basically just him. Because that's all the other two are afraid of: Him, and him alone."

Erich knew that much.

Gravity hissed with annoyance that he wasn't getting it. "So, what does that mean for you? If Sarah thinks you've got the potential to be stronger than Hard-Light?"

Wha...I couldn't.... Could I? With the right tools? Some time? Some very expensive parts...

Maybe... Probably... Definitely.

"She wants me to take over from Hard-Light?" He hedged uncertainly.

"What?" Gravity's face was incredulous, "No! She wants to expand the gang. Push out the Squares and Brotherhood - and probably me while she's at. Cement herself as Hard-Light's heir and our gang as number one in the city."

...Oh.

"Which this brewing fight with the Brotherhood is a perfect starting point for, right?"

Gravity nodded, her lips a thin line.

Shit.

CHAPTER 9

Stepping out into the basement, Grey beside her, Sarah noted the familiar scent of blood was in the air. Once upon a time that might have repulsed her, but years living with her father had removed that weakness.

Instead she felt emboldened. More alive.

There was no fancy interrogation room in the mansion. Just a surprisingly new and well-maintained pipe, tucked away in a shadowy corner of a repurposed wine cellar.

And a nearby drain.

Their prisoner for the day was an older man, abducted from his home in the middle of the day by a few of her trusted underlings. Not particularly high up in the Brotherhood's food chain – they were tightly guarded, and usually Metas to match – but the aged tattoos littering his skin suggested he was a veteran member of the organization.

As she got closer, she noted the livid bruises running along his face and she had to resist the urge to tut. She had explicitly instructed her people not to inform her father of the man's presence on the estate, but one of them must have blabbed.

Later she would have to find out who, and 'educate' them on where their true loyalties should lie. After all, loyalty to her was loyalty to her father.

Just a better directed form of loyalty.

Still, the Neo-Nazi was still alive and mostly intact, so all was

not lost. She would just have to ensure that he stayed that way long
enough for her purposes to be served.

The prisoner's face was filled with a look of loathing she was all too familiar with, his pride unbroken by the bike-lock that held him firmly against the pipe.

"Has he said anything?" She asked Francis, the nervous looking young man looking like he wanted to be anywhere else.

Which was exactly why he was down here. Boy needed to toughen up if he was going to be of any use at all to her going forward. Her little faction had no room for weakness.

"No Ma'am." The boy shook his head, "not after... the boss, got finished with him at least."

Good.

"Good afternoon, Mr. Green." Sarah spoke calmly as she directed her gaze to the glaring man, "I'm terribly sorry that we had to meet this way, but I am afraid that my father and I have a few questions. Questions we would like you to answer."

"Fuck you, and your nigger loving father, you treacherous whore. I ain't telling you shit." The man tried to spit, but it seemed fear had quite dried his throat. It came off as rather pathetic really.

Quite understandable though. Unlike in the movies, it's quite difficult to come off convincingly rebellious when faced with the possibility of torture. Not even Integrity's fanatics were immune to that. It wasn't so much a matter of bravery as sanity, after all. She doubted she would do much better were she in his shoes.

Still, she didn't plan to torture him. She had observed her father use it enough times, and more often than not, the information derived was entirely unreliable.

She had her own methods of discovering what she wanted to know. "Grey, please bring down our other guests. Francis, please help Grey, and then take the rest of the day off."

Better to get him out of here. Toughening the boy up was one thing, but she didn't want to go too far and break him. His naïve little crush would only bend him to her will so far. If she pushed too hard she could end up facing the exact opposite response from what she wanted. She'd done that quite often in the early days. When she was still learning.

Naturally, Francis was almost pathetically grateful to leave, taking the elevator up with a taciturn Grey.

Which left Sarah a few minutes to herself. Completely dismissing the glaring prisoner from her thoughts, she went over to sit on a barrel of hideously expensive wine - a holdover from the days of the estate's former owner.

Flipping open her phone, she smiled when she saw that Erich hadn't even attempted to call her after her rapid departure that morning. No doubt the young man was working himself into a tizzy and burying himself in his work trying to distract himself from the possible implications, and consequences, that might arise as a result of what they had done last night.

He was adorably predictable like that. Predictable, easily controlled, morally malleable, great potential for growth, and without any real aspirations of his own.

Not awful in bed. Just a few pointers about what I like, and he might be great.

The perfect partner really.

If she didn't know any better, she might have thought her powers
were more in line with a Machina when he all but fell into her lap. Or rather, her into his.

Now if only her cow of a sister would get out of her way, every-thing would be going perfectly.

Not for the first time she considered having her half-sibling suffer an 'accident', before dismissing it.

Too suspicious. Not so soon after Death-Shriek.

She was just finishing a 'cutesy' message to her newest 'boy-friend' when Grey reappeared from the elevator, dragging two struggling sacks with her.

"Little help?" The woman said, "That pretty boy Francis fucked right off after I got them into the elevator. Little pussy."

Sarah rolled her eyes but obligingly grabbed one and dragged it over in front of their prisoner – though, not without shocking one painfully into submission first.

"Sorry for the wait, Mr. Green." Sarah said as she looked turned back to her prisoner, whose face was turning rapidly pale as realization started to dawn in his eyes. "Just had to get your wife and brother over here before we continued."

As she spoke, she reached down to unzip the bags, revealing the gagged and tearstained faces of the man's loved ones.

Even bad men had loved ones. Maybe not as many as most, but some. No one was an island. Everyone needed some connection.

And connections can be weaknesses. And weaknesses can be lever-aged.

"Now, let's try this again." She said, trying to keep the visceral excitement from her voice as her lips pulled back into a lustful smile. "Tell me everything."

ΔΔΔ

Sarah slowly started to adjust her outfit as the elevator ascended back up to ground level; her cleavage was tucked away, her hair pulled up and the ever-present sultry smile was smoothed away into something colder.

More commanding.

"One of the bags is leaking." She pointed out, stepping away from the slowly pooling puddle of blood.

Out the corner of her eye she saw Grey roll her eyes, but she dutifully reached over to firmly zip up the bag in question.

"You're just going to see your dad." Grey scoffed, dragging all three bags over toward herself.

Sarah had to resist the urge to roll her eyes in turn. It was moments like this that she had to remind herself that Grey was her second because of her dogged loyalty and talent with a gun, not her social skills or intelligence.

"Every action or inaction might sway Daddy's choice in choosing his heir. Appearances count."

Grey scoffed again, "Death-Shriek's gone, none of your other siblings have developed powers, and Gravity's Gravity."

Yes, and Sarah thanked her luck for that small mercy every day. Because if her half-sibling ever showed even the 'slightest' inclination toward leadership of the gang, Sarah knew that all her plans would be rendered utterly worthless.

Along with me. She scowled, smoothing her hair out as the slightest crackle of static electricity threatened have it rise up.

"Just get those bodies disposed of and get down to Erich's shop." She snapped, "I want you to make sure that it's only 'my' people watching over Mechromancer going forward."

Grey nodded, giving a jaunty faux military salute, before painstakingly starting to drag the body-bags out of the elevator with her. Sarah frowned in distaste at the long smear of blood they left on the floor.

Someone will need to clean that up quickly. She thought, *Last thing we need is an outsider seeing it.*

Walking toward the stairs, she directed one of the nearby lounging toughs to grab a mop and bucket to get the elevator cleaned up, and to put out the word that she was looking for another source of information. If any of the crew happened to pick up a reasonably high ranking member of the Brotherhood, then they could expect a hefty cash deposit to find its way in their bank account.

That perked the surrounding goons up. So much so that they didn't even grumble as they jogged off to find a mop.

Her father wasn't in his office, which she had half expected. She could count on one hand the number of times she had found him in there over the years. And two of those times he had been in the middle of having sex with one woman or another. Women she later had eliminated. Over the years she had stopped keeping track of the man's mistresses though.

Too much effort to reduce a risk that never really existed.

To her utter lack of surprise, he wasn't in his room either.

Which left his workshop.

When she arrived, she found him stood over some metal contraption of no immediate purpose, his powers in full swing as he moved almost entirely without conscious thought, slapping bits of metal and wire into place with seemingly little rhyme or reason.

She had heard Erich's complaints about tinker work often enough over the last few days, and seeing the slapdash mess of wires and cables - and comparing it to Erich's nice neat minimalism - she couldn't help but agree just a little with his way of thinking.

"Daddy?" She called out not entirely sure if the man would be cognizant enough to hear her.

Fortunately for her, the man looked up immediately, his hand's still moving even without his eyes to guide them. It seemed that whatever Artificer trance he was in currently, it did not require control of his conscious mind to work.

"You find out why they were stocking that crap?" The man asked irritably without preamble.

The 'crap' in question being the crates upon crates of medical machinery and supplies they had recovered from the raid on the Brotherhood's warehouse. A fact which had only further stoked Hard-Light's anger after he was informed about Chavez's death.

She shook her head, "He didn't know much more than rumors and hearsay."

Which they had half expected to be the case, given the man's relatively low place on the Brotherhood totem pole. It had always been a long shot.
Still, it hadn't been an entire waste. Rumors and gossip were still better than nothing.

Which her father knew.

"Well, let's hear it, then." He sighed.

"Many members of the Brotherhood believe that the medical equipment is being used to create new cyborg soldiers, using a new Artificer with a particular skill set."

"Possible," Hard-Light shrugged, "but unlikely. Integrity would struggle to get any great number of volunteers for the procedure. Or at least, not enough to make it worth the heat it would bring down on his head."

Sarah agreed. The drawbacks and lack of longevity of Artificer constructs were well known. Cyborgs made using them even more so. One might gain an arm cannon and the ability to jump over buildings, but within a year or two you were likely to end up in a wheelchair with one arm.

"I thought as much." Sarah agreed, "Though, I can also see why such a theory might prove popular among the Brotherhood's rank and file."

Propagating the idea that members of the Brotherhood were putting their limbs, and very lives, on the line for the glory of the gang would definitely be something the gang's higher-ups would want, not just as an added smoke screen. It would serve to raise the ranks and files morale and drive them to work harder themselves to ensure their comrades 'sacrifice' was not in vain.

"Anything on the fuck that took out Chavez's team?" Hard-Light growled, shaping the metal beneath him with his bare hands.

"Some new Meta from out of town." She said, happy to have some more concrete information. "Apparently one of their more remote branches sent him over here to make better use of his skills."

Hard-Light sighed unhappily. "Powers? Skills? Appearance? Costume?"

Sarah shook her head. "Nothing I would consider reporting. The only other thing he knew worth mentioning was the usual complaints about the Meta being arrogant, but that's nothing new. Locals don't like it when new guys muscle in on their 'turf'.

"Great." Hard-Light hissed, "An unknown new Meta in my back

yard, Brotherhood performing some kind of freaky experiments, and I've got a bunch of medical equipment my piece of shit power has no idea what the fuck to do with!"

As he finished, the bizarre contraption beneath his fingers snapped, prompting the man to throw it away in disgust. Sarah was more than familiar with the sight of a failed Artificer trance, and she also knew he father would be snappish and irritable for days because of it.

"I might be able to find a seller for the supplies." She suggested, in an attempt to assuage his anger.

"What does it matter!?" The man huffed as he stood up, veins throbbing in his neck. "I've got money. More than I know what the fuck to do with!"

He roared, throwing tools onto the floor. Sarah didn't flinch. This was something she was also more than familiar with. It might have terrified her as a gangly teen who had just been abducted from her home, but she was an adult now.

She'd survived the crucible that was her father and come out stronger for it.

"What I don't have is prestige. Is power. Is any Metas worth a damn!" The man roared, directing an accusatory glare in her direction.

She took it without flinching. It was an old pain. One she was well accustomed to.

Still, she wasn't about to stand around to be bitched at. "Right. Well, I will get out of here and see if I can't find any more information."

Hard-Light snorted and looked away, and for a moment she thought that was that. Only as she reached the door did he choose to speak up.

"Call in with that new kid. Erich. See if he's got any ideas we can use for this shit. Shifty little bastard, but he's decent enough at fixing shit I can't be bothered with."

Sarah thought that was massive understatement, but she kept her peace.

"Of course, Daddy." She said as she shut the door, leaving her father alone to brood. No doubt he'd emerge in a few hours, looking for women or drugs. Likely both.

Huffing, she flipped open her phone to check her messages and saw that Erich had already responded to her earlier one. It was a messy ramble with little in the way of a point, but it brought a small smile to her face.

So easy to push him in the direction I want him to go. She thought, luxuriating in the sensation of power and security it gave her.

With him at her side there was no limit to how much her power could-

I'm an idiot. She thought, her grin growing almost manic as her father's last words came back to her.

Excitement thudded in her chest. How had she not thought of it already?

"Stuff you couldn't be bothered with indeed, Daddy." Sarah all-but purred.

ΔΔΔ

"Sure." Erich said distractedly as he attempted to thread a cool-ant line through the suit for the second time in as many weeks.

Another woman might have been offended by the fact that he didn't even look at her as he spoke, but Sarah was well used to the peculiarities of Artificers. And while Erich clearly wasn't one himself, he shared a great many of the same traits.

It also helped her that with his head stuck inside his suit, he wasn't thinking about their current vaguely defined – for him - relationship status, and could actually answer her questions without overthinking every response.

More important than all of that though, she was overjoyed.

"Really?" She said breathlessly, "You're absolutely sure."

Erich stopped to give her a funny look, "Absolutely sure? Not a chance. I barely even know how your powers work, or what your big hang up about them is. Bloody typical, if I'm honest. You Metas are always so quick to show them off, but ask one of you to explain them and you totally clamp up."
Sarah rolled her eyes as she handed him the tool he was reaching for, "Because if someone knows how it works, then they can come up with a counter for it."

Many a Superhero or Supervillain over the years had been brought down by being a little too glib about that information. Hell, dozens of them had their strength and weakness listed on goddamn Wikipedia.

Not that hers was any great mystery. It was pretty obvious if you looked. "But if I explained it? You think you could do something about it?"

He nodded absently, "Sure."

CHAPTER 10

"So, you have to be touching someone to use your powers?" Erich asked as he sat with a notepad. "Which are electrical."

He noted with some pride that he managed to keep his voice level as he spoke. Likely helped by the fact that he was talking about work. Otherwise he wasn't too sure he would have been as calm as he was while in a room with a woman of dubious mental health, and with whom he was also involved in a vaguely defined relationship.

Sarah, in an entirely uncharacteristic move, shifted uncomfortably on one of his work benches, "I don't *have* to be touching someone, sugar. But if I don't have something to channel into, then the electrical current is likely to arc out and ground itself on whatever's convenient.

Much like conventional lightning Erich surmised. Which meant she could generate a ton of power but had no control over it. Which meant that in a fight she either had to be right next to her target or become a threat to everyone around her.

Friend or foe.

And even then, she's not guaranteed to hit her original target.

He could see why that would be considered a 'shit' power.

The entire history of human warfare could be considered an arms race in the field of attaining 'reach' after all. He who had the longer reach struck first. Even in the days of medieval warfare, it was the pike that was king of the battlefield rather than the more commonly depicted sword. After that came bows, then guns, then artillery, then intercontinental missiles. Nowadays someone could

kill a man on the other side of the planet with a satellite deployed laser orbital strike.

Yes, in all things violent, reach is king.

"Alright, I've got a pretty good idea of what to do." He said as he clambered to his feet.

"Really?" Sarah asked, skepticism and hope warring in her voice.

"Positive." He said as he started pulling the components he thought he would need out of storage. Or rather taking stock of what he had in storage. Only once he knew what he already had, would he be able to start working on blueprints.

"Gauntlet or helmet?" He asked as he examined a capacitor, before throwing it away in disgust.

"Sorry?"

"Gauntlet *or* helmet." He repeated, "As the platform for the weapon system? Which do you prefer?"

"I... gauntlet, I guess?" The woman said hesitantly, giving him a strange look as he started sorting through strands of copper wire.

"Gauntlet it is." He grunted. "Should only take a few days. I reckon it should have an effective range of a few hundred meters and be somewhere around Gunner Three. Although I won't know the exact numbers until I see it in action."

"You can make something that can fire a cable that far?"

"Easily." He said without thinking, only to pause as the Metahuman's words finally registered with him.

A cable? What does she mean by a cable?

After a few seconds thought, the penny dropped.

"I would never use anything that crude!" He said indignantly. "Far too unreliable. The reload speed alone would be horrific."

Hell, if they were going for ridiculous concepts, he might as well create some kind of electrified whip. Honestly, the nerve. Might as well have just asked him to make some kind of crossbow like that charlatan Blue Archer.

Utterly useless waste of space that he is.

His unvoiced complaints about the bow-wielding hero were cut off as two soft, and all too familiar breasts pressed into his back.

They weren't particularly large, but god were they perky.

"If you really *can* do what you're saying you can." The villainess whispered hotly into his ear, "You better be ready for me to fuck your brains out afterward."

Erich coughed, accidentally throwing his neatly stacked pile of components into disarray with his arm in the process.

"Yes... quite." He managed to muster up, before firmly clamping down on his raging libido.

She's crazy. Totally crazy. He reminded himself over and over. "Insane, crazy, cuckoo...and totally unbelievably hot..."

"Thirty grand, all up." He managed to get out.

"What?" Sarah said, partway through softly crooning.

"Thirty thousand. For parts and labor."

"The sex isn't enough?" She asked in disbelief.

Not even close.

"I don't do pro-bono work." He said after a few moments of awkward silence.

Sarah continued to stare at him, tension mounting, before finally a tiny laugh trickled out of her.

"Thirty thousand it is then."

Erich managed to stifle a sigh of relief, even as a bead of cold sweat dripped down his neck.

ΔΔΔ

"I heard you're making something to upgrade my half-sister's power."

Erich resisted the urge to slam his head into the dashboard.

Of course she waited until I was stuck in the car with her before asking.

Gravity might have liked to come off as lazy and generally absent minded – and for the most part she was – but when she put her mind to it, she could be just as slippery as her half-sister.

"I am not *upgrading* her power." He sighed in the end, "I am creating a device to better facilitate the usage of her power in the manner she desires."

In short. For murdering people.
"That's what I said."

"No, you said 'upgrading' her power." He pointed out, "Which I wouldn't even know how to start doing."

"Just jam around with her DNA, right?"

Erich frowned, "First, I'm an engineer, not a geneticist. Second, no one even knows if the Meta-gene is real."

Gravity gave him a funny look, "Of course it is. That's what everyone calls it."

Erich shook his head, wincing as one of their escort cars cut off another motorist, eliciting honks and general discontent amongst other vehicles.

"No one knows what creates powers." He said, watching the general melee forming, "When they first started appearing, a lot of people suggested that it was a result of some undetectable form of radiation. One guy even dubbed it 'Meta Radiation'."

Erich watched out the window as one honking motorist finally saw who had cut them off, and very wisely went silent once more, hunching over in his car in an attempt to seem small.

"Of course, the newly formed Heroes Guild wasn't too happy about that. The first atom bombs had just been dropped on Japan, and lots of people were suddenly very wary of anything even remotely related to the word 'radiation'. So of course, the Guild hushed up that first guy, and started to rebrand powers as being a result of the 'Meta-Gene'."

He shrugged, noting that Gravity was listening intently as they cruised down the street.

"Not that it makes much difference. Powers are powers. We still have no clue what causes them. We know children of Metas are more likely to have an Event, but that their powers tend to be weaker than spontaneous ones."

He felt his hand subtly clench as he thought of that, "But that's no argument here or there. It could be genes, it could be a result of radiation from the parent affecting the child in the womb, or it could be something entirely different."

Gravity nodded along as if all of this was news to her. Which it probably was. It wasn't exactly common knowledge.

"Wait a minute!" Gravity shouted, shearing years off his life as she accelerated slightly at the same time. "That still doesn't explain why you're making some gadget for that my bitch of a sister. Make one for me too!"

"Can't." He gasped, heart racing in his chest.

"Why not? Because she's sleeping with you?" The woman snorted, "If that's the barrier for entry, I'll pull over right now. We can find a quiet alley and I'll show you what real fucking is."

"Charming." Erich groaned, "But no. The reason I'm making one for her, and not you is because a lightning delivery system is easy. Some mystical tech that manipulates Gravity is not."

Not that there weren't Artisans out there *with* that technology, Dr. Moon came to mind as the most obvious example, but until Erich got a chance to look at a piece of said tech, he had not a clue as to how any of it worked.

Gravity mulled over his words for a few moments, and her face went through a number of emotions. Irritation. Frustration. Sadness. Irritation again, before finally, acceptance. Grudging acceptance.

"Fine." She huffed, "but I want dibs on the next cool gadget you build."

Erich resisted the urge to scoff. The next cool gadget he built was going to *him*, thank you very much. Criminal affiliation aside, he had a business to run.

Still, he was wise enough not to say that aloud. At least, not until the woman had delivered him to his favorite lunch spot - and safely escorted him back home afterward.

Irritating as she could be at times, he couldn't think of anyone else he would rather have between him and a room full of Neo-Nazi thugs.

That was also the reason he put up with his newfound shadows in the form of Hard-Light's goons. Sure, he who sacrificed free-dom for security might not *deserve* either, but he who gave up security for freedom wouldn't live long enough be enjoying it for long either.

△△△

"Do you ever think about what your life would be like if you'd been one of the 'good guys'?" Erich stopped as Gravity spoke, another spoonful of vivid red and steaming mapo tofu halfway toward his mouth.

"What, like a hero?" He asked incredulously.

"Yeah." Gravity murmured, her own meal left almost completely untouched after the first tongue scorching bite.

Immediately, Erich felt the need to look around to where Hard-Light's goons were loitering around outside, looking rough and generally making a nuisance of themselves. More importantly, too far away for them to hear anything he might say.

"When I was younger. Much younger." He said conservatively, depositing another spicy spoonful into his mouth, luxuriating in the sublime burning sensation upon his palate.

Truly, no one made mapo tofu like Mr. Lin.

"Really?" Gravity asked, ruining the moment with her skepticism.

Still, she wasn't wrong to be so. Though for different reasons than she probably suspected.

To say, even as a child, that he thought about being a hero might have been too strong. It had simply been a given. An expectation. As inevitable as the rising of the sun.

Until it wasn't.

In the end, he simply shrugged, "Even I was young and idealistic once."

Patently untrue, he reflected, but he figured that it didn't hurt to say.

"Me too." Gravity gave a sad smile, "I think most kids are."

Eric nodded in confused agreement.

"When do we grow out of it though?"

"When we realize that life is a little more complicated than 'good' and 'bad'." He said, scooping up another scorching mouthful.
"I suppose," Gravity muttered, leaning back precariously on her chair. She almost put her feet up on the table before she saw his pointed look. With a resigned grunt, she kept them on the floor.

"What started all this off anyway?" He asked offhandedly.

Gravity startled in her seat, eyes widening, before a slow lazy grin stole over her features.

"Oh? Is the great Mechromancer taking an interest in the goings on of us mere mortals?"

"Don't change the subject," He said, discreetly glancing around the room.

Gravity's smile remained in place, but the emotion slowly bled out of it, until finally she sighed and leaned back even more.

"That thing with Chavez's team." She said, "It really got me thinking about... everything."

"Really?" He asked, "I would have thought deaths weren't all that uncommon in this line of business."

"Not as common as you might think," She said, before correcting herself, "At least, not for *us*"

Erich could see that being the case. The other two factions had been tiptoeing around Hard-Light and his organization for a very long time. So long, that this sudden aggression from the Brotherhood was almost entirely out of the blue.

"So, what?" He said around another mouthful of mouth searing goodness, "You're thinking of giving up the crime game?"

"Were it so easy..." She murmured, before glancing at him, "You better not repeat what I just said."

He rolled his eyes. As if he would? Who would he tell? His many friends and acquaintances?

"I'm serious, Erich." Gravity hissed with sudden heat.

"Fine. Fine." He said, raising both his hands in surrender, "I promise not to say a word."

"I'll hold you to that." She said, giving him a long hard stare.

A comfortable silence reigned between the two as Erich continued to eat, and Gravity studiously avoided her own meal. Occasionally she would bring a fork up to her lips, only to find herself reaching for her water the moment the red concoction so much as grazed her taste buds.

It was most entertaining.

"So, you don't think about it anymore then?" She finally asked, eyes watering from the heat.

"Being a hero?" He prompted.

"Yeah." Gravity nodded.

"No." He said flatly, "My recent criminal enterprises aside, the Guild is very clear on precluding non-Metas from its ranks."

He tried not to sound resentful about that, but he was sure he was entirely unsuccessful.

"What if that didn't matter though?" She said, leaning in, "What if all the crime and the Meta shit wasn't a factor?"

He raised an eyebrow at her, but nonetheless deliberated over the question for a few lengthy seconds.

Be a hero? Like his older sister? His parents and his grandparents?

"No." He said flatly, ignoring the wince that passed over Gravity's eager face.

"You going to elaborate?" She asked after a few seconds passed.

He looked her dead in the eyes as he answered.

"No."

The ride back was mostly silent. Erich didn't mind. His belly was full of delicious food. He had money in the bank. And he had an interesting project on his workbench. His relationship status could do with a little less complication, but he could live with that.

Hopefully.

Compared to all that, the strange mood that had come over Gravity was hardly worth worrying about. If his friend - and he couldn't believe he used that word – was having some sort of crisis of faith, then it was up to her to work through it. He doubted any words he might have to give would be of any help. He could only hope she worked through whatever conundrum she was suffering before they were invariably drawn into the next gang related shootout.

He half expected a shot to come ringing through the window as he thought those words; an inevitable result of him tempting fate. As luck would have it though, nothing happened, and the pair made it back to the shop without incident.

Things must have been looking up for him.

CHAPTER 11

"I can't believe this shit." Frank sighed as he threw his cards down onto the tipped over fridge they were using as an impromptu poker table.

Jack wasn't much better, the younger man audibly grinding his teeth as he dropped his cards.

"Believe what? That you're losing so hard?" Rose, the sole female present at their little poker game, grinned as she leaned forward to scoop up her winnings.

"Yes. No!" The older man hissed, running a hand through his jet black hair in irritation. "What are we even doing here?"

Rose sent a confused sidelong glance at Jack, who just shrugged in his taciturn way.

Zero help there. She thought, taking a deep breath of the cool night air.

"Guarding the junkyard?" She said slowly.

It wasn't the most glamorous or exciting work, but it had to be done. The boss would be furious if anything happened to one of his premiere sources for parts. Never mind the fact that the guy owned at least two other sites just like this one, that were either equivalent or larger.

Not that Rose would ever voice that opinion aloud. Dissenters in Hard-Light's organization had a nasty tendency to disappear when they got too vocal. If the mad-dog that was his daughter didn't get to you, then the old man himself did.

Which was why Rose felt more than just a little nervous as Frank continued to speak.

"Why are we here, when we could be out there? Showing the Brotherhood who really owns this city."

"We hit that warehouse of theirs the other week." She pointed out, hoping to quiet the man down before someone overhead him. "Even brought that new Meta along."

"Mechro-something." Jack said.

"Yeah, that." Rose said, game thoroughly forgotten as she attempted to keep her erstwhile friend from killing himself via pissed off Meta.

Unfortunately for her, Frank just shook his head. "So, what? We get this new Meta, and we kill, eight, maybe nine of their guys tops?"

It didn't need to be said that they had lost far more than that in return. The news of what had happened to Chavez's team had shot through the ranks like shit through a goose. No one wanted to say it, but people were nervous.

For years they had thought themselves invincible, but recent events had firmly shattered that illusion.

"We got a bunch of machine shit though." She pointed out, more to convince herself than anyone else, "The boss could use that to whip up... something."

"Medical equipment." Jack said. "Friend of mine says the boss has been raging around the mansion all week. Everyone knows that means he hasn't been able to build anything."

Rose scowled. "That's got to be bullshit. Why the fuck would the
Brotherhood be stockpiling medical equipment?"

J. R. Grey

They were Neo-Nazis, not the Red Cross.

Jack was about to respond when the lights went out.

Not just in their little clearing, but all over the junkyard; shouts of surprise coming from their fellow gang members as their guard posts were plunged into darkness.

"Fucking cheap ass generator." Jack growled, pulling out his phone and turning on the flashlight. "Got an Artificer for a boss, and still can't get shit to work properly."

Rose agreed wholeheartedly, but wisely kept her thoughts to herself.

"Sam isn't answering her phone." Jack said sullenly as he glanced at his own.

Because she's probably already trying to fix the generator. The twitchy mechanic wouldn't be sitting on her ass when it was her ass on the line.

"Well, fuck it." Jack said, already moving off in the direction of the generator. "I'm not waiting around in the dark for her to *maybe* start fixing it."

Rose felt a bit leery about leaving their post, but seeing Jack start striding off after the other man got her moving.

Better than sitting in the dark alone.

She could hear voices from all over the junkyard, and lights moving around as people tried to figure out what was going on. No one was particularly alarmed though. This wasn't the first time this had
happened, and probably wouldn't be the last.

Still, Rose couldn't deny that the Junkyard was pretty freaky when illuminated just by the light of their phones. Jutting junk and cars took on a distinctly ominous tone as shadows twirled

134

to and fro in the gloom.

Despite the ridiculousness of it, Rose found herself reaching for the comforting grip of her pistol. Sure, it wasn't one of the fancy laser ones that Hard-Light's inner circle got, but it had served her well enough in the years since she had joined the gang.

Not that she'd ever had reason to fire it.

The few times she'd been called in to force a belligerent business owner to pay up, just waving it around had been enough to get the job done. To be honest, she wasn't entirely sure she could shoot someone if it came down to it. She wasn't in the criminal life for a love of violence. She'd just kind of... fallen into it. A not uncommon story in this line of work.

"Someone talk about something." Frank said from ahead of them as they wandered through piles of rusty junk.

"About what?" Jack asked.

"I don't know... How are the kids?"

"Fine." Jack responded in his typical way, killing the conversation before it even started.

Despite herself, Rose chuckled.

It was just so ridiculous. Here they were, three hardcore 'criminals' getting nervous because of a little darkness. Why she-

"Fuck."

She'd almost walked into Frank after the man had come to a sudden stop. "What's the matter? Stepped in shit again?"

She'd told the patrols time and time again to pick up after the guard dogs, but they never did.

"No." Frank said, deadly serious.

Stomach sinking, Rose looked over to see what the man was

looking at.

"Christ!" She shrieked, tripping over as she stepped backward.

It was Sam and her boyfriend. Dead and swinging in the breeze. High tension cable wrapped round their necks, before being strung up from a crane.

"Just like Chavez." Jack breathed.

Rose agreed. She hadn't seen it, but she heard about it. Everyone in Hard-Light's gang had. Blood running cold, she clambered back up to her feet, gun in hand.

"We've got to get back to the others."

They would be safer with numbers. Not a fucking chance they were dealing with this alone.

Ahead of her, the two men nodded, drawing their guns. Determinedly the trio started going back the way they had come. Unfortunately, they'd only traveled a few meters when it started up; Screams. Shouts. The occasional burst of gunfire. Coming from all over the junkyard.

Like something out of a bad horror flick. Rose thought.

Barely a minute later they started coming across bodies. Sometimes alone. Sometimes as part of a group. Throats sliced open, strung aloft with cable, or simply run through with a blade, the handles still sticking out of them.

Just like with Chavez's team.

It was the third such gruesome tableau that finally broke her will.

"Fuck this." She hissed. "Let's get the fuck out of here."

"Right," Frank nodded from ahead of her, "We're going to pick up the- Where's Jack?"

Rose's light and gun whipped around to show artificial alleys made from discarded junk, but no man.

He was right fucking there!

"Do... do we go look for him?" She asked.

The look Frank gave was totally incredulous. Instead of answering, he simply turned around and started jogging in the direction of the exit, only a few errant steps away from sprinting. Rose took off after him, heart racing in her chest as her breathing echoed in her ears.

There was no warning before it happened. Just a low whistle of something flying through the air, and Frank collapsed. He let out a wet gurgle as Rose jumped over him, the woman not bothering to look back as she sprinted for the exit.

She only made it a few more feet before something hit her in the head, sending her sprawling to the dirt. It was a small miracle that she managed to hold onto her phone, but her pistol went sailing off
into the darkness.

Arms skinned and bleeding, she started to crawl toward where she thought it had fallen, only to groan in pain as something slammed into her back, pinning her to the floor.

"Please." She gasped, trying to move despite the foot pressed into her back.

"Poorly balanced mass-produced garbage." A voice above her snorted in disgust. Whoever it was, their voice was totally distorted, almost as if they were garbling marbles when they spoke.

Just to her left, she saw what had hit her; a throwing knife, now lying in the dirt.

"I surrender." She cried, "Please... Please don't kill me."

"Why do the scum always whine so much." The voice asked rhetorically. "You're all so content to strut around, proclaiming yourselves rulers of this city. But when you're down on your luck, and at someone else's mercy, you all say the same things. 'Mercy. Don't kill me. I have rights.'"

"At least try and die with some dignity."

"No, wait-

△△△

Sarah couldn't help but feel slightly disappointed when she wandered in to find Erich working on the suit. Never mind the fact that she'd been dreaming of having a more powerful ability since she'd been a little girl.

With deliberate calm she walked over to the man, who was yet again fiddling with the coolant system.

"Hello Erich," She said, "Any progress on my gauntlet?"

The man didn't respond, and for a second she had to resist the urge to shock him to attention as his torso remained firmly inside the suit's.

Fuck it.

"Erich!" She said, letting rip with a small jolt of power.

A loud thunk, and a few curses later, Erich emerged from the suit, rubbing his head and looking more than a little irate.

"What!?" He groused, staring daggers at her.

Normally she knew he would never summon up the audacity for such an act, but when around his tech she knew he had the tendency to be... shortsighted.

"The gauntlet?" She repeated, "What progress have you made?"

With any luck he would have gotten the parts he needed together and could really start his planning in-

"Over there. On the table." He motioned, before clambering back inside the suit. "And don't fucking do that again."

For just a moment, Sarah was struck dumb. Only for a moment though, and the second it passed her feet were clattering along the floor as she all but sprinted over to the table.

There they were. Just as he said they'd be.

More than that, there was not one, but two shiny new gauntlets, rife with technological components.

They weren't exactly stylish or eye catching, but they did have a rustic utilitarianism to them. Not that she much cared how they looked, just so long as they worked.

With almost indecent haste she started pulling them on, only to realize once they were on her hands that she had no clue how they worked.

"Erich." She called, "How do I activate them."

"Just aim in the direction you want them to go and push your power into the palms." The man said automatically.

It was almost two seconds later that he realized what he had just done.

"Outside! Outside!"

"Too late." Sarah sing-songed.

Aiming at the wall of the workshop, Sarah excitedly pumped as much power as she could into her hands.

With instant results.

The sound and light were deafening, as honest to god lightning leapt from her very fingertips to lance against the wall with all

the fire and fury of a bolt from Zeus himself.

It was awe inspiring. An entire thunderstorm encapsulated in her very palm.

Then it was over, and they were left with cherry red and partially melted walls, small residual arcs of electricity sparking across the
place, and the overpowering stench of ozone in the air.

Sarah collapsed to her knees, too overwhelmed with emotion to stay standing.

Erich felt like doing much the same, only for entirely different reasons.

"Again." He whined, seeing the second hole to be punched into the wall of his shop. He still hadn't fixed the one left by his first meeting with Gravity.

Sarah didn't care. She was overjoyed. Beyond overjoyed. The power, the smell, the sensation of it all. It was ecstasy. Beyond ecstasy.

"How does it work?" She breathed huskily.

There had been no cable. Nothing launched from the glove. No delay either. Just a long uninterrupted stream of unyielding electrical power.

Power felt without limits. She thought, heat blazing in her chest. *Unlimited power.*

Erich was not nearly so enthused, turning away from the hole in his wall with a sigh.

"Basically, the lightning gets shot down a laser beam." He said, bringing his shirt up over his face to protect against the stink. "The fingertips of the gloves have very small laser lenses in them, which can't do much by themselves, but combined with your power, they can shoot an incredibly short pulse of high energy light. One powerful enough to create an electromagnetic field around it."

Sarah didn't really understand the science of what he was saying,
but damned if the words weren't passing right through her and down to her... core. Almost of their own accord, her hands started to roam.

"The electromagnetic field is so powerful that it can rip electrons in the air, creating a needle thin pathway of plasma." Erich continued, not even looking at her to notice what she was doing.

"And since plasma is a better conductor for electricity than air, the lightning travels along that instead." Sarah all but moaned, marveling at the elegance of it. "Straight to the target."

"Yeah," Erich shrugged, missing the heat in her voice as he preened. "That's basically it. Pretty simple application of basic science when you get right down to it."

Maybe to him.

Sarah knew Hard-Light wouldn't have thought of such a system in a hundred years, and she knew she certainly hadn't. And she'd had more than enough incentive to try.

She watched with glazed eyes as Erich threw a tarp over the suit, before walking over to open the sliding doors. A gentle breeze blowing through the room as he did, dissipating some of the stench.

Sarah sighed as it caressed her heated and sweaty skin. The things she could do with these gauntlets. The power she held.

Ignorant of her thoughts, Erich was still chattering away. "Honestly, it was pretty easy to do. Didn't need to add in batteries or a power source of any kind. Which helped me keep them small. Honestly, the hardest part was finding a conductor for the palm that wouldn't melt with the sheer amount of juice you were going to be putting through it."

She was halfway through tearing her top off, entirely ready to act on her earlier promise of fucking the insufferable genius's brains out, when Gravity ran in. Dripping wet from the shower, and without a shred of clothing to protect her modesty.

"We under attack!? What the fuck was that noise!?" She shouted, gun ready, only to recoil as the smell hit her, "Ugh, what the fuck is that smell?" Then her eyes finally alighted on Sarah.

Or more specifically, the gauntlets on her hands. Then, almost of their own accord, her eyes tracked toward the massive blackened crater in Erich's wall.

"Oh, for fucks sake." The nude woman groaned. "That's just fucking unfair."

At which point, Erich finally noticed that no one was listening to him, and was stuck between looking indignant, and goggling at the nearly naked, and entirely naked, women on display.

Which was the exact scene Hard-Light's goons ran in to see, having been drawn by the sound of the gauntlets going off.

"Holy shit." One man whispered as he surveyed the entirety of it, although whether it was the nudity on display, or the damage that drew the oath, no one could say.

Though more than one man and woman agreed with him on both accounts.

CHAPTER 12

"I call dibs on the strip club." Erich said, firmly putting his finger over the building's location on the map.

Across from him he heard a hastily aborted laugh from Gravity, though Sarah and Hard-Light looked far less amused. Erich found himself regretting his spontaneous outburst, as the air in the hastily converted war-room started to grow ever more tense.

He firmly kept his finger on the map though.

"Fine." Hard-Light eventually sighed, bringing up a hand to massage the bridge of his nose, "The kid gets to hit the titty bar."

Inwardly fist pumping, Erich deliberately didn't look at Sarah, who had quickly turned her glare on her father.

"Daddy!" She cried.

"We're all hitting different targets anyway, so it was going to be one of us going. May as well let the kid have the titty bar if he wants it so much." As the man spoke, he deliberately glanced down at Sarah's gauntlets; which were still on her hands even though there was no need for them in the middle of Hard-Light's mansion. "I figure he's earned that much."

Sarah looked like she wanted to complain, but after a few moments thought, she settled down. Though not without a final seething glance in Erich's direction, which the Engineer studiously pretended not to see.

All the while, Gravity watched on with barely contained mirth.

Erich didn't care. He was content to let his three compatriots believe his choice in target was for an entirely puerile reason.

It wasn't.

He got enough bare tits flashed his way at home as it was. No, he had picked the strip club because it was likely to be the least defended of the available targets.

Hell, if it had more than a bouncer or two for security, he would be surprised.

"Right, so Erich's hitting the titty bar. I'm hitting another warehouse. Sarah's hitting a drug lab. Where are you going?" Gravity asked, directing a speculative glance at Hard-Light.

"I'm hitting Integrity's little club house." The man grunted.

Sarah gasped, and even Gravity looked a little taken back. Erich didn't have any reaction at all. He didn't know what the 'club house' was – or more importantly, care.

"Daddy you can't!" Sarah pleaded, her hair rising as static crackled through it. "Half the Brotherhood's Metas could be there."

"Much as I hate to agree with her, she's right." Gravity chipped in. "Not even you can just waltz in and out of that place."

"Doesn't matter." Hard-Light ground out. "If we're going to find the fuck who killed my people, we need to search the most likely spots."

The man shrugged, "Besides, I think you're both underestimating me. In fact, I think everyone is, including the fucking Brotherhood." There was a light hum in the air as the man's iconic energy swords came to life, "I think it's high-time I reminded those Nazi fucks who the scariest Meta in this shithole of a city is."

This time it was Gravity who looked like she wanted to argue, but much like Sarah before her, ultimately kept her peace. She didn't even bother with a venomous look either, as she moved over to sprawl out on a chair once more.

"Whatever. It's your funeral old man." She muttered.

"What was that?" The man in question asked, a dangerous edge entering his tone. One that sent shivers up Erich's spine.

"Nothing." Gravity said, paling as she suddenly sat up straight.

"Fucking right." The Artificer said, swords dissipating into motes of light. The tension in the room dropping back down to normal levels only a few moments later.

That was not quick enough for some though.

I think I might need a new pair of pants. Erich whimpered in his mind, and judging by the look on Gravity's face, he wasn't the only one.

"Alright, now that Olivia is quite done wasting time," Sarah said, completely unflustered by her father's show of force, and apparently over her earlier horror, or at least hiding it. "I would say we need to move onto picking out teams for this little operation.".

"Right," Hard-Light grunted, "The kid can take Smith's team. You can take Grey's. Gravity can take Lopez's, and I'll take Grant's and Tyler's."

Sarah thought it over for a second.

"Actually, I think I'll take Smith's team. With Sam gone he's still pretty new to leadership, and I'd rather keep a close on eye on him for now. Grey's team can go with Mechromancer."
Hard-Light just waved his hand as if to say he didn't care. Which he probably didn't to be honest. Hard-Light was bit more 'reality focused' than most Artificer's tended to be, but not by much.

In the two months or so that Erich had been in the gang, he

had discovered that the actual 'running' of the place was pretty much left to Sarah. Hard-Light was ironically, both a cornerstone of the gang and a figurehead.

"What are we doing if we encounter the 'Ghost'?" Erich asked, as he turned his thoughts back to the situation at hand.

Gravity quirked an eyebrow at him. "How do *you* know that name?"

"...by talking to people?" He said uncertainly.

"Yeah right." The woman snorted, "You don't talk to anyone. You barely talk to us and we *live* with you."

Erich wanted to point out that Sarah didn't live with him, but she was over often enough that it was kind of a moot point.

"Grey probably told him." Sarah said distractedly, eyes still firmly on the map, "I put her on his guard detail, and I've seen him talking to her once or twice."

"Oh?" Gravity smiled, "Has a new woman entered our dear Mechromancer's life? Trying to turn yourself into a real Mech-Ro-mancer?"

"If I had a gun on me, I would shoot you for that god-awful pun." Erich deadpanned. "And *she's* been talking to *me*."

And for the life of him he couldn't figure out why. The tall and gangly tattooed woman had even less in common with him than the sisters with zero mechanical aptitude at all. From what he could tell,
she wasn't even enjoying it.

"Sounds about right." Gravity grunted, slouching back into her seat. "God forbid you sought out human companionship yourself."

Erich shot a glare at her before talking a calming breath. "My incredibly small social circle aside, I can't help but note that none of you have said what to do if we encounter the Ghost."

Which probably wasn't the guy's Cape name, but it was what Hard-Light's goons had taken to calling him. The slaughter of Chavez's team, and then later at the junkyard, had made more than a mark on all their psyches.

"The whole purpose of this operation is to smoke them out of hiding, and yet I've heard zero comment on how we plan to actually take them down once we do." He continued.

Sarah looked slightly uncomfortable as she finally looked up from the map, Gravity's grin had turned decidedly wooden, and even Hard-Light's surly scowl had faded somewhat.

"We don't know." The old man grumbled. "They haven't left any survivors, so we don't know what his or her powers are."

Sarah bucked up a bit, "But on both occasions they were active, it was at night, and only against human targets. So we are striking during the day, and keeping our Metas with our teams."

Great. So they were winging it and hoping for the best. Once more he praised his foresight in picking the strip club.

Sarah look him dead in the eyes, "I would also remind you that this operation has a secondary purpose. In the event that we do *not* encounter the Ghost, it's almost a given that we will find other members of their senior leadership."
Who *would* have information on the new Meta in the Brotherhood's ranks. Along with a host of other useful bits of information vital to prosecuting the continuing conflict. Sarah had already stressed to all of them that she wanted at least *one* of those people alive.

"Fine." Erich sighed, running a hand through his hair, "I guess I'll just have to improvise something."

Gravity smirked from her position at the back, "Chin up, Erich. You've already taken down two Metas. What's one more?"

Two too many. He thought.

△△△

As Hard-Light's small army got loaded up and ready to pile into vans, Erich couldn't help but notice one small fact.

It hadn't gotten any smaller. Or at least, not appreciably smaller given the slaughter at the Junkyard the other week. Never mind the various small conflicts between rival gangs' members that had been occurring sporadically over the course of the feud.

He almost instinctively turned to ask Gravity what the deal was, only to realize she was over with her own team. So instead, he reluctantly turned to Grey.

"Irregulars." The woman said as phlegmatically as ever.

Which then lead onto a particularly long discussion on the exact make up of Hard-Light's gang. Or at least, long for both individuals involved. Erich loathed social contact as much as any put-upon genius, and Grey just wasn't particularly talkative, despite her apparent irrational desire to be in his presence at the shop.

Which ironically, despite his words at the briefing, was one of the reasons he rather enjoyed her company. When Sarah was around, the woman could be positively chatty -if a little crude, but when her boss was gone, Grey could be relied upon to stand in stoic silence, occasionally handing him tools, while watching him work on whatever project needed doing.

It was almost as if the life went out of her whenever the blonde left her general vicinity. Which was a positive change as far Erich was concerned. It certainly made her more tolerable to him than most people he came across.

ΔΔΔ

"...So you're saying that Hard-Light's organization only really has about fifty core members? The rest are more or less just menials and hangers-on? Bodies to crew his facilities?" Erick summarised.

The tall woman nodded, absently listening to her earpiece, much as she had been the through the entire explanation. Not even once on the entire ride over had he seen her switch channel or turn it off.

"We're here." She said without preamble, clambering out of the van and onto a non-descript, if a little rundown, street.

Erich trooped out after her, his suit whirring as the synthmuscles within warmed up again after the long drive over. It had been uncomfortable sitting in complete stillness within the immobile suit for the entire car-ride, and he found himself luxuriating in the sensation of being able to move his limbs once more.

"How are things going with the other teams?" He asked as he turned around to get a good look at the area they were in.

"Fine." Grey said, as she watched her people disembarking from their group's second van – a concession that had to be made given
the size of his suit. "Gravity and Sarah are still en-route to their destinations, and Hard-Light has engaged three Meta individuals at his."

Erich nearly choked on air at the woman's casual utterance that Hard-Light was currently fighting *three* enemy Metas.

Scary motherfucker or not, that was still a tall order.

"Is he going to be ok!?"

The tattooed woman gave him an incredulous look – or at least, as incredulous a look as she seemed capable of mustering.

"He'll be fine."

Erich wasn't quite so sure, but he figured it would be wiser to keep his doubts to himself.

Besides, he figured. *I should probably focus on my own task.*

No matter how much of a cake walk it was going to be.

It was at that moment that the van across from him exploded.

The sudden fireball sent panicked goons hurtling, either to the floor, or the nearest bit of cover. Erich wasn't much better, ducking pointlessly as a flaming chunk of debris whipped past his armored head.

Rocket. He thought numbly. *That was a rocket.*

The emotion swept back in once more, filling his world with sight and sound. Why did they have a rocket launcher? Why would they use it? Surely that violated *some* unwritten rule of street gang violence.
More importantly, could his suit survive a rocket to the chest?

Probably. Though it wouldn't be much fun or leave me with much in the way of shields afterward... He guessed.

Could his suit survive two rockets to the chest?

Not a fucking chance. He snarled as he looked around for the nearest piece of cover, only to realize that there wasn't any. Or at least, not any that wouldn't detonate violently when struck by a fucking rocket.

"Did anyone see where it came from!?" He asked franticly over the comms, struggling to be heard over the frantic chatter of the thoroughly surprised squad of criminals.

"Second story window of the target location," Grey's calm voice answered back, somehow perfectly clear over the noise.

Erich's eyes panned over to the spot, and sure enough, there was a rocket launcher poking out the second story window of the strip club.

What was even more surprising, even than the choice of weapon, was that the woman holding it was clad – or unclad – in clothes that left little illusion as to how she made a living. From other windows he could guns emerging, as more women, and some scantily clad men, joined the fray.

"Nazi strippers," Erich murmured in disbelief before he raised his arm. "Aim assist on."

"Acknowledged." Gravity's somber voice came though the speakers, just before Erich fired. The force blast took the rocket wielding young woman straight in the forehead, which whipped back with what was likely an audible crack if he'd been close
enough to hear it.

Only, as she fell, one of her colleagues ran over to deftly scoop up the weapon, bringing up to his shoulder with surprising competence. Erich was about to fire again, buoyed by the fact that his own allies had started to return fire.

"Shield at ninety percent." Cursing, he realized that he was still standing out in the open like an idiot. Firing again and taking out the second rocket wielder, he searched around for cover, only to belatedly realize there was none. Or at least, none that would hide his massive bulk.

Even the still reasonably intact van was starting to look like swiss cheese as more and more shots peppered it.

Which left him only one option really. No matter how much he didn't want to take it.

"I'm going in!" He yelled through the suit's massive external speakers, suit humming as he charged toward the closed purple doors of the strip club.

Fire redoubled against his shields as the occupants within realized what he was doing, Gravity's voice informing that his shields were now at eighty percent.

But it was too little too late. He slammed against the building's doors with the force of a runaway train, shattering them as he crashed inside.

The sudden muting of the gunfire outside was odd, as he was left only with the humming of his suit and his panting breaths. It was an odd effect. Perhaps a result of some clever sound proofing with the places garish lilac curtains. It felt almost like he'd just stepped into another world. An effect only reinforced by the fact that the
entranceway was completely empty of defenders.

How peculiar Erich thought. *Shouldn't the entrance at the very least be guarded?*

Still it gave him a moment to catch his breath and survey the place. In truth he had never actually been in a strip club before, and despite himself, his eyes wandered just a little over the place's cheesy décor. That which he could see through the hall's second set of interior doors, gloomy interior and high intensity spotlights. Of course, that was the moment one particularly brave, or stupid, employee emerged from them to blast him full in the chest with a shotgun.

It achieved little beyond create a negligible decrease in his shields, but it did serve to remind Erich that he was here to destroy the place, not critique it's interior. Not matter how in need of critiquing it was.

Erich blasted his attacker with casual ease, ignoring the crack as the man flew back through the doors. Only, as he stepped forward to continue his assault once more, he heard it.

Squelch?

Heart filling with dread, he looked down to where the offending noise came from.

"It would seem the entrance was not entirely undefended after all, He thought with growing resignation. *I'm going to have to break out bucket again.*

Assuming he lived long enough to do so, he thought, as he heard the sound of trampling feet heading his way.

"Death by Nazi strippers." He muttered, "Sis, if only you could see me now."

CHAPTER 13

"Could you, uh, quit doing that boss?" Smith asked, the blonde young man stuttering from his spot on the van's bench. "Your kind of making the rest of us nervous."

Sarah gave him a considering look, eyes roaming over the rest of his team as she continued intermittently releasing sparks from her newest toys.

"Bronte." She said.

"...Bronte?" The team leader asked in confusion, eyes intermittently flitting towards her hands.

"My new cape name is Bronte." Sarah smiled happily, "After the Greek goddess of lightning."

Now that she finally had a power worthy of having a title, she'd been doing some research on what one she wanted. In the end she'd narrowed her choices down to the two divine hand-maidens of Zeus. It had been difficult choosing between the twin goddesses of lightning and thunder, but eventually she decided that Bronte had less unfortunate overtones to it than her sister, Astrape.

Seeing the skepticism on the team leaders face, she let loose with another crackle of power, enjoying the way those in the van with her leaned away from the noise and the smell.

"You don't like it?"

The chorus of affirmations for her new name was music to her ears.

Of course, she knew it was entirely fear talking, but that was fine. The novelty of it being her own power to elicit it, not fear of reprisal
from her father, had yet to wear off.

Still, it did her little good to terrify her entire team into puddles before the mission even began. She needed them to be in some state to fight when they finally disembarked. So, with more than a little reluctance, she finally stopped flaring her powers. Though she did enjoy the barely audible sighs of relief that passed through the van as she did.

"Five minutes out," the driver's voice called through the grill connecting the back to the front cabin. The man's fear was tangible, but it was only to be expected. He wasn't part of the organization's core. Just another nobody grabbed from one of their fringe businesses.

A part of her wondered if the man even knew he was working for a supervillain before today.

Absently, she started to check over her equipment. Her barriers were functioning fine and her laser pistol was sat on her belt, fully charged.

Most importantly though, her gauntlets were ready.

Oh, how excited she was to finally put them to use.

A few moments listening to the organization's communications told her that her father had already engaged the enemy... and to her surprise, so had Mechromancer.

Ha.

She wasn't a great believer in karma - it was a bit hard to be a supervillain if you were - but she certainly felt there was some greater cosmic force at work there.

Still, as amusing as it was, it was also alarming. Strip clubs being defended by sex workers wielding rocket launchers was not the norm.

Nor was Integrity's home having only three Metas present.

Something very peculiar was going on with the Brotherhood, but she had not a clue what it was. Which only reinforced the need for these missions. They needed some information on what was going on with the Neo-Nazis.

"Equipment check!" She barked out to the team with a vicious grin, receiving a number of affirmatives from the group.

As core members of the organization, they were fully fitted out with barriers and laser rifles. Some even had masks designed to imitate Hard-Light's own skull theme, as well as provide some minor vision enhancements in low light conditions.

Not that they would be needing them today, given that the sun was high in the sky. Perfect for ambushing an opponent who had only operated at night thus far.

"My barrier's not working properly." A young woman near the door called out, "It keeps flickering on and off."

Sarah cursed.

Typical Meta-tech unreliability, She huffed. One reason amongst many that not everyone was running around with the advanced technology. An Artificer could only create so much stuff before maintenance became a full-time affair.

Still, nothing she could do about it now.

"Then I would advise not getting shot." She shrugged.
"Yes, ma'am." The girl swallowed nervously.

"We'll be pulling up any minute." The man said, "I can see people out front... I think they know we're coming."

Sarah scowled. Either the Brotherhood's communications were

more on the ball than they had anticipated, or someone had blabbed. And given that a strip-club of all things was apparently putting up stiff resistance against what should have been a surprise attack, she knew where she was putting her money.

"Pull over here then." She shouted back, "No point in is getting to the originally planned point if we all die before even getting out the van."

"Will do." The man said, utterly failing to hide the relief in his voice.

Sarah shifted in her seat slightly as the van decelerated with the sound of shrieking brakes.

"Out." She instructed before they had even fully stopped moving.

Newness of their leader aside, this team had done a number of raids just like this over the years - albeit usually against softer opposition - and obligingly piled out with a promptness borne from experience.

Sarah piled out last, keeping low to the ground so best to use the wall of shields created by her underlings personal barriers. Gangster usually weren't much for 'training' as such, but the 'shield wall' technique had certainly been drilled into them over the years.

Rounds started to ping toward them, but Sarah was already glancing through the press of bodies toward likely spots for cover. Patting individuals on the shoulder to get their attention, she started directing people towards the best positions available. When
there were only two people left, she used them as mobile cover to get to her own position, moving along by guiding them both by the shoulders while they continued to shoot.

During her brief time out in the open she'd counted about three dozen Brotherhood goon's moving about, though as she peeked out from cover again, she saw that a good eight of those had been downed already.

Her own people had taken zero losses in return; more a result of their superior equipment than any great disparity in skill. Barriers allowed her people to peek up and shoot for longer, and their laser weapons burnt through all but the hardiest of cover. Even a glancing hit from the overpowered weapon systems could be debilitating.

Though not nearly as debilitating as being hit by one of my new toys.

She was tempted to just start blazing away with her own powers, but she resisted the urge.

She had to keep her mind on the tactical situation, not get caught up in the thrill of a firefight. Her time would come, it was just a matter of waiting for that ideal moment. One where she would get the maximum impact from unveiling her new ability.

Despite the fact that the firefight had started with her people outnumbered almost three times over, it was the Brotherhood who broke first; retreating back to the rundown apartment building that they had repurposed both as a safehouse and drug lab.

Sarah drew her pistol and aimed a few leisurely bursts at the retreating figures. Once upon a time she would have been forced to use single shots, but Erich's upgrades had done a lot to nullify the weapons inevitable overheating issues.
I really should get him to look at the rifles too. She thought as she observed one of her people plinking away with single shots. *It's such a waste to not be able fire automatically when the weapons are almost entirely without recoil.*

Of course, dragging Erich away from the suit would be a task in and of itself. As would negotiating him down from whatever extravagant fee he would no doubt charge for the service itself. It would be more than worth it, but it was still more than she was willing to spend.

Hard-Light might have thought that money was of no importance to the organization, but he wasn't the one who balanced the books. They were well off, yes, but that was no call to spend money recklessly.

Sarah watched dispassionately as one final fleeing figure tumbled to the pavement just outside the doors to the apartment complex, her back torn open and steaming where it had been struck by a laser.

By her count, only about ten had made it inside, but it was possible there were more skinheads who had not taken part in the outside skirmish.

"Let's get moving." She said as she rose up, "We don't want to give them time to barricade the doors."

"We've got wounded, boss." Smith trotted over, "Jenny took a round to her shoulder."

Sarah looked over, *Ah, the young girl with the faulty barrier.*

"Will she survive another half hour?" She asked, returning her gaze to the door.

Smith furrowed his brows, "I'm not a doctor so I couldn't…"
Sarah sighed, "Is she screaming and spraying blood everywhere? Or clammy and unconscious?"

"No, ma'am." The leader said. "She's awake and complaining about it."

"Then she'll live." Sarah said decisively, "Have someone help her back to the van and then catch up with us."

Smith frowned, but conveyed the orders to one of his teammates.

A token attempt was being made to barricade the door from the other side when they arrived at the entrance of the apartment complex, but a few rounds through the flimsy metal doorway discouraged the defenders from continuing.

"Break it open." She said as she heard the sound of rapidly retreating footsteps.

One of her people shot open the lock, and then broke the door open with a few well-placed shoulder bashes.

Letting a few of her people go in first, she stepped inside to discover the corpse of one unlucky defender, and no other members of the Brotherhood in sight.

"They must be either waiting for us further inside, or they're trying to escape out the back." She surmised

Part of her wished she'd put people around the outside entrances to prepare against exactly that, but she didn't have enough people to maintain a proper assault and surround the place. Not if they encountered an enemy Meta.

"Right, let's get moving," She said.

As it turned out, the Brotherhood had hunkered down on the second level of all places - likely as a result of panic and the location of the lab. The end result of which was that the new firefight was taking place in a myriad of rundown halls and apartments.

Sarah and her people were pulled into a drawn out game of cat and mouse as they were forced to hunt the skinheads down room by room.

Which was actually to her people's advantage. Sure, the Nazis had the home field advantage, but the tight confines of the building's hallways acting as a natural funnel. And within the concrete jungle the Brotherhood were utterly incapable of bringing their superior numbers to bear.

And even if they managed to get the drop on one of her people, their hard-light barriers were more than sufficient to let them sustain the surprise blow and turn it around on the unfortunate ambusher.

As was the case when Sarah stepped into a room and physically collided with an assault rifle wielding young man, bowling them both to the ground. As she clambered to her feet, she noted that under different circumstances she might have considered the man across from to be very attractive.

In a bulkier, more muscular, Erich sort of way.

Of course, knowing that he was a Nazi did quite a bit to sour the appeal of his obvious muscles, chiseled jaw and high aristocratic features.

Such a waste.

With a sigh she launched forward to grab at him, one hand around his bare wrist, as he tried to bring his gun around.
"Do me a favor and don't shit yourself." She hissed, looking into his startled eyes, just before she let rip with her power.

Nothing ruined the elation of a good kill like the smell of freshly cooked human faeces.

ΔΔΔ

"We're done! We're done!"

Erich sighed in relief as one stripper threw down her weapon. Then another. And another. Until finally every weapon not being held by a member of Hard-Light's crew was on the floor.

The eight odd members that remained.

Two of them had caught bullets during the firefight and definitely weren't getting back up. He assumed. He hadn't really looked if he was totally honest. He had his own problems at the time.

Speaking of which...

Cautiously, he looked over at the readout on his shields.

Thirty two percent.

Too low. Much too low.

Even *with* the shields still up, his left leg was moving a little slower than it should, which made him think something had managed to slip past the barrier system and damage the delicate joint. More importantly, his left pulse blaster was entirely out of commission after he overheated it barely five minutes into the fight.

Not that I had much of a choice.

Operational safety limits were one thing when you were drawing them up in the safety of your shop, quite another when some madwoman ran at you with a primed grenade.

He deliberately looked away from the blackened smear that remained of said woman, along with much of the wall that had been behind her.

Not that it was particularly out of place given the state of the building. The club, and the state of its occupants, reflected the carnage that had taken place there. If there was a single chair still intact or wall without a hole in it, he would be hard pressed to find it.

"On your knees. Hands on heads." Grey drawled lazily, weapon still raised.

The tired and bloody denizens of the building were slow to comply, but once they realized Erich's people weren't going to gun them all down on the spot, they moved out into the open.

As they did, Erich belatedly realized they weren't all sex workers. Some of the men who he had mistaken for male strippers originally were just more gangsters in the classic Brotherhood style. Either that, or they were the least sexy looking strippers he had ever seen. Not that he was any great expert on strippers, male or female.

And it's not like anyone's looking sexy at the minute, He thought as he looked over the tear stained, bloody and traumatized faces staring back at him.

As the surrendering defenders finally started to settle down, he noted one man had remained behind.

He was an older geezer, one Erich hadn't even noticed prior to this moment. Likely because he wasn't armed, a scantily clad woman, or
even standing up.

Instead he sat in a wheelchair, a look of irritated disgust written all over his face.

"Well this turned out to be a pretty fucking useless hiding place." The man said as he turned to look at Erich's suit.

He looked expectant, as if waiting for Erich to react in some way, but Erich had not a clue why.

Instead he was debating the merits of threatening the wheelchair bound man into moving out into the open like everyone else.

"And of course, you don't even recognize me. Just typical." The man snorted after a few moments had passed.

At which point, one of Hard-Light's goons, who had been in the act of collecting up the discarded guns, happened to glance over.

"Holy shit!" The man said, dropping the weapons with a clatter as he shakily brought up his own. "Integrity!"

The shout brought the attention of all the others present, and they were just as quick to turn their eyes away from the other prisoners to focus their guns on the wheelchair bound man.

Erich didn't blame them. As soon as he heard the man's name, he had been just as quick to bring up his own weapon.

"Now that's more like it." The man grinned, eyes flashing in the clubs dim light, utterly uncaring of the way his people were squirming uncomfortably as the threat of imminent violence rose.

"What the fuck are you doing here?" Grey asked, the most calm of the bunch, but not by much.
"I don't answer to the help." The man sneered, turning his eyes back to Erich. "Surrenders should happen villain to villain."

Erich could care less.

"Why are you here, Integrity?" He repeated, keeping a stutter from his own voice only through sheer force of will. "Why's the leader of the Brotherhood hiding out in a shitty strip club... and using strippers for muscle?"

Rocket launcher armed strippers. Of all the ways he might have gone out.

Besides, the defenders here had been reasonably competent, but not nearly competent enough to justify the sheer amount of hardware he could see strewn around the room. This was the kind of stuff you gave out to your core membership, not some recently press ganged sex workers.

And that didn't even address the fact that Integrity hadn't entered the fray. The man was supposed to be an incredibly powerful speedster.

Although, not anymore, clearly. Erich realized as he looked over the man's wheelchair bound state; more or less answering his own question and feeling like an idiot in the process.

"Why, I would have thought it was obvious." The man chuckled, arms going wide to encompass the room. "This is one of the last remaining strongholds of the True Brotherhood in this town."

The man's smile faded slightly, but Erich could still see some bitter amusement in his eyes, "Although, I imagine if Hard-Light's newest pet is here, my other operations are receiving similar visits. Would fit right in with everything else our new mutual friend has done."

Erich said nothing, but somehow the man seemed to take that as an affirmative.

"Well done then," The crippled supervillain sneered. "You've done the Hangman's dirty work for him."

Erich frowned, "Who the fuck is the Hangman?"

Integrity gave him a malicious grin, "I'm pretty sure you people call him the 'Ghost'."

CHAPTER 14

"Well this is a bitch and a half." Gravity murmured as she sat at the meeting table.

Sarah sent a glare in her half sister's direction, but ultimately couldn't argue. It *was* a bitch and a half.

"Any news from Hard-Light?" Erich asked tiredly.

"Fortunately for you, no." Sarah said acidly, seeing an outlet for her irritation, as she looked over the map.

It was much changed from that morning; the red markers that had once indicated Brotherhood business and residences were now divided into yellows for New Brotherhood and black for True Brotherhood.

And there were significantly more yellow markers on the table than black.

Including a number of new ones that Integrity was all too happy to point out. Though Sarah was going to be sending out some of her own people to confirm that fact. The events of the last two days had only served to reinforce that they needed far more information about what was going on in the city.

"You really think he's going to be that pissed?" Erich asked, a tinge of worry piercing through his lethargy.

"He's not going to be happy." Gravity said sympathetically, "He's usually pretty clear on the 'no prisoners' thing."

"Integrity's a valuable source of information." Erich pointed out, defending his decision to bring the wheelchair bound man back

alive. "Bringing someone back alive was supposed to be our objective."

Although he had only done so after ensuring the man really was wheel chair bound.

By breaking one of his legs.

He still felt a small shudder run through him each time he remembered the sound of bone splintering under his suit's fingers, while the Neo-Nazi had looked on with that same mildly amused patronizing look in his eyes.

"Yes, he is. Hard-Light won't have any issue with you bringing him along." Sarah's glare redoubled as she looked at him. "What he's going to be pissed about is that you let the rest of his people go."

"I took their guns." Erich defended sullenly.

"Oh yes, because it's so hard to find more guns in this city." The blonde said sarcastically. "All you've done is given us more people to fight later down the line."

Erich wanted to argue but couldn't. She was right after all.

Still, it wasn't like he'd had many options. He couldn't just... gun them all down. And neither could he bring them all back with him. It had been difficult enough fitting everyone into their one remaining van and getting out of there before the cops showed up.

"Erich's unexpected nobility aside," Gravity butted in, saving him from any further tongue lashings, "has Integrity said anything else?"

Sarah sighed, but reluctantly returned to the topic at hand.

"Plenty." She said, "In fact, it's been difficult shutting him up." Erich could see that being the case. The man was more than just a little bitter about his organization being usurped right out from under him. Being betrayed by friends and colleagues you've known for years will have a tendency of doing that to you.

"He's convinced this 'Hangman' has some kind of mind-control ability." Sarah said.

"Mind control's a myth." Gravity scoffed, "His people were bought off by this new guy. Simple as that. Brotherhood might act like they have some holier than thou 'noble mission' but at the end of the day they're all just bottom feeding scum like the rest of us."

Erich couldn't help but feel Gravity was a little biased on the subject. Understandably so though.

He doubted he would have a high opinion of a group that wanted to essentially exterminate everyone that even remotely resembled him.

More than that, Gravity had proven to be less than objective on the subject of the Brotherhood before.

Like the time she took us all out to a restaurant, despite knowing there was a good chance we would be attacked there. He thought, as he considered his second, and last, meeting with the Crusher.

"Perhaps." Sarah allowed, "But that doesn't explain one of our own people going turncoat as well. Three of the people who I have gathering information for me disappeared after we got back from the last outing."

Needless to say, they were the same three people who had helped select the group's targets for the last attack. Targets which had all turned out to be of great value to the True Brotherhood faction.

Which is most certainly not a coincidence, Erich thought grimly.

"That just proves our people aren't much better." Gravity muttered, "Show them some cash, and they're pretty quick to switch allegiances."

Sarah glared venomously at her half-sister, but ultimately was forced to once more concede that she had a point.

They were a band of criminals who were held together more by fear of Hard-Light, poor circumstances, and a love of money, rather than any great sense of camaraderie.

A Hard-Light who was currently missing, and had been for two days now.

Morale wasn't quite at rock bottom at the compound, but it wasn't far off either. It certainly didn't help that both teams accompanying the villain had disappeared with him, leaving the organization's standing 'soldiery' at a measly thirty or so people.

No one had quite suggested aloud that the organization's powerhouse, and the most powerful Meta in the city, had been taken down, but it was certainly going through everyone's heads.

"It's not a total loss." Erich said, "We now know where all that medical equipment was supposed to go."

Although not even Integrity had known what its purpose was.

"Doesn't do us much good." Gravity muttered as she scooped up one of the yellow monopoly pieces. "We don't really have the manpower to attack the place."

Especially not with the Hangman still out there.

The fact that they had a name for the guy now was nice, but given what they now knew, the name Hangman was even more terrifying for the rank and file than the enigmatic Ghost had ever been.

...Not that any of this was of any concern to Erich *anymore.*

He was playing the part, but he already had a van back at his shop loaded up with tools. Now that he had the suit, and his bank account was nicely full, he was just waiting for confirmation that Hard-Light was definitely dead. Then he was getting the fuck out of here.

No way he was going down with this sinking ship.

Still, a part of him regretted it. He wasn't much for people, but Sarah and Olivia had... grown on him. Unstable and twisted as they were.

He listened with half an ear to the rest of the meeting, saying the right things when prompted, as Sarah went through the rest of what they knew and made tentative plans to bunker down and wait for Hard-Light to resurface.

Sorry girls, He thought as he strode from the meeting room, *I'm just not the heroic type.*

ΔΔΔ

"Come on, Erich." Gravity said as she handed him a pair of pliers. "I need *something* to upgrade my power."

Erich sighed as he set about stripping a wire. "Gravity, I get where you're coming from. I really do. But do I, or do I not, look like I have enough on my plate right now?"

The teams accompanying Hard-Light had been the ones carrying his
'upgraded' laser pistols, as they had been the ones most likely to face stiff resistance. As a result the only ones still available were strapped to his, Sarah's and Gravity's thighs.

And none of them were giving theirs up to a random mook, despite being the ones who probably least needed them.

As a result, Erich was sequestered down in the mansion's garage, with a small crate of spare electrical components stolen from Hard-Light's workshop... upgrading laser rifles.

Which Gravity was ostensibly supposed to be helping him with.

"Can't you think of something?" Gravity whined, "She's calling herself Bronte now!"

Yes. Bronte. Erich thought that naming oneself after an actual goddess was a little shameless, but it was also perfectly in keeping with what he knew of Sarah's ego.

"I'm busy." He said through gritted teeth.

Mostly with planning my escape and sequestering away my earnings, but still busy!

"With this?" Gravity said, raising a half constructed laser rifle. "This'll take you a few hours if that."

"I still have to repair the suit." Erich pointed out.

Gravity shook her head. "No you don't. Sarah's having Grey look it over. She figures the woman's been watching you for the last few days, so she'll at least know how to recharge the batteries and put in fresh coolant."

Erich felt like his heart stopped within his chest.
"She didn't!" He gasped.

No one touched his suit. Least of all an... uneducated thug!

Sorry Grey, but it's true.

He was halfway through storming from the room when he felt a familiar sense of weightlessness overtake his body.

"Put me down woman!" He roared as he struggled against the strange green light.

171

"Sarah thought you'd react that way when you found out." Gravity sighed, "Look Erich, I know you love the suit. Perhaps even a little more than is strictly healthy. But we can't have you obsessing over it like you usually do. We just don't have the time to indulge it."

Obsess? Him? He didn't obsess! He gave things the exact amount of time and attention they deserved, and not a moment more.

"Don't give me that look." Gravity frowned, "She's literally just changing the coolant and shoving in fresh power-packs. Even a monkey could do it."

Erich did have to concede that point. It *was* something even a monkey could do.

"Fine." He sighed tiredly. "Just put me down, so I can finish off those rifles."

"And invent something to give me a boost over my sister?" Gravity chimed in hopefully.

Erich gave her a look as he slowly dropped back down to the ground. "You've never cared that much about it before?"

Sure, she had whined and moaned, but never for long. It was more in jest than anything else.

She shrugged, "Is it really that strange? Hard-Light's missing. Nearly half our crew is gone. And we've got some new psychopath in charge of the Brotherhood."

Well, when you put it that way...

"Fine." He groused as he returned back to his temporary worktable, "After I'm done with this."

And it's certainly not going to be cheap!

He almost instantly regretted his decision as the grinning woman wrapped him in a hug.

"No hugs!"

△△△

Erich looked over his suit with a critical eye, flicking back and forth between it and the omni-pad on the table.

"There, see?" Gravity said, Grey indignantly nodding along with her, "It's *fine*."

Erich ignored them both. Uneducated philistines that they were.

Only after a full two minutes of silent inspection did he have to concede that was right.

Probably.

"There, now get back to work on my new gizmo." Gravity grinned, gesturing at the work table where a half-constructed shoulder
harness sat.

"I am." He grunted, lifting up a partially disassembled laser pistol in his hands.

"You weren't even looking at it." She accused, "I'm not having you half-ass it after the amount you charged me for it!"

Yes. Him announcing the price for his time and effort had gone quite some distance toward cooling the woman's joviality after he agreed to even work on it at all.

"I don't 'half-ass' anything." He said indignantly as he finished tightening a screw, still not looking at the weapon in his hands.

Which was why he saw Grey rolling her eyes from off to the side. "Can I leave now? It's nearly midnight."

Erich reluctantly nodded, gesturing for her to go with a casual wave of his hand. Which the woman accepted with only the slightest of scowls.

"Would it kill you to be a bit more polite?" Gravity asked as she leaned back on a stool, watching their colleague disappear back into the mansion.

"She touched my suit. *Without my permission.*" He said, as if that explained everything.

"You originally planned to sell it." Gravity pointed out.

Yes. He thought. *And then your Dad forced me to pilot it on a whim. So forgive me if I'm a little overprotective of the only device standing between me and perforation by the next Meta-Gunner that doesn't like the look of me!*

Instead of saying all that, he just sniffed again, and turned his head away.

Gravity looked like she was about to say something else but stopped before the first word left her mouth. Instead she reached for her earpiece, as a complicated look stole over her face.

Erich watched, his guts turning to ice water as his hands slowly stopped screwing the laser pistol back together. When Gravity finally took her hand away from her ear, it was to give him a steely look.

"Drop that. Sarah wants us in the meeting room." She said without preamble.

Erich was about to ask why, but the sound of an alarm ringing through the mansion pretty much answered his question for him.

"We're under attack, aren't we?" He asked with a put-upon sigh.

Well, it was a good thing I managed to get those new rifles finished. He thought blearily, his body crying out for sleep he knew it would not be receiving any time soon.

CHAPTER 15

"It would seem the 'New Brotherhood' has decided to capitalize on our temporary moment of weakness." Sarah said as soon as Gravity and Erich joined the three other team leaders at the meeting table.

"I've received a number of reports that over the last few hours, armed individuals we assume to be part of the New Brotherhood have been trickling into public areas not far removed from the mansion. As of the last hour, a rough head count has suggested more than a hundred are now present, if spread out over a number of different locations."

Sarah placed a number of red tokens on a new, much smaller, map. "I have no doubt that this assault is intended to cripple our organization permanently while Hard-Light is... out of contact."

Two of the team leaders shared nervous glances at that, but Grey simply stared on in mute acceptance.

Gravity wasn't quite as subtle with her summary of the situation, "So we're hopelessly outnumbered and 'Daddy' isn't around to bail us out. Great. When and how are these guys planning to arrive?"

"If past habits hold true, the second night falls. And as for transport? They probably plan to walk." Lopez said as he looked over the map. "Most of these places aren't that far away."

Sarah looked a bit irritated by the interruption, but nodded.

"Yes. As far as we can tell they used their own means of transport
to arrive at these rallying points but intend to move as one mob toward us."

Erich swore. That pretty much ruled out ambushing their vehicles during transit. It would have been a handy way of staggering them, if not wiping out large numbers of them entirely in one fell swoop. He knew his force blasters would do nasty things to a truck or bus if he put enough juice into them.

Funny, He thought, *once upon a time that might have made me feel queasy.*

"Any Metas amongst them?" Asked the final team leader, a man who's name Erich couldn't quite remember. Something starting with an 'S'.

Sarah shook her head, "None that are known to us."

Which meant sweet fuck all if the New Brotherhood had been hiring new people. Some Metas developed abilities that resulted in visible changes in their body, such as scales, fur or metal skin, but most looked just like anyone else.

He also doubted a group like the Brotherhood would be willing to accept any of the poor sods who developed visible mutations.

Not that the rest of the world is much better in that regard.

"Any chance we can call in the cops to disrupt them before they get here?" Erich asked as he turned his mind back to the task at hand.

The perfectly reasonable question (to his mind), drew incredulous looks from everyone present.

"The cops will certainly show up." Sarah said finally, "but only after everything is over. They're more than happy to let us all kill each other before coming in to clean up what's left. To their mind, it's better we all kill each other than them risk their lives trying to break it up."

Erich figured that would be the case.

"Worth a shot." He shrugged, "I assume that it's the same for the North Granton Defenders?"

Gravity's scoff was all the answer he needed to that question. The local Guild affiliated hero team was even more corrupt and ineffective than the cops. It seemed that barely a week went by without one of them being caught up in at least one scandal.

"Right, so what's the plan to see us through the night?" He asked, resisting the urge to make a dash for one of the vans in the garage.

He figured he would have a better chance of escaping at some point during the coming battle.

"We've still got twenty eight experienced guns to throw at them and three Metas. That's nothing to sneeze at." Sarah said. "Plus, the mansion's automated defenses."

Erich tactfully refrained from pointing out that he wasn't a Meta. Just a dude in a set of power armor.

And how come no one told me this place had automated defenses?

He'd certainly never seen any. Though he supposed that was probably part of the design. Still, it stung his professional pride as an engineer that he hadn't even gotten an *inkling* that the place had any defense beyond the intimidating reputation of its owner.

"We can arm the staff and the bottom feeders." Grey said. "They'll all be green as hell, but even a newbie can guard a hallway and fire a few rounds downrange before they catch a bullet."

Gravity looked a bit uncomfortable, but Sarah nodded. "Good idea. If we're lucky we might be able to replenish our core membership from those who do well."

Assuming any of them survive, Erich thought cynically before another thought occurred to him. *Hell, assuming any of **us** survive...*

Just throwing caution to the wind and running like hell was looking more and more tempting by the moment.

"That's still not all that many," Gravity frowned, "We're going to have to pull completely back to the mansion if we want to cover everything."

Erich frowned, "If we completely give up the outside, what's to stop them from just burning the place down with us inside?"

Sarah shook her head, "The building may look old, but it's all superficial. All of the building materials are as modern as you can get. The place won't burn easily, if at all."

Well, that was a load off his mind. He still had nightmares about the Crusher's death, and he had no desire to experience a similar fate first-hand.

"Right, so we just have to hold out long enough for Hard-Light to return, or until the cops can no longer reasonably ignore what's happening." Gravity said.

Sarah nodded determinedly, "Grey's team and I are covering the main entrance hall. Sam, I want you to put at least two people on every possible side and servant entrance. Supplement your guys with staff if you have to. Gravity, you and Lopez are going to be part of our reserve team, shore us up wherever the Brotherhood start to push."

To Erich's mild surprise, Gravity didn't argue. She accepted her half-sister's commands without complaint.

"What about me?" Erich asked as Sarah trailed off.

He watched on in mild confusion as the blonde woman seemed to mull the question over for what felt like a very long time.

"I need you to take some of the staff and cover the escape tunnel."

Erich's heart skipped a beat.

Seeing the glances being passed around the room, it seemed he wasn't the only one who was ignorant of said tunnel's existence.

"I normally wouldn't mention it," Sarah growled, "but given that a few of our people have gone turncoat in recent days, it isn't impossible that they are aware of it, and might use it as a point of entry."

"Don't get too comfortable *Mechromancer*," Gravity sniggered,

"If the battle drags on long enough without any indication of trouble on your end, you can bet your ass Sarah's going to have you relocate to the fight's biggest hotspot."

Erich felt the grin that had been slowly growing on his face wither and die as Sarah nodded from her spot at the end of the table.

"I'm still down to one force blaster." He attempted to say, only for Sarah to cut him off.

"Then you still have one more than anyone else in this mansion has."

Seeing that there was no way he was getting out of his secondary duty, he found himself hoping for the Brotherhood to attack the escape tunnel. At least if they did, he'd be nice and hunkered down with some meat shields to hide behind, rather than being forced to wander from hotspot to hotspot.

"I'm assuming this escape tunnel is in the wine cellar?" He sighed.

Sarah nodded reluctantly.

"Great," He continued, "I'll need some help moving stuff we can use

as cover down there. I'll probably also be grabbing my defenders from the staff at the same time."

Hopefully he could grab a few that looked halfway reliable before the others scooped them all up.

Sarah waved her hands, as if to say he was dismissed. "Grey, go with him. I'll take your team with me, and you can lead Erich's.

Show him where the tunnel entrance is while you're at it."

Erich was almost offended that he wasn't trusted to lead his own team, as the taciturn woman rose with a silent nod.

He knew it was the right choice though. He had zero leadership experience, and even worse social skills.

Besides, at least this way I have one reasonably competent meat shield to hide behind.

It was all about looking out for the positives. Like the fact that he was about to be stationed right next to the escape tunnel. Possible point of egress for the enemy or not, that was some pretty amazing luck.

Though I'll probably have to kill Grey if I decide I've got to escape.

That put something of a damper on his plans for freedom in the event things started going poorly.

Could I do that? Stab an 'ally' in the back in cold-blood?

His conscious mind quibbled back and forth over the question, but in his heart of hearts he knew exactly what he would do.

Perhaps not without hesitation, but certainly without a doubt.

ΔΔΔ

"Move, or I start moving you." Erich said, his suit's speakers giving him an even more ominous tone than he intended.

The gaggle of lackeys he had collected together glanced back and forth between his massive suit and the stairs down into the cellar.

"Move." He said, charging up his single force blaster with an ominous whine. Even if the other one was still operational, he couldn't have used it at as one hand was holding a massive rucksack.

Still the sound of just one of the weapons charging up proved to be enough, and the group of five clambered down the steps into the gloom, hands fearfully clutching the weapons in their hands.

Erich had zero sympathy for them.

All of them were parasites. People that clung to core members of the gang as their entourage, basking in the second hand power it gave them to associate with members of the criminal underworld.

Besides, even as lackeys they were all members of the gang, and displayed the colors proudly. The only issue was that none of them
had ever actually had to do *anything* before besides stand around and look menacing or run simple errands for their criminal masters.

Hell, he might have been worried about one of them shooting him in the back and trying to make a run for it if he thought they had a little more spine.

Not that he was any better.

He was planning to do the exact same thing after all.

Just a few more rungs up the totem pole, He thought with cynical amusement.

The main difference between them was that he had half a ton of power armor and they didn't. Which was all that mattered in the end. Knowledge might be power. Money might be power. But at the end of the day, the only real power was power.

"You need to work on your leadership skills." Grey murmured from her position against a nearby wall, heavily tattooed arms crossed tightly over her chest.

"I'm not a leader." He said. "I'm an engineer."

She shook her head, "You're a supervillain and part of this gang. That makes you a leader whether you like it or not."

Well aren't you chatty today, he thought.

"Get in the hole." He muttered, unwilling to concede that she had a point.

Still, the way the lithe young woman smiled as she strode down past him told him that she knew she'd won that little bout.

If he wasn't about to be relying on her to keep any of their newfound unwilling allies from turning their guns on him when things inevitably got hot, he would have been half tempted to give her a little shove as he started descending the stairs as well.

He hated losing.

He could grovel, beg, and writhe in the dirt like a worm if he had to.

But losing?

Losing got to him.

By the time his slow ass thunked down into the wine cellar, Grey was already directing her surly workers to set up barricades across from what looked to be a perfectly normal wall.

Since he doubted it was supposed to be blasted open in the event it was ever supposed to be used, Erich could only assume it would slide open at the behest of some unseen command console.

"Drop the bag." She said as he thudded over, which he dutifully did, still entirely ignorant of its contents.

He watched on with mild interest as she pulled out a ballistic blanket and passed it off to a watching goon.

"Drape that over whatever barrel you're planning on hiding behind." She said, before repeating the action for the next four to wander over.

"It won't stop a laser or a force blaster." He pointed out as soon as they were of earshot. "Wouldn't it have been better to build some mobile barrier projectors?"

"Do you think any of these people are valuable enough to our employer that he would buy a surplus of equipment to build barrier projectors?" Grey said as she draped her own ballistic blanket over a barrel – before going to stand behind a much sturdier looking stone pillar.

Well… no.

Grey snorted. "There's a reason the world's still using old world tech for most stuff. Meta-tech is just too high goddamned main-tenance to be cost effective past a certain level."

Erich wanted to point out that people like him could fix those problems, but he knew that was patently untrue. Sure, he could *reduce* problems in Meta-tech, but at the end of the day, it was still Meta-tech, with all the issues inherent with it.

Not least of which is that one required a frankly incredible amount of education in a number of different fields to even con-template peaking inside a device and having the faintest clue as to what was

going on.

Which would be even more compounded by the fact that two Meta-tech devices, even from the same Artificer, could have wildly different design principles despite being made to per-form the same purpose.

Yes, he could see why Hard-Light might just grab some ballistic blankets instead of a more effective, and thus proportionally more expensive, alternative.

Now that I think about it, I'm actually amazed he even thought to in-vest in defenses at all.

The more he thought about it, the more he came to believe that Sarah was the one to buy the ballistic blankets and store them away for an occasion like this.

He started as the wall in front of him started to peel back, re-vealing a wide dark tunnel leading off into the distance. From the look of it, it must have been a repurposed part of the city's old sewer system.

"Why are you opening it?" One of the goons asked incredulously.

"It's an open tunnel." Grey said phlegmatically to the lightly clad young woman, "No cover. Good kill zone for us."

And it was better for them if they saw their attackers coming, rather than have the first indication of their existence be the door sliding open to reveal a horde of well-armed racists.

"As the degenerate half-breed said." A familiar voice spoke from the darkness to Erich's right, startling him as well as the goons. "So with that in mind, any chance I could get a gun?"

Grey hadn't reacted at all to the voice, beyond a slight tightening of her vaguely Hispanic features.

"Why would we give you a gun?" Erich asked after calming his racing heart and realizing Grey wasn't going to say anything.

"Figured it was worth a shot." Integrity chuckled croakily.

He was a sad sight. Filthy, with his unmoving legs splayed out beneath him as he sat with his back to a pole, a bike-lock of all things wrapped around his neck. Outwardly he seemed calm, despite his squalid conditions, but Erich could see the rage in the man's eyes.

He could understand it well, even if he had no sympathy for the former supervillain.

The guy had once been the leader of one of the most powerful gangs in the city, as well as one of its more powerful Metas.

Now he was crippled, powerless, stuck in a basement, chained up with a bike-lock, and there was a very real possibility that he was about to be discovered by the subordinates that had betrayed him in the first place.

Unarmed and defenseless.

Racist old scumbag or not, that has to suck.

Hell, he had to give the old bastard credit for holding it all in, rather than sitting there raging away at them. He didn't know if he would have had the same self-control in similar circumstances.

Actually, that was a lie.

He *knew* he wouldn't.

Erich might have said something else, but he was interrupted by Grey who had one hand to her ear.

"Everyone get into position." She said quietly, "Sarah says the New Brotherhood have finally started to move."

Erich checked his internal clock, and saw that it was nine o'clock on the dot.

Like clockwork, He thought uncomfortably, charging up his force blaster once more, if only to hear its soothing hum.

I don't know whether to be relieved or horrified, Erich wondered as he saw lights bobbing in the distance.

It seemed that true to form, the New Brotherhood had far more information than they should, and were entirely aware of the 'secret' escape tunnel.

Either way, the prospect of imminent violence was a welcome reprieve from sitting in the dark waiting nervously for something to happen.

For the last few minutes, he'd been listening to the sounds of fighting going on above.

By all indications it was going well for the defenders. All of the entry points were holding, and so far, there had been no indications of a Meta-human presence amongst the attackers.

Whether that meant that the New Brotherhood had none remaining beyond the Hangman, or that they were being held in reserve, no one knew. Either way, it was giving Hard-Light's crew ample time to cut down the attacking chaff.

Should I even call it that anymore? He pondered as he trained his weapon on one of the flashlights bobbing in the distance. *With Hard-Light missing, isn't it Bronte's crew?*

He supposed, if the man really was missing, there wasn't much point in renaming the gang. Even with Sarah's leadership, it probably wouldn't be around long enough to warrant a name change anyway.

"*Wait for them to come into range.*" Grey's voice whispered over the comms. "*With any luck we can take them all in the first salvo.*"

Just like his, her hard-light barriers were offline. The powerful protective system would have been obvious in the pitch black of the cellar, and would have given away their planned ambush.

Normally, that would have been a perfectly fine trade off, but given that none of the other people with them had the advanced barrier system, Grey decided that blanketing everyone with concealment was better than leaving two people with great protection and everyone else without any.

Erich didn't quite agree with that line of thought, but he was willing to concede that he was a less than objective observer,

189

given that he
would have been one of those amply protected people.

*The **most** amply protected,* he thought grimly as he watched the lights come ever closer.

Not that they were all he could see. His suit had built in night-vision as a given, so he could see the approaching Brotherhood gangsters in reasonable detail.

Despite being part of what should have been a surprise attack, they were little different from the other thugs he had come across in his time with Hard-Light. They were dressed in casual clothes, wielding an assortment of weapons, and moving as more of a mob than a disciplined unit.

No rocket launchers, he noted with relief.

Just the usual assortment of small-arms. Which he promptly relayed to Grey, along with a rough count of their numbers.

The olive-skinned woman nodded, *"Get ready."*

Erich whispered into his suit, "Aim assist on."

"Acknowledged." Gravity's voice intoned through the suit's speakers, Erich's arm locking up as the limb moved to follow the reticule linked to his eye.

Erich centered it on a young woman who was near the front of the pack. She was covered in tattoos affirming her allegiances and prejudices to the world, but in that moment, he could only think of how young she looked.

He would be surprised if she was even a day over eighteen.

"Fire." Grey's voice echoed loudly through the darkness.
Erich felt the recoil shoot through his arm as his weapon fired, the bolt of energy released striking the young woman straight in the midsection. Given the tightly packed nature of their foes, he had overcharged the weapon in advance, so the resulting

blast struck not just his target, but people behind her as well.

He found to his surprise that he felt nothing as he surveyed the gore. No shame. No horror. No guilt.

Even the nausea was a tired, muted thing.

Humans are such adaptable creatures, he thought.

Still, he felt some small tinge of envy for the lackeys to his left and right. Given the darkness of the tunnel, they saw none of their handiwork as they opened fire. Hell, they didn't even really see what they were shooting at. They shot at distant lights rather than people. Intellectually of course, they would know they were shooting at people, but it was still a very different sensation to see a light falling in the distance rather than a human being.

By the time he was ready to fire again, the short firefight was all but over. Caught completely out in the open, the Brotherhood members had been massacred to the last within moments of the first shot ringing out. A group of ten reduced to zero in seconds.

He had to give credit to her, Grey knew what she was talking about.

I wonder what her history is?

He dismissed the idle thought as soon as it came up. It didn't matter. He was going to be gone soon enough. A new identity.

Perhaps he would go by John this time?

"Right." Erich said once he was sure every one of their attackers were dead - something only he could confirm with his night vision, "That's that."

Rather anti-climactic really.

"Don't." Grey said as she heard the telltale sounds of someone fumbling for a torch. "More may show up."

Which meant the lackeys were going to be sitting in the dark for even longer. Alone with their thoughts.

Erich wasn't totally sure that was a good idea.

The people with them weren't soldiers. They hadn't killed before. Even with just a quick glance around, he could see similar symptoms to what he experienced after his first kill. Fear. Nausea. Disgust.

Not the kind of things you wanted the people you might need in a few minutes to be dwelling on.

"Don't you think it might be a good idea to give them a breather?" He asked as he heard the telltale sounds of someone throwing up.

Hopefully they didn't do that right next to their cover, otherwise we're all going to be stuck with that smell for a while.

And considering the stagnant nature of the air down in the cellar - and the fact that they had an open door to an old sewer system right next to them - the air quality was pretty piss-poor where they were at to begin with.

Grey shrugged, "They don't have to be happy. They just have to shoot when I tell them to, at what I tell them to."

Well, I tried.
If Erich could have shrugged within the confines of his suit, he would. It wasn't like he cared about anyone's mental health beyond his immediate needs. He just didn't want an emotional breakdown taking one of their fighters out before the next attack happened.

Although we might get lucky and have there be no next attack, he hoped.

Although given that *he* was stationed down here, he doubted that would be the case. It wasn't like Sarah would keep him out of the fight as a result of their 'relationship'.

The suit was now the gang's heaviest hitter, given that Hard-Light was gone. Sarah didn't have the luxury of keeping it out of the fight even if she wanted to.

Which she definitely didn't.

Tentative feelings of... affection he may have felt for the unstable woman aside, he was well aware that she was using him. Any affection she might display was probably faked. A ploy to pull him over to her side.

There just wasn't a hell of a lot he could do about it besides ride it out.

...or get the hell out of dodge, he thought as his mind swung back around to his burgeoning escape plan.

A plan he could put into motion the second Hard-Light was confirmed to be dead.

...Maybe Gravity might want to come with? She's not exactly enamored with the whole villainy thing?

He ruthlessly slapped down that line of thought as soon as it registered.

It would be a stupid risk. An unneeded one that could have dire consequences if Gravity was even slightly more loyal to her father's organization than he thought.

Never should have thought of it, he groused.

All this... social contact was making him strange.

Weak.

"We've got another wave incoming." Grey hissed as more lights filled the tunnel.

"Great." Erich sighed.

I really need to get out of this place, he reaffirmed in his mind, as his targeting reticule centered over another person's face.

An older man this time.

△△△

Gravity sighed as she gunned down another target, which proved to be enough to send the rest scampering back into the trees surrounding the estate. Around her, other members of Lopez's team continued to fire at the fleeing skinheads, but Gravity refrained.

She hated the racist punks as much as the next guy, but she found something inherently distasteful about shooting someone in the back.

"This is Gravity, we've repulsed the assault on the west servants entrance. Still no sign of Meta presence." She said into her comm unit.

"Confirmed." Sarah's business-like voice answered, *"They're pulling back from the main entrance hall as well. No Metas here, and Grey says it's much the same down in the cellar."*

So, they had known about the escape tunnel. That was worrying. She had always known the gang was something of a sieve when it came to information, but the escape tunnel's existence was very much on a need to know basis.

Still, that was Sarah's problem to worry about. Not hers.

"Stay vigilant everyone," Sarah said over the mansion wide line, *"That first attack was probably a probe to test our defenses. We can expect whatever Metas they have to come in with the second attack."*

Still, it took a good five minutes of tense waiting for the second assault to come.

It was an unusually long amount of time given that most conflicts between criminal factions were brief and bloody affairs. An inevitable result of the attacker's need to be in and out before a police or Guild response was mustered.

The cops might drag their feet when it came to responding, but they would show up eventually; if only to maintain the rapidly disintegrating fiction that law and order was being maintained within the city.

"Should we redeploy?" Lopez asked deferentially as shadowy figures flitted through the tree line across from them.

"Nah," Gravity shook her head carelessly, "If Sa-*Bronte*, wants us to move, she'll tell us. We can pull out when that happens." Besides, she'd much rather be doing something useful, as opposed to sitting around waiting for the call.

This time their enemies were far more cautious on their approach. Rather than striding across the lawn as if they owned the place - assuming it to be all but defenseless with Hard-Light missing – they mostly stuck to the cover of the tree line and took potshots.

"Not going to do you much good though," She said as she eyed one particular figure who seemed to be yelling orders to the others. "John, you ready?"

The team's best marksman nodded, bringing his scoped laser rifle smoothly up to his shoulder as he rested the cruck of it against the window frame.

Gravity felt her power pass through her, her mind turning blank as she focused on the sensation of lifting the distant body up into the air. As her power worked, the world became simpler. Not a place of humans, grass and trees. Just mass.

Mass and movement.

Distantly she heard a crackle of ionized air and felt the mass she was lifting lessen as some of it dissipated explosively into vapor.

Recognizing the signal for what it was, her power faded, and once more she was back in the regular world. Things were more than abstract concepts of shape, size and weight once again.

"Good job," She breathed, as she spied the distant downed figure that mere moments ago she had lifted into the air.

"Ready for the next one?" She grinned.

The man nodded.
"Right," She said, firing up her power once more as she spied her next target.

It was around the fifth such repeating of this pattern that Sarah's voice came over the comms, disrupting her concentration and sending her target clattering to the ground before he had even really been lifted.

The blonde woman yelled, *"Trucks incoming! Approaching the front entrance at speed! Mechromancer and Gravity, get the fuck over here!"*

Gravity hissed with irritation, before scooping up her gun.

"That's our cue people!" She yelled, crouch walking back toward the hall, "Reserve team, relocate to the main entrance immediately!"

ΔΔΔ

"Fucking run!" Sarah yelled as she realized with horror what the truck's plan was.

Already her people were scrambling back, and she joined them just in time.

The first truck crashed into the front steps of the mansion and continued onward, momentum carrying it into the front door of the mansion with enough weight and force to crash through them, and much of the wall they were attached to.

The entire mansion shook with the impact, Sarah and her people being sent sprawling as dust and debris flew through the air as the truck – now tipped onto its side – slid to a screeching, agonizing, stop.

Just a few meters from where Sarah had fallen.

"Everyone, ok?" She shouted as she tried not to cough from all the dust that had been thrown up.

There were a barrage of 'yeses' to her question, but there were a few pained noes interspersed throughout.

Cursing, she brought her gun up to peer at the now thoroughly wrecked entrance hall, and truck wedged within it.

"Gun's up people, get to cover!" She yelled, "They'll be coming through any minute."

To their credit, her people were quick to react, moving to nearby bits of cover while dragging their wounded allies with them. She noted as she dived into her own bit of cover, that most of their injuries were centered around the legs; a place the vests barrier system didn't cover.

Well, at least they can still shoot, she reasoned as she aimed her laser pistol at one of the two places one might squeeze past the wrecked truck to gain entrance to the mansion.

"Christ, I thought were fighting Neo-Nazi's not the Yakuza!"

Sarah whipped her gun around in alarm, only to curse as she saw who had spoken.

"Gravity get your ass down here!" She hissed, zero tolerance for his sister's mildly racist remark, "I need every gun I've got squared on the entrance."

"Yeah, fine." The woman in question huffed as she started directing Lopez's people to spread out. "Where's the second truck?"

Sarah shrugged, "It pulled up short of the mansion. We expected the second one to do the same, which was why we were caught off guard when it accelerated instead."

She had been expecting many things from this 'New Brotherhood', but a kamikaze attack was not among them. Olivia's Yakuza remark certainly held a small grain of truth to it.

We're criminals for god's sake, she raged. *It's hard enough to get ahold of decent fighters in the first place, let alone ones willing to* **martyr** *themselves.*

Gravity clattered into cover next to her. "Seems that Mechromancer's not-"

A loud clang interrupted whatever Gravity was about to say, drawing gun barrels from all over as her people honed in on its origins.

The turned over truck.

"Hose it." Sarah said without preamble.

Gunfire ripped into the truck from all angles in a continuous spray of laser fire and bullets, filling the vehicle with holes.

This wasn't the movies. The vehicles exterior provided zero protection from small arms fire.

Which was why, only after a full ten seconds of continuous fire, did Sarah raise a hand for people to stop.

Even then it took a few extra moments for the last trickle of fire to die down. This was not a room full of disciplined soldiers, after all.

Silence filled the room, broken only by the clangs of metal cooling
after being rapidly heated by high intensity beams of light.

"No one's coming in." Gravity said warily.

Yes, Sarah had noticed that as well.

"The question is wh-"

The weakened metal of the truck's bed burst open as a massive furry *thing* leapt out of it.

"Shoot it!" Sarah shouted with alarm, putting actions to words as the thing bounded towards her.

Gauntlets, she thought, dropping the gun even as the creature bore down on her.

The gunfire started, but the shock of the creature's reveal had delayed it for too long. The creature was right on top of her, teeth glinting in the light as its maw opened wide.

She wasn't going to be fast enough.

CHAPTER 16

"That all of them?" Grey asked as she peered out into the darkness.

"That's all of them." Erich responded as he peered at what remained of the second wave.

They'd done the exact same thing as the first wave and died just the same. Which didn't make much sense to him. Everything they'd seen and heard about the Hangman suggested, if not a tactical mastermind, then at least someone with a degree of strategic acumen.

Sending waves of gang members at them achieved nothing. It didn't even put an appreciable dent in their ammo reserves, given that this was Hard-Light's main base of operations, and thus stocked to the gills with weaponry, both mundane and exotic.

"Can the Brotherhood even afford to sustain these kinds of losses?" He asked.

Grey shrugged, "Perhaps before they had their little split. They could have just shipped in more guys from branches in other cities."

But now that this city's branch has deviated from the main organization, that might not necessarily be true anymore, Erich realized. *It depends on the internal politics of the Brotherhood.*

And he supposed, how many losses the *New* Brotherhood had taken in the course of their little coup.

He was about to turn around and ask the shackled Integrity about exactly that when Grey shouted, "Everyone brace!"

Brace for wha-

It was fortunate that the suit's internal motors did much of the stabilizing for him, because he would have been sent flat on his face as the entire *room* shook as something *heavy* smashed into something upstairs.

Everyone else was not quite so lucky, as they were thrown from their feet. Not that Erich really cared about that, his focus was primarily on the way that dust fluttered down alarmingly from the ceiling.

His suit could withstand many things. A mansion falling on it wasn't one of them.

"What the hell was that?" Erich shouted over the comms as the initial surprise faded, only to receive static in return. "What's the hell's going on up there?"

Nothing. Just more static.

Frustrated, and more than a little alarmed, he turned to Grey as the woman clambered back up to her feet. "You getting anything?"

"Not anymore." The woman said, in the process of her shaking her head when a bladed disk slammed into her neck.

Erich stared in numb incomprehension as Grey reached numbly

J. R. Grey

up to the implement, from which blood was already streaming, before she silently collapsed to the ground.

Brain kicking back into gear as the woman's body hit the ground, he was vaguely aware of alarmed shouts from the lackeys as he brought his blaster up in search of a target.

Nothing came up though. All he saw was the green tinted interior of the tunnel and the bodies that occupied it.

No.

As he watched, something glinted in his display for but a second as it flew past him.

There was a meaty thunk just to his right, and the distinctive sound of another body hitting the floor.

"Thermal." He shouted, adrenaline spiking higher as another glint flew from the tunnel to strike another lackey.

"Acknowledged." The suit responded, bathing his sight in oranges and blues.

There!

An orange blob hidden amongst the cooling corpses of the second wave, some blocky and cold instrument strapped over the figures crouching shoulder.
'Got you, fucker!' Erich thought triumphantly.

"Root Command Charlie-Epsilon-Zulu." A voice shouted just as he prepared to fire.

Erich's triumph vanished; to be replaced with dread as his limbs seized up utterly, the hum of the force blaster dissipating as the suit entered an emergency shutdown.

The three remaining lackeys were still in the process of turning back from their downed ally toward where the voice originated from, when three more palm sized deadly disks flew from the darkness to take them in the throats.

Each collapsed with a wet gurgle, one barely managing to turn on their torch, before leaving Erich as the only one still standing.

Utterly immobile in his suit.

"Fuck. Fuck. Fuck." He swore as he desperately tried to wiggle out, knowing in his heart of hearts it was useless.

"Oh, the irony." A computer modulated voice chuckled from the darkness. "Caught out by your own paranoia."

Erich barely listened. He was still trying desperately to move limbs that wouldn't budge.

"Give it up, Jason." The voice continued as the speaker emerged into the light cast by the fallen torch.

The person's form was utterly enshrouded in a gender concealing black bodysuit. "You designed that protocol to stop *anyone* from using that suit after the voice command was given. Your fallback in case anyone ever tried to use it against you, right?"

How!? He thought furiously.

How did they know his name!? How did they know about the root command!?

He had told no one about it.

No one.

Wait, if they know about that-

"Yes." The voice interrupted his thoughts, "I know all about the shutdown system in Sarah's new gauntlets too. Such an elegant, if gory solution to a possible threat. I really must give you credit for that. It really is quite inspired."

If Erich thought he was worried before, that comment drove his fear to new heights.

"Such a shame. All that genius. All that talent. And you're just as greedy and petty as even the worst bottom feeder." The figure said, "Your sister would be so disappointed."

As if having lost interest in him, the figure started to leisurely walk forward, a device coming to life in one hand. Even as he was forced

to crane to look from his immobile suit, Erich could clearly see the timer emblazoned on the side.

"Honestly," The figure sighed, "I expected more from the brother of the Blur."

Fear momentarily took a back seat as Erich snarled, yelling in impotent rage as he cursed and struggled, desperately trying to shift the immobile suit as the explosive device clamped onto him with a metallic clang.

The featureless face plate of the figure peaked in front of the suit's grill, "So, I think I'll do her a favor by-"

The sound of a gunshot had never sounded so sweet, as the figure dodged to the side with surprising agility for someone that had just been shot in the gut.

"Gagh!?" They shouted with very human sounding pain, even through the distortion of their mask.

"Fuck you, Hangman. You Jew loving mother fucker!" The distorted and high-pitched voice of Integrity rang out.

It was barely audible it was spoken so fast, but Erich had spoken to his sister many times when she chose to accelerate herself, and even as his heart leapt into his throat, he was able to parse through the hyper-fast curse.

Peering round as far as he could, Erich could see that somehow the Neo-Nazi had shattered the collar holding him in place, and had

crawled over to pick up a discarded gun.

A gun he was blazing away at the now named Hangman with, as the black suited figure ducked and weaved.

"Steal my gang!? Steal my men!? Break my fucking spine!?" The former gang leader cursed with hyper speed as he continued to shoot.

Erich watched on, expecting any moment for a disk to fly out from the fleeing Hangman's form and finish off the escaped skinhead, but it didn't happen. Instead he watched incredulously at the figure fled into the tunnel, clutching at their gut as blood dripped to the floor behind them.

"Come back here you piece of shit!" Integrity swore with superspeed as he continued to fire down the tunnel until his gun clicked empty.

Erich waited with bated breath for the figure to do exactly that, but as the minutes passed, interspersed with the noise of gunfire overhead and the sound of Integrity's labored breathing, the Hangman did not return.

"Cowardly fuck." Integrity hissed, his voice returning to a more normal speed.

Erich didn't disagree, but he figured he had bigger concerns.

"Little help?" Erich asked, not entirely sure whether it was wise to make the man aware of his presence, but also quite desperate to

get out of his claustrophobic prison.

"I've got it," A familiar voice rasped with an unhealthy sounding wet gurgle.

Erich sighed in relief, all but sprawling out of the suit as it opened up. Turning around, he saw that Grey was not as dead as he had thought, and that she had crawled over to pull on the suit's emergency release lever.

An impressive feat for a woman who was rapidly turning grey from blood loss.

Erich hurried over to pull out the disk, only for the woman to flinch back.

"Leave it." She croaked, "Pull it and I'll bleed out in seconds."

Erich looked at her blankly, mind running a mile a minute - then he pushed her weak hand aside and yanked.

"I know." He said tonelessly as the woman's eyes widened with surprise, moments before she collapsed into the growing pool of blood.

"I'm so sorry." He hissed.

Feeling numb, and running more on autopilot than conscious thought, Erich reached over to pull the rifle from the dying woman's body.

"I would like to say that this is mind control." Integrity chuckled from his spot behind them, "but I've seen enough witnesses being silenced over the years to know when someone doing it to me."

The man pinned Erich with a thin smile as the engineer aimed his gun at him.

"Isn't that right, Jason?"

"As you said," Erich grunted, before unloading a dozen shots into the prone Neo-Nazi's form.

The man collapsed with a wet thud, steam oozing from his corpse.

Still running on autopilot, Erich walked over to pull a clip from one of the lackey's corpses, making sure they were all dead as he did. As he worked, he kept a wary eye on the tunnel mouth.

Magazine in hand, he placed it into the open hand of Integrity's corpse, ejecting the spent clip from the man's gun.

Job done, and hands still shaking, Erich looked at his suit. From overhead he could still hear the sounds of battle going on, but it was gradually petering off. Now that the Hangman was gone, whatever jammer they had brought had gone with them, and Erich could hear muted chatter from the earpieces of the corpses around him.

Hurrying over, he moved to clamber back in... only to stop.

Idiot.

The explosive the Hangman had put in place was still there. It was a small miracle the assassin hadn't set it off as they fled out of sheer spite. It was what he would have done.

Must have been rattled, Erich thought.

Not particularly surprising given what he assumed the figure's power-set to be. Being taken by surprise was probably as shocking as being shot itself. He sincerely doubted it happened to them often.

Still, rattled or not, the explosive probably had some kind of anti-tampering mechanism on it. Fingerprint scanner or something.

It was what he would do.

With time and resources he could probably get it off without blowing himself to hell in the process.

...Unfortunately, he didn't have that.

The suit's undamaged.

That was suspicious. He had no ready made explanation for

why, and he was far from sure he could make some convincing battle damage before someone upstairs came to see what was happening.

Hell, they could be on their way to 'reinforce' them while he was

standing there.

He was still deliberating over what to do when the roof started to collapse above him, admitting a veritable inferno of flaming debris from the floor above.

Shit.

"You made me sleep on the couch? In my own home?" Erich asked from his position on said piece of furniture.

Gravity, who had been slumped over the breakfast counter, woke with a snort, and her bleary eyes instantly focused on him.

Then she laughed. Or tried to.

"I drag your bruised and battered body from that cellar, and that's the first thing you say to me?" She chuckled, "Just typical."

Erich studiously pretended not to notice the way she wiped a tear from her eye, or the sheer relief in her features.

He did direct a meaningful look at her helmet on the floor next to her. Not even upright, it looked like she'd torn it from her head and simply dropped it. He might have been offended on its behalf, were it not for a far more pertinent detail taking up his attention.

Claw marks.

Three gouges had torn through the helmet, and by all appearances had missed Gravity's head only by the slimmest of margins.

"We lost then?" He asked.

Gravity shook her head, genuine mirth replaced with a far more cynical variety.

"No." She said, "We won. We killed the freaks they sent after us and the rest of the Brotherhood's goons retreated."

Erich had no idea what she meant by freaks, but he could guess they were some kind of Meta.

Likely the ones who did in her helmet.

"Then why are we here?" He asked, before adding, "And why am I on the couch?"

He had been living in the mansion after Hard-Light's disappearance for a reason, and it certainly wasn't the company.

His home was not well defended.

"We might not have lost, but we didn't win either." Gravity said ruefully. "The crew's gone."

"Gone?" Erich repeated.

Gravity nodded, "Gone. Disappeared. Fled. Those that were still alive at least. Hard-Light's little faction is no more."

Erich was incredulous, "Sarah didn't stop them?"

Gravity snorted again, but there was no real humour in it. In fact, he could almost hear a slight break in her voice.

"Who do you think's using the bed?"

That was what finally did it. The dam broke and tears started to slide down Gravity's face as her body was wracked with quiet sobs.

Erich had no idea what to do.

Comforting people was not his strong suit. People in general were not his strong suit.

Clambering painfully off the sofa and tallying the litany of aches and pains that ran through his body as he did, he walked over to his... friend.

Slowly, ever so slowly, he patted her on the shoulder. Not unlike a man gingerly petting a particularly strange and dangerous beast.

Fortunately, it seemed to work, after a few minutes of excruciating awkwardness, Gravity stopped crying long enough to aim a tired grin at him.

"Smooth." She croaked.

He shrugged uncomfortably as he stiffly retracted his hand.
It worked didn't it? He felt like saying. Although, god knew, he hadn't expected it to.

"Come on." Gravity grunted, sniffing and wiping tears from her face as she stood up. "You're up, so with any luck sleeping beauty will be too."

Erich steadfastly made no indication that he heard the way her voice hitched toward the end of that sentence.

Erich nodded, glad that the... emotions, were over. "How long have I been 'out'?"

"Two days." Gravity said, not even looking at him as they strode to 'his' room.

Erich nodded, pulling up his shirt to see the patchwork of blue and purple bruises that covered his torso.

Yes, he could see that being the case.

Idiot, he added reproachfully as Gravity cracked open the door and they both stepped inside.

Although, it seems I got off much better than Sarah.

'Bronte' was not in a good way.

"No doctor?" He asked, as he took in the sloppily applied nature of the bandages covering the woman.
Particularly around her face. She looked more like a mummy than a person from the waist up.

Gravity shook her head, eyes firmly on her sister, "We're persona non grata now. Real doctors would turn us into the cops, and the back-alley kind would inform the Brotherhood."

She shrugged as she slumped into a chair that had been placed beside the bed, "The Brotherhood's won and everyone knows it. If there was any doubt that Hard-Light's gone, last night put a nail in it. We can't rely on his reputation to protect us anymore. Not from the gangs or the cops."

Erich's thoughts immediately went to the collection of gear he had stashed away in one of the vans. This was his chance to make a getaway.

"What happened?" He asked, brow furrowing as he felt an entirely unexpected pang of shame, "Last I heard things were going well."

"I could ask you the same thing." Gravity sighed, surprising him by tenderly gripping her unconscious sibling's hand. "A truck slammed into the building. Which would have been fine were it not for its cargo. Three freaks. Fast, strong, and with a freakish regenerative factor. Werewolf looking motherfuckers."

That caught his attention.

"Three? All with animalistic features?" He asked.

"Yep." Gravity nodded, "Like something out of a fucking horror movie."

"Three?" He repeated, Sarah's state and even his own plans forgotten. "You're sure it wasn't a single Meta with animal traits and two in a costume or something?"

Gravity looked at him, as if offended, "It definitely wasn't a fucking costume."

Erich didn't care, "And they all had the same powers? All three of them?"

His heart sunk when she nodded.

That's not statistically possible. Not all in one country, let alone one city.

"Shit." He cursed, hands running frantically though his hair. "Shit. Shit. Shit."

The medical equipment, he thought.

Still, a part of him held out hope.

"I need to see the bodies."

Gravity gave him a funny look, but answered nonetheless, "that'll be pretty hard. Mansion was on fire when I left. Won't be much left seeing after you dig through all the rubble."

That... that was good. Inconvenient, but good. At the very least it bought time. Unless the Brotherhood were less than subtle with their newest members.

Still, any plans to flee were gone now. This was the kind of trouble that followed you to the ends of the earth.

Escaping Hard-Light would have been a cakewalk compared to trying to outrun the Guild.

And he had no illusions the Guild wouldn't follow him. Anyone involved in this now had a target sign painted over their back.

"Erich, what's going on?" Gravity asked, noting the way the

blood drained from his face.

"I... I need to... I'll be in my workshop." He finally settled on, rushing from the room.

Gravity was left alone with Sarah once more, hand still holding hers.

"What the fuck was that?" She muttered to her sister.

Sarah remained as still and silent as ever.

△△△

Erich let water run over his shaking hands as he stared into the mirror after throwing up into the toilet.

Which had been distinctly uncomfortable given that he had not eaten anything in some time.

Even amidst his recent worries and revelations, his mind kept going back to that moment. Right when Grey's eyes widened in surprise as he plucked the disk from her throat.

She would have died anyway, he reasoned. *Or she would have gotten you killed.*

Yes.

She would have died anyway, he reiterated.

They were far from a hospital and the mansion was going to burn down around them within the hour. She would never have made it. All that would have happened was that she would have gotten him killed by informing Sarah of something she really didn't need to know.

You didn't know that at the time though, his reflection pointed out. *You just... acted.*

His hands still shook.

Striding out into the kitchen, he grabbed a can from the fridge. One of Gravity's beers. A low carb one he noted with surprise and dismay. Still, he wasted no time in popping the tab and guzzling down the drink.

Not nearly a high enough alcohol content.

Still, it satisfied the craving. More of a habit than a physical need, but the development of that craving was just a matter of time at the rate he was going.

"Work to do." He muttered, striding downstairs towards his shop.

Work would take his mind off things.

It always did.

ΔΔΔ

"Huh, you're still here?" Gravity murmured tiredly as she wandered into his shop.

Erich didn't even glance up from his assorted parts pile. Long since expanded from his days fixing toasters. Hard-Light had been more than happy to send all of his cast-off Meta-tech components his way.

"Why wouldn't I be?" He asked distractedly. "It's my home."

Gravity walked over, plucking up a memory processor as she did, "I don't know about *that*. I figured you would have taken your little van and skipped town by now."

Erich froze, partially disassembled omni-pad in hand.

"You knew about that?" He said with deliberate calm.

Gravity shrugged, "You were both out cold these last two days, and I kept expecting the Brotherhood to come bursting through the door at any moment. Figured it was a good idea to have an escape plan. Imagine my surprise to find your van already stocked up and ready to go."

Erich felt a drop of cold sweat run down the back of his neck, and it took a considerable amount of will not to reach for his laser pistol.

"Oh, chill out." Gravity laughed, swatting him lightly on the shoulder. "I'm not judging. Sarah might, but she's not really in any position to make it known, and I'm not about to tell her."

Erich let out a breath he hadn't realized he was holding.

"...Thank you." He said finally, and to his surprise, he found he meant it.

"Damn. I should have brought my camera. Not often I get to hear something like that from you," Gravity smiled, a much more genuine one than she'd had not twenty minutes earlier.

It would seem that just having someone to talk to had done her some good. Which was good for him because he would have had no clue how to help her otherwise.

"Quite." Erich said, a small smile of his own gracing his features despite his best attempts to stop it.

"Another rarity. Will wonders never end?" Gravity laughed before leaning over the table, "So, what's got you so excited that you practically ran out on me and my poor half-sister?"

"Our way of striking back at the Hangman." Erich said as he inspected a few loose strands of synth-muscle.

And just like that, Gravity's good mood was gone.

"No!" She practically spat.

It was so loud and surprising that Erich nearly dropped the strand he was holding.

"No?" He asked finally.

"No." Gravity reiterated. "It's over. Done. We lost. The best thing we can do now is get out of this town while we still have our lives."

It was funny. If Erich had heard that said even a few days earlier, he would have been jumping for joy.

"I would love to." He admitted, "but even if we run now, it won't save us. The Brotherhood have let the lion out of its cage, and if we're not quick, it's going to devour us all."

Erich was well aware that he was being more poetic that he needed, but what could he say? Imminent danger had a way of bringing out his inner thespian.

"What are you talking about?" Gravity said, having picked up on his obvious fear.

"How do you think powers are formed?" He asked, running a hand through his hair, "not the actual mechanics, but the catalyst for the event?"

"Stress?" Gravity said uncertainly.

"Exactly." Erich said as he was once more drawn to the pile of components before him. "Stress is what starts the change, but what most people don't realize is that the source of that stress, and how an individual perceives it, affects the resulting power more than anything else."

Gravity nodded.

"That's the problem." Erich continued, "you said that these 'werewolves' all had the same powerset. That's not a natural occurrence. In a modern society, stress comes about as a variety of different factors. More than that, people's subconscious solutions to these differing factors vary."

Erich pointed at her, "I'm willing to bet that your power came about as a result of a need to escape. A sensation of being 'crushed' physically or emotionally."

Gravity scowled at his bluntness, but ultimately nodded.

"More than that, it didn't affect your outward appearance." He paused. "Or perhaps it did. There's a lot to be said about Metas being more 'attractive' than average. Perhaps as a result of it being a benefit in a modern society. As opposed to something more grotesque but functional, like claws, scales or fur."

He shook his head, "The point is, that situations where Meta develop powers that make them look inhuman are rare. Situations where three individuals develop the *same* powers and the *same* appearance are statistically impossible as a result of circumstance."

Gravity gradually tacked onto what he was saying, "so someone forced people to have an Event that resulted in that powerset."

"That's the problem." Erich continued, frustration rising, "it's always been theoretical. The kind of stress needed to trigger an Event... it's massive in people who aren't already directly related to a Meta. Even then, you have no idea who might even have the traits needed to have an Event in the first place. So in order to test for it..."

"...You'd have to effectively torture a massive number of people in the hopes that one or two of them *might* have an event." Gravity finished, a look of nausea coming over her face.

Erich nodded. "You can see why it's remained just a theory so far, and why we don't have governments churning out Meta superheroes all over the place. A 'Meta Farm' isn't just morally repugnant, it's expensive and incredibly risky. Even if it works, you've essentially created a Meta with an unknown powerset and level with an ingrained desire to destroy the facility that created them."

Gravity still looked nauseous, "but clearly the Brotherhood have found a way around that problem, because those three who

attacked us were under their control, and had the same powers. Which means they have some way of controlling the outcome."

Erich wouldn't say they had the artificial Metas under control.

From what you told me, they basically threw them at you and then got the hell out of there.

"So why's this a problem?" Gravity asked finally. "Let's call the cops and have them take down the Brotherhood for us. There's no way they can bribe their way out of this."

"No!" Erich shouted, almost jumping up from his seat, "Don't you see! *We* know it works now. *We* can spread that knowledge. Could you imagine what would happen if the ability to create Metas on demand spread to a warlord on the West Coast?"

Gravity's dark complexion paled, "it would upset the power balance."

"Upset it!?" Erich said, "It would goddamn shatter it. It wouldn't be like the government could use the same technique to even the odds. Could you imagine the public outcry?"

Erich saw it was finally sinking in for her.

This isn't the kind of problem that heroes or cops sent to resolve, he thought. *This is the kind of problem that gets resolved with a black ops team and a bullet for everyone even peripherally involved.*

Including him.

"Shit." Gravity said, effectively summing up the situation.

CHAPTER 17

"Any improvements?" Erich asked as Gravity slunk back into the shop.

She didn't say anything, but the way the woman slumped into a seat was all the answer he needed really.

The more days past, the clearer it was becoming that Sarah needed an actual doctor. Her condition had yet to improve, and they were rapidly approaching the limits of his and Gravity's medical knowledge.

Hell, we had to google how to hook up an IV, he thought.

It was fortunate for them that Sarah had been unconscious at the time, because they hadn't gotten it right on the first try.

...or the fifth.

"How are things coming on your end?" Gravity asked tiredly.

Erich shrugged, "They're coming. At this rate I should be finished before the end of the month."

Gravity shook her head, "that's not fast enough. The Brotherhood could start on the Red Squares any day now."

Now that Hard-Light's faction was out of the way, it only made sense for them to start on their primary rivals now that they knew their new 'weapons' worked.

Can't help but wonder if we were just a trial run?

Erich shook his head. It didn't matter in the end.

"I am well aware of how close we all are to getting put on a government hit list," Erich deadpanned, "but I'm already going as fast as I can."

He gestured to the half-built torso in front of him.

"Once I get the first one set up, it should be able to act as my assistant. That should speed the process up."

If not to any appreciable degree. A fresh AI would be about as intelligent as a particularly bright dog, albeit in different ways to an actual dog.

'Intelligence' is a spectrum after all, he thought.

He was a prime example of that very fact. Brilliant in all things engineering, but he was all too willing to admit to a number of deficiencies in other areas.

People most of all.

"It would go faster if you were actually willing to help me." He pointed out, not for the first time, and likely not for the last.

Gravity sent a tired glare his way. "If I did, would you start helping me clean up Sarah's shit, sponge bath and feed her?"

No. Not in a million years.

He was a genius, not some kind of menial. He didn't deal with people... or their *fluids.*

"The robot could do it." He said offhandedly, as he started installing what used to be a webcam into said machine's head.

"You think I'm about to trust your mechanical contraption with my sister?" Gravity asked incredulously.

Erich might have been offended by the insinuation that his creation would be anything less than perfect, were it not for the grain of truth informing the woman's words.

AI could be... finicky.

There was a very good reason they hadn't sparked the next technological singularity, after all.

Even the fairly robust Omni-Systems Artificial Intelligence template he was going to pirate from the web was far from foolproof.

*And that's before I start installing some **very** illegal combat sub-routines into it.*

"Fair enough," he grudgingly acknowledged.

"Why are you even building those things anyway?" Gravity groused, gesturing at the collection of limbs and synth muscle strewn about the workshop, as well as the fabricator in the corner, which had been churning out more components almost non-stop since he'd started.

Again, Erich didn't begrudge her skepticism. A well-designed combat droid was usually only about as effective as a reasonably competent soldier, a few times more expensive, and not half as adaptable.

Of course, the fact that he was building them for himself cut down on the price considerably, but even then they wouldn't be as cost-effective as a brand-new suit.

"The Hangman's a mind reader." Erich reiterated for what felt like the third time, "If I go after him with just a suit again, he'll tear it apart with the same ease he took out my first one."

Which was true, even if he'd lied about exactly *how* the mind-reader had taken him out. Even if Erich didn't include a system of fail safes this time, the meta would still know every move he planned to make three steps in advance.

"That's why Integrity was sure the guy had mind control powers." He explained, "it's not difficult to get people to do what you want if you know their every want, need and weakness within moments of meeting them."

Gravity stared at him for a few moments, before deflating "so you
say. I still think we had a leak."

Erich didn't doubt they did, but it didn't change the situation with the Hangman, "He knew shit. Shit I told no one. He's a mind reader."

"So how did Integrity get the drop on him in the tunnel?" Gravity asked, referring the altered version of events he had told her.

"I'm pretty sure he sped up his mind sufficiently that the Hangman would have only registered it as a blur or 'white noise'." He theorised, "If he registered it at all."

Erich had no idea how the mechanics of the guy's mind control worked, but that was his working theory. It didn't help that Integrity probably hadn't planned for that to happen. The guy had probably just wanted to slow down his perception of time so he could launch his surprise attack at the perfect moment.

"And this happened after you had your suit taken out?" Gravity reiterated.

"Throwing disks with explosives attached." Erich shrugged, "Got the drop on me, on all of us, when my shields were down. Which only reinforces my mind reading theory. He knew *exactly* when our guard was down."

Gravity stared at him for a few more seconds, before shrugging, "you don't seem nearly as upset about losing your suit as I thought you would be."

Of its own volition his mind went back to it. The darkness. The heat. The suffocating claustrophobia…

"Bigger problems right now." He spat as he shook his head to dismiss the phantom sensation of metal pressing down around him.

Frowning, he gestured to the half-finished combat droid hung up on the rack in front of him. "Pass me that wrench, would you?"

Erich sensed his friend's eyes watching him for a few more pregnant moments, before he felt the cool metal of the tool settle into his hand.

"I'm going to make *another* adult diaper run." Gravity sighed as she stood up. "You want anything?"

"Carton of milk. We're running low." He said shortly.

It was only as he heard Gravity walk away, that he noticed that his right hand was shaking.

Did she see? He wondered, panic flaring in his chest.

Almost of their own accord, his fingers brushed across the laser pistol on his belt. He wanted to take it and run. Far and fast. He'd done it once and he could do it again.

Can't run, he reminded himself. *They'd catch you. Quickly. You've got to stay. Strangle this problem in the crib.*

Still, it was difficult to calm the racing of his heart.

Need to get back to work.

He deliberately ignored the suit blueprints sitting on his table as he returned to the drone in front of him.

Still, the sensation of metal closing in around him remained at the back of his mind. Pressing at the very edge of his senses.

He scowled, fear morphing into anger as he redoubled his efforts.

Keep working.

ΔΔΔ

"Why'd you make it look humanoid?" Gravity asked as he welded the latest unit's torso armor on.

He shrugged as he lifted his goggles to inspect the seam, "it's convenient."

"Yeah, but like, isn't it less efficient?"

Erich stepped over to the workbench to grab a drink – a non-alcoholic drink. Budding alcoholism aside, he'd never indulge while working.

"Sure, compared to say, a four-legged box with a gun on top." He admitted, "but eventually I'm going to have to transport these guys across the city. I need them to fit in the van, and I need them to be relatively inconspicuous during our assault. That's why we're going to be making a run to thrift store when it's finally time for the assault. Need to buy some baggy clothes to outfit them."

Gravity giggled, "We're going to put clothes on them?"

Erich nodded, "Just enough to fool someone at a distance."

In the dark...

The need for discretion wouldn't have been a problem in the past, but like Gravity said, they no longer had Hard-Light's reputation to hide behind. And rogue AI constructs tended to draw a lot more heat than comparatively more dangerous constructs. Like his old suit.

Which is something we have the Master to thank for.

Sure, the man had worked with other supervillains of his time, but at the end of the day, it was him and his endless legions of Meta-tech constructs that conquered the West Coast and split the country in two.

The stigma toward AI of any description still ran deep because of it.

Got to be more subtle now, he thought as he looked at the finished robot.

"If you were going to do that, couldn't you have made them more... human looking?" Gravity wondered as she looked at the machine's hard angles and boxy shape.

"You were the one who wanted me to go faster." Erich pointed out, "this is the compromise."

And even with the compromise, he'd like to think what he'd done had been pretty damn impressive.

Sure, security bots weren't amazingly rare, and he'd already had all the parts he'd needed on hand, but that didn't change the fact that he'd churned out ten of them in the course of a week.

Well, pretty much alone, he amended, as he glanced at two of his utterly still helpers. The soft whining of their motors and the blue glow of their headlights were the only things indicating that drones were active.

"Bring in the next unit," he said, watching with no small degree of satisfaction as the two units leapt to obey, their eye pieces flashing yellow as they moved.

"Acknowledged." The two units said in unison, their voices echoing with artificial distortion.

Which anyone listening to will hopefully pass off as a voice changer, he thought.

"That's another thing I don't get." Gravity said as she watched the

two robots clatter over to the next unit; one that had been entirely assembled but for its armored components. "Why the lights? You just said you wanted to be subtle."

Erich frowned, "it's a safety feature. They turn off when they enter combat mode."

"Why'd you need a safety feature?" Gravity asked, still eyeing the two drones.

He shrugged uncomfortably, "If your computer glitches, you might end up losing some files. If one of *these* glitches…"

Well… it went unsaid.

Personally, he would rather have a few seconds warning if his creation's threat recognition software decided to fail.

"You aren't filling me with confidence here." Gravity deadpanned as she glanced at him.

"I built these things in a week." He said, "if they *didn't* have a few issues, then I'd be goddamn surprised."

He'd had to cut a few corners; one of which was the origin of the drones combat-subroutines.

Here's hoping the unit AI from 'Call of Destiny' is as good as the reviews said it was.

It was a cheap trick, but he wasn't an amazing or particularly fast programmer. It was easier for him to simply crib from a preexisting model. He could only hope it wouldn't come back to bite him in the ass later.

Gravity's frown softened as she ultimately conceded his point, "I guess you're right."

He nodded, about as happy as she was about relying on something that was, in all likelihood, unreliable.

"They're just disposable muscle anyway." He said.

Gravity turned back to eying the units as they dragged their skeletal brother over.

"I guess." She said, before changing tact entirely, "So, how are things coming with suit 2.0?"

It was an innocent question, meant more to change the topic than anything else. Nonetheless, Erich felt his stomach drop out from under him as his mind turned towards his suit.

Grey's disbelieving eyes staring up at him. The scent of blood in the air. The sound of her lifeblood dripping to the floor.

"I haven't had time." He said, his hand clenching into a fist, "the drones have been keeping me busy."

ΔΔΔ

"I think I wanted this, you know?" Erich murmured to Sarah's comatose form.

Even as he made his confession, he whispered under his breath. All but silent even in the quiet of his room; if only on the off chance his captive audience regained consciousness.

Even if his paranoia had come back to bite him in recent days, he found it difficult to shed the habit of a lifetime. He wasn't even sure he wanted to.

Gravity was out. Another shopping run to refill their meager stash of food and drink. She had charged him with watching over her comatose sister, refusing to accept his exclamations that one of his robots could do it.

So, there he sat, looking at the woman who for a short time had been his lover, and in some small way, his jailer.

"Sure, it was mostly at the back of my mind, but I knew from the moment I showed you that suit, you would want me to build more." He admitted, more to himself than anyone else. "How could you not?"

In the corner of the room one of his sec-droids watched over both of them, a laser rifle cradled in its cold metallic hands.

"And, you know what? I enjoyed it. Even the piloting." He murmured, Especially the piloting."

He smiled bitterly, "I never admitted it. Not even to myself. But I
think I *was* enjoying all of it. The money. The power. The respect. The... sex. But most of all, I think it was the sensation of being one of the 'big' people."

That had been new. And so intoxicating. To be noticed for his talent. To not be a footnote in some else's story for once. To be judged on his own merits rather than be drawn up against the example his sister set.

"I think it was my way of finally beating her. Sad as it is." He mused, "Taking on Metas with a suit *I* built."

Proving that he, a mundane man, had the power to do battle with the metaphorical demigods of the new age.

"And I'll be honest." He nodded, "for all my plans to run. For all my plans to escape this life. When I get right down to it, I don't think I can."

Lord knows, if he had been willing to make just one or two sacrifices, he could have escaped from Hard-Light.

If he *really* wanted to. But he hadn't.

He'd made excuses in his own mind and continued down the path, complaining all the while.

"I think Grey's death is what's driven it home for me." He admitted, "what I'm willing to do to keep living this lifestyle. Who I'm willing to hurt for my own gain."

Not without hesitation, but without a doubt, he repeated in his mind.

That was the crux of it, wasn't it?

He'd never thought himself a bad person. Greedy, vain, callous, cowardly and more, but never... villainous.

Hell, he'd even managed to convince himself he was somewhat heroic. In some small way he'd been living out a fantasy of his youth; fighting Neo-Nazis on the streets of North Granton in a suit he had built himself, surrounded by people with powers.

A beautiful woman on each arm...

Proving to himself that he was *one of them.*

Then he'd met the reality of his situation; powerlessness.

Hangman had mastered him as easily as one might an unruly child.

Because they cheated. Because they'd done something Erich had never even considered. Because they'd acted in a way that would have gotten anyone but them killed.

And they'd not just survived, but thrived.

Because they had a *power.*

And powers did not conform to the laws of reality as science understood them. They were the ultimate wild card. The ultimate trump. A way of overturning any given status quo.

And because of that, Erich had been forced to confront a second truth.

Grey's eyes staring up at him as he plucked the blade from her neck, as if silently pleading to know why.

He knew why.

Because you were a threat to me, he responded from across the gulf of time. *Because it benefited me more for you to be dead rather than alive.*

That was the conclusion he had come to.

What did that make him? To inflict pain on others for one's own gain? What else could that be but the act of a villain?

He had to accept that.

He couldn't afford to keep being so... halfhearted about all this.

"Get well soon Bronte," he murmured as he gently squeezed one of her bandaged hands. "I think I understand you more now than when all this began."

Certainly not *all* of her... but more.
"Engage sentry mode," he said as he stepped out of the room.

"Acknowledged."

Gravity wouldn't be happy about it, but he found he didn't care. She would get over it. His presence in that room wouldn't help Sarah.

It wouldn't help anyone.

No, he had work to do.

He had to take the Hangman down.

Not because he'd wronged him. Not because it was the right thing to do. Not because hundreds of people would die in horrific ways if he didn't.

He was going to do it because the mind reader's existence was a clear and present threat to him.

At least, that's what he told himself as he strode down the stairs to his shop.

"This may be more difficult than I initially gave it credit for." Erich surmised as they looked over the plans for the abandoned hospital that the New Brotherhood had converted into their 'Meta Farm'.

"You can say that again." Gravity frowned.

The place was massive. So big that Erich had no idea how a place of that size had been built in a city that desperately needed more
hospitals, and yet was now sitting 'abandoned'.

"Do you know why it was abandoned?" He asked curiously.

"The usual," Gravity shrugged. "Corruption, mismanagement, politics and budget cuts. It was pretty big news back when I was a kid."
That sounded about right.

"Right, so what did you manage to find out yesterday?" Erich said, getting back to the topic at hand.

"Saw at least two dozen Brotherhood gang members lounging about outside yesterday, but there's definitely more inside."

Definitely, Erich thought, *support staff at least; doctors, nurses, orderlies… guards. Not just to protect the place, but to keep the prisoners in line as well.*

And given the kind of work he thought they were doing in there, he was willing to assume that anyone present was an enemy combatant.

Which is just as well, because I need to silence them all anyway… including the prisoners.

That was going to be rough. No two ways about it.

Not for the first time, he considered just flattening the place from a distance and calling it a day.

"I know that look," Gravity said. "The cops will ignore a lot of things, but they won't ignore people using heavy artillery in a city. If we're going to do this without drawing *too* much attention, we need to be careful."

Which translated to putting a few pounds worth of explosives in the right places to make it look like the place was destroyed by something else. Like two Metas duking it out inside.

Erich sighed, and nodded.

Looks like I'm was going to be looking a lot of people in the eyes when I murder them.

"You think your bots are going to be up to it?" Gravity asked.

Erich glanced over to where the silent machines, now twelve in number, stood lined up against the back wall of his shop. He'd initially had them patrolling the place but watching them prowling about at all hours had swiftly got on his nerves.

"One bot for ten gang members, assuming the same level of equipment and competence we've seen thus far." He guessed.

The bots casing could shrug off most forms of small arms without much trouble, but like his suit, the design's weaknesses were the joints. If you threw enough bullets at them, they would go down.

"That many?" Gravity whistled. "I thought you said they were about as good as a competent soldier?"

"I did." Erich shrugged. "And that makes them worth at least a dozen street thugs by my reckoning. Besides, ten's an ideal situation. Heavier weapons or Metas will scrap them without much trouble."

It took a certain level of creativity to deal with whatever craziness a Meta might throw out, after all. Modern AI just weren't capable of it.

"Alright, so I assume that's our job then?" Gravity asked, a hint of nervousness entering her tone. "Dealing with any Metas that pop up?"

Erich didn't blame her for being nervous. He knew he certainly was, and he'd only heard about these 'werewolves' from her second hand.

Prior to her more detailed explanation of the brutes, his running theory had been that Hard-Light had been caught off guard by the
Hangman's mindreading powers and taken out that way. But the more he heard about these new artificial Metas, the more he worried that the man had simply been overwhelmed by a horde of the slobbering monsters.

Which did not bode well for their own chances, given that they were about assault the place they originated from.

No, he thought. *If they had more than three available, they would have used them during the assault on the mansion.*

And given that those three had perished – at the expense of nearly all of Hard-Light's *very* well equipped goons – he was hoping that the Brotherhood had yet to create more.

Still...

"It is." He admitted to Gravity's previous question.

Gravity looked like she wanted to swear, but in the end nodded stoically.

"Look on the bright side," he said as he ran a hand through his hair, "there's one Meta there that we can leave to the bots."

"Who?"

"Hangman." Erich said, "If you encounter him, direct the bots to take them down. If I'm right, and they're a mind reader, the bots have an infinitely better chance of catching him off guard than we would."

Integrity had proven that.

In an ideal world, Erich would have whipped up some kind of anti-mind reading device now that he knew what the Meta's power was.
Unfortunately, this was reality, and he had no idea how to even start on such a project.

How does one even 'read' minds?

That was the problem with powers. They didn't play by the same rules that the rest of reality seemed to abide by. Speedsters should be pancaked by their own acceleration. Bruisers should crack concrete with their sheer density. Shooters should melt the skin of their own hands.

Hell, even chunks of my own tech is cannibalized from parts created by Hard-Light, Erich thought grimly.

Erich might have had a better understanding of technology than the old man ever did, but even he had no clue how the ultra-compact Meta-Tech batteries that powered the whole ensemble worked.

It just did.

"Well that's a good. I wouldn't want to mess with him after the pounding he gave you." Gravity grinned, pulling him from his thoughts.

Metal closing in. Blood in the air. Screams in the dark.

"Quite." Erich faked a thin smile at the woman's small attempt at
levity, ignoring the tightening of his chest.

Of course, Gravity noticed immediately – his acting skills were atrocious.

"You sure you're going to be ok with this, Erich?" Gravity said. "You haven't even started on a second suit yet."

"I'll be fine." He said, ignoring the hairs rising on the back of his neck as he thought of clambering once more into a... suit.

"You don't look fine." Gravity pointed out calmly. "You're turning paler than usual."

"I'll be fine." He glared.

If he thought that would make her back off, he was sorely disappointed. Which only made sense really; she'd lived her whole life surrounded by villains with short fuses and generally unstable personalities.

"You're not fine." She said. "You're practically shaking."

Erich firmly gripped his treacherous right hand to his chest, stopping its quivering by smothering it against himself. He glanced away from Gravity's concerned gaze, shame blooming in his chest.

Which was morbidly funny, now that he thought about it.

I've never pretended to have any great moral fortitude, he thought.

He'd never pretended to be more than he was. A selfish and vain coward, desperately scrambling to save his own skin.

"I'll do it." Gravity said finally.

"What?" He said, taken completely off guard by the random statement.

"I'll do it alone." She said, resting a hand on his shoulder. "You don't have to go. Me and the bots should be enough."

No. They weren't. Not even close. Even *with* him, this was liable

240

to fail and get them both killed.

I want to accept though. So very badly.

"...No. You won't." He sighed, "you fail, and I'm toast anyway."

Gravity stared at him, eyes roaming over his, if not determined, then no longer terrified, expression.

"And here I thought you would say something inspiring about always having my back," she chuckled.

Erich shrugged.

He wasn't that guy. He never would be.

"Well," she said, "if you're determined to come on this little suicide mission, you really need to get a suit of *some description* up and running."

She gestured to the map.

"Otherwise we're going to end up getting pinned down at the first bottleneck we come across. We need *something* to act as our breacher."

Erich nodded tiredly, "give me a few more days. I'll get something together."

Gravity grinned.

"Good. I'll see if I can't drum up some extra manpower in the meantime. Hard-Light's guys might have all gone to ground, but there should still be some smaller gangs roaming about with more balls than brains. Just a matter of waving some cash in their direction really."

Erich wondered for a moment why she hadn't mentioned this idea
prior to now, before deciding it wasn't really worth it.

"Just try and get a few that will wait until *after* we've destroyed the horrific torture factory before they stab us in the back."

Gravity gave him a jaunty salute before she strode out of the room, one of the sec-units peeling off to join her.

Erich sighed, before turning back to his worktable.

A few days to put together a new suit? Yeah right...

ΔΔΔ

Erich sighed as he looked over the initial designs for his new suit.

"Well... It's prettier than the first one was," he muttered.

It was also smaller and faster.

...With weaker shields, weapons and armor, as well as a shorter operational time, he amended.

Which was only to be expected when one considered that he planned to assemble it over a few days with half as many parts as his first attempt.

Still...

Erich heard the telltale beep of his drones entering combat mode and immediately dropped his Omni-Pad as he reached for his laser pistol.

"Report." He said to the nearest yellow eyed sec-unit as he kept a wary eye on the door.

"Asset 'Gravity' has returned with an unknown individual." The machine intoned with its artificial cadence. **"Permission to engage unknown individual?"**

"Permission postponed." Erich instructed as he started walking toward the shop's entrance, "All available units accompany me. Escort mode."

"Acknowledged." The drones said as they fell in around him with machine like precision.

Erich had a vague idea of what he would find outside: Gravity being denied entrance by the sec-unit at the door, accompanied by some two-bit gang-leader.

Probably a low-level Meta of some description.

Which likely meant a woman, given the disparity in Event rates between the genders.

Of course, there was also the possibility that she had been captured and was being held hostage at gun point. Which was why he was being accompanied by an entire compliment of his drones.

He had also taken to wearing one of the few remaining hard-light vests at all hours, so he was reasonably safe from being sniped the moment he stepped outside.

All in all, it was nothing to get particularly excited about, and he was far more interested in returning to the 'suit' that was taking shape inside his shop.

Which was why he was caught almost completely off guard when he saw who – or what – was standing beside Gravity on the street.

Or rather, looming over Gravity on the street.

"Yo, Erich." Gravity's voice called, no doubt taking pleasure in his poleaxed expression.

Not that he really noticed her, focused as he was on the seven-foot-tall purple skinned woman standing next to her.

"Who's your friend?" He asked as soon as he recovered.

"Myra." The woman in question answered. "Leader of the White Tigers and your ally in seeing the Brotherhood driven from this city."

"As she said." Gravity grinned, "her and her people are pretty eager to give the Brotherhood a bloody nose."

"But not so eager as to forgo payment." Myra said as she crossed her massive arms over her *equally* massive chest.

"That won't be a problem." Erich put in as he surreptitiously waved for the drones to stand down. "I think you will find us quite well suited to remunerate you for your assistance."

No matter how much it pained him to do so.

"Good." The woman said, "because if I'm going to be throwing my people into this meatgrinder, then I expect to be well compensated for the loss."
Gravity frowned at the woman's words, but Erich found himself looking at the statuesque woman with a newfound respect.

This was someone he could work with.

CHAPTER 18

"So, it's true that Hard-Light had another Artificer with him." Myra said as she glanced around the shop. "I assume that makes you Mechromancer then?"

"In a manner of speaking." Erich responded as he gestured to the drones standing sentry along the walls, "I'm without a mech at the minute though, so it doesn't quite feel right to keep going by the title."

"You're still Mechromancer. Suit or not." The woman insisted. "These little toys you've got keeping an eye on me are proof of that."

Erich shrugged. He had hoped to be subtle about the fact that his guards were all still armed, but it seemed the gang leader had seen right through his wafer-thin deception.

"As you say." He said for lack of anything else to say.

"Although, if you're still hankering for a suit, you can come work for me. Me and my people could really use an Artificer. Might not have access to the same shit Hard-Light had, but with him gone... well, we have room for expansion." The woman offered frankly.

"Let's stop right there." Gravity jumped in, cutting the woman off before she could say anything else. "You're here to help plan out this assault on the Brotherhood and negotiate your pay, not try and poach away Erich."

"Worth a shot." The woman shrugged, utterly unabashed. "Would take you too if I could."

Erich coughed, getting his mind back on track after being caught off guard by the offer.

It wasn't like he would have accepted anyway. It had been risky enough running with Hard-Light, who had been considered pretty much invincible before everything had gone south and proven that to very much not be the case.

Even if we still have no idea what happened to the man...

No, he wasn't about to sign up with a small-time gang. Especially one that thought it was a good idea to piss of the same group that had done in the former most powerful Meta in the city.

"Right." Erich said as he handed both women an Omni-Pad. "I've been looking the place over, and I think our best chance is to use the same approach against them that they used on us. A lightning fast assault initiated by a kamikaze strike from a truck or equally heavy vehicle right through the front doors. From there we go in, slap down some explosives, and get out."

"Who's going to drive the truck?" Gravity asked, "one of the bots?"

Erich shrugged, "In a manner of speaking. I can rig up a simple drive system, if we can grab the vehicle we're going to use an hour or so in advance."

"Too risky." Myra chimed in as she looked over the hospital map.

"Look at this hallway. Much too thin. There's a good chance we'd just end up creating an obstacle for ourselves and jamming the whole place up."

Ah. He hadn't thought of that. Then again, he was well out of his comfort zone, so it wasn't really all that surprising. He was an engineer, not some kind of strategic savant.

Really, he would have preferred to pass it all off to Gravity, but it seemed that even with the loss of her father's organization, she was far more content to be a follower rather than a leader. She was also far better at deflecting tasks than he was...

"How accurate are these bots of yours in a shootout?" The massive purple skinned woman asked.

He shrugged, "They're machines so... very. So long as they get a second or two to acquire the target they should be accurate up to the range possible with their weapons."

Which was a mishmash of different guns, given that Gravity hadn't exactly had time to scoop up a dozen laser rifles while she dragged both Erich and her sister from Hard-Light's burning mansion. Erich had been forced to arm his security force from whatever Gravity could buy from the various illicit arms dealers that roamed the local neighborhood.

Myra hummed in thought before tapping a few locations on her pad. "How about we place a shooter here, here and here in advance of the attack. From there they could take out any door guards before keeping those entrances suppressed."

Erich watched as a number of red icons appeared on his own pad where she'd tapped.

"Won't they notice us getting the bots into place?" Gravity asked as she took a sip of her drink.

Myra shook her head, "My people are familiar with that area, even if we didn't know what was going on there. We figured it was just another drug lab, not a... what did you say it was again?"

"Trafficking ring." Gravity put in before Erich could speak, belatedly remind him that the whole reason they were going through with this was to keep what was going on in that hellhole quiet. "We're also expecting a Meta named 'Hangman' to be there. He was injured in our last engagement, so with any luck, he should still be there recuperating."

Because this was going to get really complicated if he wasn't. Given that all these changes had only come about *after* Hangman showed up, Erich was betting that the telepath was the source of them.

If they could take him *and* the hospital out at the same time, it would hopefully put a lid on the entire 'Meta-Farm' thing, before it managed to spread.

"Right." Myra nodded, "The guards stick to the building itself rather than the surrounding street."

She gestured at the watching drones, flashing them a mouth full of teeth that definitely weren't human. It hadn't been all that long ago that Erich had pointed out how rare it was for powers to come with visible 'defects' and for just a moment, he wondered what had

caused the woman before him to have her powers develop in such a way.

Myra continued heedless of his thoughts, "Put some clothes on them like you did with the one at the front before sending them out at night. None of those skinhead fucks will pay them any attention. Probably just assume they're another bunch of vagrants."

Erich tapped a finger to his chin, drawn from his thoughts. "Sounds like a good idea, but that doesn't exactly give us a way to gain *entry* to the place. We're not exactly running a surplus of energy shields here."

Hospitals were tall and had lots of windows. Perfect places to snipe from. Even with his bots providing cover fire, he wasn't eager to make a dash across that much open ground. Especially in a new, weaker, and entirely untested suit.

"Energy shields?" The woman scoffed, "Shit, you rich folk and your fancy pants shit. We don't need that. My guys can whip up a few smoke cannisters. All you need to do is chuck them out and run like hell for the doors."

Erich didn't like the sound of that, and from the look on Gravity's face, she wasn't a massive fan of the idea either.

"And what's to stop them from gunning us down when we're all nicely bottle necked at the door in this mad scramble?" She asked skeptically.

Myra grinned, razor sharps fangs peering out from between her lilac lips, "That's what you've got me for."

ΔΔΔ

"Do you trust her?" Erich asked as he felt the third automated arm settle onto his suit's back mount with a satisfying clunk.

Myra had left to gather her people after another hour or so of planning their assault on the hospital. At least she said she was gathering her people.

For all they knew, she was selling them out to the Brotherhood as they spoke. Which was why Erich had his drones on high alert, with four of them dressed up in casual clothes and standing sentry just outside the shop.

Gravity pursed her lips as she lazily nursed a beer. A low-carb one. Erich thought they were gross, which was probably why she kept buying them. It was a good way to keep him from raiding her stash.

"Trust is a strong word." She said finally. "Everyone has their price, and in this business those prices are pretty damn low."

"Not exactly a ringing endorsement." Erich muttered as he tapped the screen on his Omni-Pad.

"I wasn't finished yet, and don't use me to test your suits tracking software!" She said, ducking as the arm swung towards her. It was pointless anyway, the arm unnervingly followed her every movement.

Erich shrugged, powering down the arm with another couple of taps to the Omni-Pad.

"As I was saying." Gravity continued as she returned to her seat with a pronounced pout, "Myra will sell us out if she thinks it's in her best interests. Fortunately for us, those interests align far more with ours than the Brotherhood's."

Erich could see that being the case. The woman's inhuman features would put her on the Brotherhood's shit list no matter what she did.

And somehow I doubt the New Brotherhood's use of 'werewolves' has changed that stance.

From what Gravity had told him, the Brotherhood had deployed the Metas that attacked her in a manner more fitting for disposable ordnance than a living asset to the organization.

"We also go back a fair way," Gravity continued as Erich checked to see if the new connection had messed with the suit's shielding system. An actual shield, rather than a barrier system, given the decreased size of the suit's generator.

He was a bit concerned that the long length of the new automated arms would mean that they poked outside of the shield's protective bubble.

"Surprising." Erich said as he noted with satisfaction that there was no unnatural drain on the shields. "I would have thought hanging out with another gang would have been a big no-no while you were with Hard-Light."

Gravity shrugged, "In case you didn't notice, he and I didn't exactly see eye to eye on a lot of things."

Yes. He definitely had noticed that.

"So do you know just her, or the rest of her crew as well?" He asked, more to continue the conversation than out of any real

251

interest. Gravity had already answered his initial question after all.

"I know a few of them. I imagine the memberships changed a fair bit since I last ran with them. Small-time gangs tend to have a pretty high turnover rate."

Erich could see that being the case.

"So you didn't just hang out, you were actually part of the gang for a while?" He asked with not-a-little surprise.

"Hard-Light wasn't really in the picture back when I was actually a part of the gang." She said, not that it was even really a proper gang back then. Hell, we probably had more in common with those vigilante groups you hear about."

That caught Erich's attention.

"You? A vigilante?"

Gravity actually flushed.

"Only a little!" She protested, "and only because we mostly hit other gangs. Small time ones like us, but ones that were into the really shady shit. Trafficking and the like."

"And Myra was in on this?" He asked, trying to reconcile the massive woman from before with a youthful vigilante. She had seemed like many things, but altruistic wasn't one of them.

The grin that had been forming on Gravity's face died.

"As I said. We were a lot younger then." She said finally, "the White Tigers are just another gang now. Not the worst around, but not much better either. The only good thing I'd say about them is that actually do provide some protection for the people they extort."

Obtuse as he was, even Erich could tell it was a sore spot for the woman.

"So, why'd you leave?" He asked as the silence started to drag.

Gravity frowned, "My powers developed. Which was also when I finally found out who my father was."

Ah, Erich thought, *now I get it.*

It wasn't an amazingly uncommon practice. For villains or heroes. All one had to do was start leaving bastards all over the place. Which was easy enough for men of means, which most villains and heroes tended to be.

Sure, it was an investment that wouldn't see any results for something like sixteen years, if ever, but it wasn't like it was any great investment of effort on the part of the man either. All one had to do was keep tabs on the kid every other year and see if any powers developed.

For Heroes it meant easier access to protégés, and for villains it meant Meta underlings.

His thoughts must have shown on his face, because Gravity gave him a dry smile.

"Yep," she said, "suddenly I'm no longer my own woman. I'm part of Hard-Light's little organization. Sarah doesn't talk about it, but her story's pretty much the same. Death-Shriek too, before he got on the wrong side of Grey Hood."

J. R. Grey

Erich didn't know what to say to that.

"Pass me the next arm would you." Was what he finally settled on.

Gravity looked dumbfounded for a moment, before sighing and reaching over to grab the appendage.

"I don't know what else I was expecting." She said as she passed him the arm.

△△△

Erich twitched slightly as he felt the suits four automated arms shifting on his back. It was an unsettling sensation to feel them moving independently of his will. Not unlike having a particularly large and cumbersome animal strapped to him.

"Nervous, kid?" Myra grinned over at him, mistaking his discomfort for nerves. Which wasn't an entirely incorrect assumption to make.

He *was* nervous as hell.

"Uncomfortable." He said, thankful that the suit's comm system meant he didn't have to yell over the noise of the van. "This suit was a rush job, and I can feel it."

"Doesn't look like a rush job." Myra said, eyes running admiringly over his latest suit. "I've seen plenty of Artificers use worse for much longer."

"Which says more about the low standards of Artificers than it does my suit," he pointed out.

254

The purple skinned Amazonian still looked skeptical but nod-ded anyway.

"Fair enough." She said before turning toward the rest of her people, who were so tightly packed into the vehicle that it was standing room only. An unfortunate side effect of working with such a low level gang was that the vans that Erich had taken for granted while working with Hard-Light were now far fewer in number.

Two to be precise. And one of those was his. Or rather, Hard-Light's, but possession was nine-tenths of the law.

Besides, it's not like he'll be needing it anymore, he snarked as he thought of the likely long dead supervillain.

He would have preferred to go in the van with the drones rather than be crammed in here with the rest of Myra's gang, but he doubted it could have taken the extra weight, even with Grav-ity riding along to try and alleviate some of it.

He was drawn from his lamentations by Myra beginning her pre-battle speech. Unlike him and her, the rest of her people didn't have earbuds to communicate, so she had to yell.

"Right kiddy-winkles you know the plan. Mechromancer's drones are going to be the first on station, and they're going to be the ones to deploy smoke. That means we should have some cover when we arrive. Don't think that means you can stand around scratching your ass when you jump out. The second your feet hit the ground I want you running for those hospital doors. Let's get inside, get these explosives planted, and get the hell out."

"How will they know where the doors are if there's smoke everywhere?" Erich asked, the idea only just occurring to him.

"This ain't our first rodeo," Myra grinned, "my driver's done this a hundred times before. He's going to point the rear of this truck directly where we need to go. All we need to do is start running when we get out."

Seemed a little slapdash to Erich, but Myra seemed confident, so he withheld his skepticisms. It wasn't like it mattered to him. The visual filters in his helmet would be more than capable of seeing through a little smoke. So long as enough of Myra's goons made it to the front door to pull off the attack, he didn't care if a few got picked off while they were stumbling through the smoke.

Erich dismissed them from his thoughts as he turned toward his own suit's diagnostics window.

Shields, full strength. Synth-Muscle, primed and ready. Coolant system, operational. Back-Arms, functioning.

For good measure he had the system run its own check.

"Lasers Online. Shields Online. Targeting Online." Gravity's computerized voice announced, the familiar rhythm a balm to his worried mind.

Fuck it, he thought with an eerie sense of déjà vu. *Let's do this.*

The rest of the White Tigers were either more used to their drivers insane driving style, or steadier on their feet than Erich, because he was the only one who stumbled as the vehicle pivoted.

Or they don't have enough room to fall over, Erich noted with grim satisfaction as he saw the strained look on the faces of those goons who were pressed up against the wall.

Still, the moment the van swerved to a halt, the back doors were swung open and people were piling out onto the smoke-filled street.

"Time to go, kid." Myra grinned as she easily pulled his heavy exo-suit to its feet with a single massive purple hand before leaping out herself, the van swaying violently on its suspension as the purple Meta left.

Erich wasn't much slower as he charged out of the van, his suits sensors allowing him to see across the car-park despite the clouds of smoke obscuring everything.

Which was why he got to see in great detail as one of the White Tigers took a stray round and collapsed mid-charge. Nor was she the only one, as he could see two other prone figures face down in the smoke.

Myra might have disdained the use of energy shields as a rich man's crutch, but he imagined those of her posse who weren't bulletproof might have felt differently.

Besides, it wasn't like the defenders were having it entirely their own way. From behind him he could hear the methodical gunfire of his drones as they advanced on the building. Rather than the mad dash of their organic counterparts, his mechanical underlings fired as they advanced, forcing the defenders to duck back into cover in those few moments where the smoke shifted enough to give either side a vague view of the other.

"Erich, second floor, third window from the right!" Gravity radioed.

Through the gloom of the smoke, Erich watched as a figure was dragged up into the air, flailing madly as they were illuminated in green.

Ignoring the occasional spark of bullets impacting his shield, he focused on the figure.

"Weapon Three. Manual Control. Eye Reticule." He murmured as his targeting system interposed a targeting reticule over his vision.

"Manual Control Engaged." Gravity's automated voice responded.

As soon as the reticule was in place, he thumbed the activator on his wrist and three shots cracked out from over his shoulder.

The glowing figure jerked in the air, before going still.

"Target down." he said simply, watching as a moment later the glow faded, and the body slumped against the parapet of the window.

"Nice." Gravity shouted, *"the rest are keeping their heads down now. Get over to Myra before a Meta shows up."*

"Drones on me." He instructed, running forward as the machines around him stopped firing to jog after him. One lagged behind as a result of sparking leg, but he paid it little heed.

The situation at the door was about as he expected, with Myra's gang hunkered down in front of a doorway with the woman herself battering away at the doors.

Shit, he thought as he noted that they'd been reinforced. Not enough to withstand the enthusiastic battering of an angry brute for long, but enough to have delayed their plan for a quick breach.

"Drones. Sentry mode." He said as he ducked into cover, inwardly acknowledging that this suit had that one advantage over its predecessor, in that it was actually small enough to use cover.

Well, that and the fact that I could still move in this one in the event it stopped working, he thought, acknowledging the not insignificant degree of claustrophobia he now suffered from his time spent

immobile in his last suit.

"Weapons one, two and four. Independent targeting." He murmured as he saw the first defenders sortieing from the hospital's other entrances.

The arms on his back leapt into motion, whirring away as their targeting systems honed in on the distant figures who had started to exchange fire with his own group. The three arms fired in unison, although whether or not they hit anyone, Erich couldn't say given the general confusion of the battlefield.

Fortunately, their Brotherhood goon's aim seemed to mostly be on the drones. Which was understandable, given that they were all still standing out in the open.

It seems 'Call of Destiny' lacks a cover mechanic, Erich grumbled as he watched one of the drones stumble back from a shot before rebalancing itself. *Need to rectify that.*

Fortunately for him, the drones were not so weakly armored to be brought down by a few stray rounds. It would take a good number of shots in the same general area before their armor was compromised.

It also helps that Gravity and her drones are still on overwatch, he thought as a distant figure was lifted into the air, to be perforated by gunfire a moment later.

"Kind of need those doors open, Myra." Erich shouted, wincing as gunfire thudded into the pillar he was hiding behind.

Myra didn't grace his complaint with a response, but she did seem to redouble her efforts to batter down the metal entrance. As he watched, the steel entrance continued to deform under the woman's enthusiastic blows.

"Ammunition reserves: eighty percent." Gravity's automated voice helpfully announced, causing Erich to wince.

"Selective fire mode." He hissed, wary of expending his anti-telepath weapons ammunition reserves before he even encountered them.

Or any Meta for that matter, he thought, before wincing at tempting fate.

"Doors down!" Myra shouted triumphantly as the metal door collapsed with a crash, "get the fuck-"

The woman was cut off as a figure from within smashed into her, sending both of them to the ground in a tangle of cursing limbs.

"Shoot it!" the woman shouted as she pried the creatures teeth away from her throat.

She needn't have bothered. While Erich and the rest of her people might have been stunned by the arrival of a goddamn werewolf, the drones and the weapons on his back had no such compunctions.

They had just been waiting for an appropriate firing solution. A needless precaution given that Myra was a brute, and thus could shrug off most small arms, but Erich hadn't thought to program in

an exception.

Which was why, when Myra lifted her assailant into the air, the werewolf yowled in pain as dozens of rounds were fired into its back from behind. Which was then followed by a second barrage of fire as the gangsters and Erich recovered from their shock.

"Yuck." Myra cursed as she clambered out from under the creature's corpse, her front liberally smeared with werewolf blood. "What the fuck kind of Meta was that!?"

Erich didn't deign to answer the dangerous question. Doing so would defeat the point of coming in the first place. Instead, he promptly put another two rounds into the werewolf's head.

Don't want that regenerative factor coming back to bite me in the ass, he thought, ignoring the surprised looks from the White Tigers.

At least, those who weren't busy firing back at the skinheads trying to flank around them.

"Drones, follow mode. Drones two and six, sentry mode." He instructed before gesturing for Myra to get inside the building. "Let's get this done."

The woman scoffed, rubbing blood from her chin, but strode into the building nonetheless. Hearing no gunfire from within, Erich, the White Tigers, and his remaining drones followed after her.

The interior was nothing special. Little different from any other hospital really, if a little more wind worn from lack of maintenance.

There was also the remains of the Brotherhood goons who had been guarding that particular entrance spread out quite liberally around the lobby. Erich didn't need a degree in criminology to see that they'd been done in by teeth and claws.

It would seem that the Brotherhood's method of controlling their test subjects is far from foolproof, Erich grimaced as he turned away from the gory tableau. And he wasn't the only one who did so, as he heard someone throwing up behind him.

Although, he thought, trying to understand the implications of the scene, *it's possible they don't even **have** a control method. Which would explain why the Brotherhood retreated after delivering the werewolves to the mansion. They didn't want to be eviscerated by their own weapons.*

Shaking his head, he brought his mind back to the task at hand. None of this would matter after he brought the entire building down and put an end to the creatures.

"What the fuck?" Myra repeated as she surveyed the carnage. "Seriously. What the fuck?"

"Get the explosives ready," Erich instructed, "we're on the clock here."

Every second they wasted brought New Brotherhood reinforcement closer. In the form of goons, other Metas...

...or cops and capes.

Myra glanced suspiciously at him, but nonetheless instructed one her people to pull out the bundles of explosive they had brought with them.

"On that pillar there." She said, after quickly consulting the map on her omni-pad.

"Let's keep moving," he instructed.

They found a few more bodies as they passed through the halls, Myra in the lead. It was enough to make him wonder if the earlier werewolf had escaped rather than been released. Perhaps as a result of panic in the face of their attack?

Still, even with a werewolf on the loose in the interior, he would have expected more defenders about the place. They couldn't have all been killed or gone to defend outside.

"How are things looking outside?" Erich radioed.

"We're down to three drones. A speedster showed up and took out the two you left on the doors. I took care of him by canceling his gravity and letting him splat into a wall."

Erich grimaced at the mental image. Myra, who had been listening in, directed three of people back the way they had come. A wise precaution against being flanked now that their exterior defenders were out of commission.

Graivty continued on, "*I think he was the leader on site, because now most of the Brotherhood out here are keeping their heads down. They seem pretty content to hunker down and wait for reinforcements.*"

That made sense, but Erich wasn't quite ready to believe it. Every time they'd encountered the New Brotherhood before, they'd been played like a fiddle. He couldn't believe that everything was going his way now that he'd engaged in an insane assault on one of the Brotherhood's main facilities.

Still, it did no one any good to for him to voice those misgivings aloud.

"*Right, try not to get complacent.*" He radioed, "*we know the Hangman's a sneaky bastard, and we've already encountered two Metas.*" He resisted the urge to curse as he nearly said werewolf, giving away to Myra that this was more than a trafficking ring. "*I'm willing to bet there will be more.*"

"*Roger that.*" Gravity acknowledged, the faintest hint of nervousness in her voice.

He didn't blame her. He wouldn't have been too happy with the possibility of encountering another one of the creatures that nearly caved his head in.

As they advanced further into the hospital, they started to find where the first of the test subjects were held.

"What the fuck is this!?" Myra grunted as she peered into a room with half a dozen men and women cowering in the back corner. *Likely the 'medical' staff,* he thought.

That wasn't what had drawn Myra's eye though. It was the rows of cots filled with people strapped to their beds.

Their very bloody beds...

He had no doubt if they looked around, they would find a torture room, equipped with all the tools needed to induce an Event, as well as some system to associate that pain with some kind of animal.

He made it sound simple, but he was sure the execution was quite a bit more complex, given how simple the theory behind it was. Otherwise he was sure there would be artificial Meta humans all over the place.

They're all members of the Brotherhood though, he noted with both relief and surprise as he noted the tattoos strewn about. *Perhaps captured from the True Brotherhood, or volunteers from the New Brotherhood?*

It didn't really matter in the end. The knowledge that he was about to blow up a horde of Nazis made the act slightly more... tolerable.

At least, more tolerable than blowing up a horde of innocent people.

Slightly, he thought as he deliberately looked away.

CHAPTER 19

"Let's keep moving." Erich said, as he started walking down the hall.

Myra looked like she wanted to argue, eyes leaping between him and the hospital room. In the end though, she rolled her eyes and followed after him. It seemed that whatever questions she had, she was willing to put them aside, or at least wait until they weren't waist deep in Nazis before raising them.

Which is good, because I know exactly what I'm going to have to do if she gets even a hint of what she's actually looking at.

He didn't want to do that. But he would.

Not without hesitation, but without a doubt.

The fight from there became kind of rote. Myra's people split off down the varied catacomb of hallways to deploy their explosives.

Every now and then Erich could hear gunfire as they came across roaming members of the Brotherhood, but given the briefness of it, it seemed that Myra's people were winning.

With any luck, they'd find Hangman soon. If not, well, he was willing to settle for dropping an entire hospital on the guy.

It would be suitable payback for their last meeting.

Assuming the guy's even present, a voice niggled away at the back of his mind.

He dismissed it.

It didn't matter if he wasn't.

They had to take out the hospital anyway. At the very least, it would weaken the New Brotherhoods position. Perhaps enough for the

Red Squares to get involved.

Which wouldn't be a total disaster once the werewolf menace had been taken care of.

"Still alive then, Erich?" A familiar voice echoed through the hospital's scratchy old intercom. *"I must admit. That was an oversight on my part. I had assumed Hard-Light's organization crippled and the survivors fled."*

Erich felt his blood run cold, even as he wondered why the Hangman wasn't using his 'real' name. It would have been a convenient way of muddying the waters with his allies.

"What can I say?" He responded over an open channel, utterly sure the telepath was listening, "I'm tenacious. Like a cockroach."

"Quite." The voice responded, *"not unlike that worm Integrity. Why you've even managed to build a new suit."*

Erich glanced over to see one of the hospital's cameras watching him, before he blasted it.

"Spoilsport." Hangman chuckled, *"I wonder if this one has the same fail-safes as the last one?"*

Erich scowled, banishing the phantom sensations of his suit closing in around him with anger.

"Why don't you show yourself and find out." He snarled, glad that Gravity wasn't present to hear this. Not that he thought she would do anything about it.

With the revelation that she was unbothered by his escape plan, he figured she was pretty safe. The only people he really had to fear learning the truth of his previous contributions to Hard-Lights organization was the man himself, and his daughter.

Neither of which still posed a threat to him.

"Perhaps I will?" The voice laughed, sending a shiver down Erich's spine. *"It's not often I get to kill a rat twi-"*

The man was cut off by a loud gunshot.

"I think that's enough of that." Myra said as she lowered the smoking barrel of her machine pistol from the sparking remains of the nearest intercom speaker. "If you're quite done chewing the fat, perhaps we can get out of here BEFORE more Brotherhood goons, or the cops, show up."

Momentarily stunned, Erich nodded slowly, almost slapping himself for being baited like that.

"Yeah, let's get out of here." He huffed, getting his head back in the game. "Are all the explosives in place?"

The purple woman nodded, "last of my people just radioed in. We're good to go."

"Then let's get the fuck out of here." Erich said, resisting the urge to insist that they stay to hunt down the telepath now that he knew the Meta was here. He'd have to settle for dropping the blowing the place up, hopefully before he esca-

Actually... he thought as an idea came to him.

"Drones. Search and Destroy. Priority Target."

"Acknowledged." The machines intoned, splitting up to head off in different directions, the one with the sparking leg lagging behind.

Myra, and the two goons of hers that hadn't split off to place the last of the explosives, watched them go.

"Damn waste." The woman said, the barest hint of frustration in her voice as 'limpy' disappeared around the corner.

Erich shrugged, as he started walking back the way they came. "Always more where that came from."

Although, with Hard-Light no longer acting as a source of Artificer parts, he didn't know exactly when he would be able to produce *more*. The competition for Artificer created parts on the black market was totally cutthroat. Hell, most of Hard-Light's income came from selling off his own failed experiments.

"For you maybe." The purple woman sighed as she jogged forward to act as the groups point man. "Unless you're willing to reconsider my earlier offer?"

Erich shook his head. In other circumstances he might have seriously considered the woman's offer of more work, but his recent criminal experiences had served to more than put him off.

No. He was getting out of this city, and he was taking his hard-earned cash with him. What came after that... well he'd think of it when it came to him.

Maybe open another tech store?

Might even take Gravity if she's interested, he amended, deliberately not thinking of Sarah's current state.

"I'm sure the veritable piles of cash Gravity is paying you will soothe your offended sensibilities." Erich pointed out.

To his surprise, the gang leader did perk up at that, "True."

"How are things looking outside, Gravity?" Erich radioed.

"Same as before," Gravity responded, *"Though I'm now down to just the one drone. No idea what happened to the other one. It just started smoking before keeling over."*

Erich grimaced, "a bullet must have gotten in or shook something loose."

He could almost hear the woman's shrug over the line. *"Maybe. Either way, be careful on your way out."*

She didn't need to tell him twice. He was very conscious of the fact that he was in a building that was rigged to blow at any moment.

"Your people ready to leave?" He asked, turning to the massive purple bruiser as some of the gangsters who had peeled off to place explosives earlier trotted back into the room.

"Mostly." She said after a few moments listening to her own comms, "one of my teams has stopped reporting in."

Erich felt a shiver run down his back as a sense of déjà vu ran through him.

"Do you want us to go look for them?" He asked reluctantly.

Myra just looked at him like HE was the crazy one. "Fuck no. They're either dead or too dumb to use their radio. Either way, if they're not here when the rest of my teams arrive, we're leaving them."

"Roger that." He grinned, remembering why he liked the foul-mouthed gang leader.

"Movement!" One of Myra's gangers shouted, drawing them both from the moment as they turned their weapons towards the double doors the man was aiming at.

"Our people?" Myra asked, only to receive a shrug in return.

"Great," she hissed, "everyone start moving. Me and the tin-man are staying behind to act as rearguard."

Myra's people needed no further prompting, dashing from the room even as Erich directed incredulous eyes at the woman.

"Oh, don't give me that look," the woman said without even having glanced at him, "you and I have the most protection. Makes sense for us to bring up the rear."

The fact that neither of them would have to perform the role if he hadn't sent off his bots on a search and destroy mission went without saying.

Sighing, Erich acknowledged her point, slowly walking backward with the woman while they both kept their eyes on the set of double doors at the end of the hall.

Which was why the pair of them got to see in detail as the doorway exploded off its hinges as another werewolf burst through.

"Another one!?" Myra roared in disbelief, even as she yanked the trigger on her oversized gun, sending masses of lead at the creature.

Erich wasn't any slower, as he let rip with all four of his weapon systems at the creature, even as it kept coming. It charged mindlessly down the hall as round after round pelted into it, sending Erich's heart leaping into his throat as it bore down on them.

Not going to kill it fast enough! He thought, hands raised ineffectually as Myra tackled it, casting her gun aside.

The pair of massive figures slammed into the hospital wall with enough force to smash straight through it, leaving Erich in an empty hallway as the sounds of violence echoed from the newly formed hole in the wall.

He considered running. Given that Myra had just talked about abandoning her own people, he doubted she would have held it against him. They weren't friends. She hadn't just acted to save his life. The werewolf had been a threat to both of them.

He half turned, ready to move.

And stopped.

He tensed again, willing his legs to act, but they stayed pinned in place. Motionless.

Grey's face flashed before his eyes. Pleading. Betrayed.

Angry.

He shook his head, as he cast aside the memory.

...He'd done the right thing. The smart thing. He kept telling himself.

His legs refused to move though.

"...Shit." He cursed as he turned back around and dashed into the hole that Myra and the werewolf had passed through.

...and nearly got his head taken off by a stray swipe from the creature's claw.

"Shit!" He cursed as he fell back into the hallway from which he'd came. Still, he got a great view of the battle going on a few feet away.

Myra and her foe hadn't traveled far after busting through the wall. The pair were duking it out in the way only bruisers could as they thoroughly demolished the bathroom they were in. Even as he watched, Myra, blood streaming from claw marks across her face, slammed half a toilet over the werewolf's head.

Her eyes widened in surprise when she saw him, no doubt wondering why he hadn't run away. Still, she was pragmatic enough not to question her good fortune.

"Shoot it!" She roared.

Erich didn't need to be told twice. He also didn't need to worry about friendly fire.

Myra was bulletproof. The werewolf was not.

It did have a mean regenerative factor though. Which meant he had to be... surgical about this.

"Weapons One, Two and Four. Manual Control. Eye Reticule." He hissed, not even waiting for the suit to acknowledge before he started firing.

It was difficult to keep track of in the frantic melee going on in front of him, but he determinedly kept his eyes on the creature's head as his weapons started firing.

"Hesitate a little asshole!" Myra hissed as bullets pinged off her steely skin, leaving marks that would no doubt blossom into impressive bruises with time.

"Hold it still, woman!" Erich roared back as his guns stitched massive holes across the creature's body as it struggled in her grasp, claws digging into her as it scratched madly at her arms. "I need to get off a headshot!"

Which was made all the more difficult by the fact that there was a minute amount of lag between the movements of his eye and the reticule.

"I'm trying, ah, fuck!" The purple woman hissed, grimacing in pain as the creature suddenly latched onto her throat with its teeth.

Perfect, Erich thought as the act momentarily stilled the monster's head.

Four guns fired at once, practically obliterating the werewolf's head, and spraying Myra liberally with the contents of its brain pan.

The woman still held on for a few more moments to the twitching corpse, before realizing that it was in fact, a corpse.

Dropping it, she slumped to the floor, taking massive gulps of air. Erich wasn't much better, as he slumped against the bathroom wall, blood rushing in his ears as his legs shook from left-over adrenaline.

"You didn't run?" The woman finally asked.

Erich shrugged.

The woman grimaced as she gingerly probed at her wounds with

her fingers, "didn't take you for the type to be a White Knight."

"I'm not," he muttered as he checked his ammo counter.

Twenty percent remaining, he frowned. Not good.

"Your gun's in the hallway," he said, "grab it, and let's get out of here."

"Don't have to tell me twice," the purple woman said as she clambered to her feet, wincing as her wounds made themselves known.

"You still able to walk?" He asked as he noted how stiffly she was moving.

It would be just his luck that after going out of his way to save the gang leader, she would end up too wounded to move, and he would end up having to abandon her. Because he sure as shit wasn't going to be able to carry her, even if she did help. His current suit could barely sustain its own weight, let alone someone else's.

"I'll be fine." The woman huffed as she pushed past him and out into the hall. "I already owe you for saving my ass. No chance in hell I'm about to own you another."

Despite himself, Erich felt a chuckle slip out of him as he stepped out after her.

A chuckle that turned into a choked snort as *something* slammed into his side and sent him sailing through the air.

He lay sprawled across the ground for a moment, dazed by the blow even as he choked for air.

I think I may have cracked a rib, he thought blearily.

Not that he knew what that sensation felt like given that he was more of an 'indoor child', but he reckoned the sensation of raw bone deep fire running down his side was a pretty good indicator.

"Shields Down. Weapon Two Disabled. Weapon Four Disabled." Gravity's robotic voice informed him. **"Power Core Compromised."**

Something grabbed him, by one of his remaining weapon mounts he thought, and dragged him to his feet.

"Move, Erich!" Myra's voice roared in his ear even as she put action to words by bodily pulling him with her, sending more pain stabbing through his side.

He didn't complain though, instead he focused on putting one leg in front of the other as he tried to jog along side her, a feat made more difficult by the pain in his side and the sudden sluggishness of his suit's response.

As they reached a corner, Myra spun while running to fire a few rounds back down the hallway. Erich used the opportunity to glance back himself, and when he did, he felt his blood run cold.

"Oh," he said, with a voice that held only the slightest hint of hysteria, "it seems that the Hangman has my suit."

Then he ducked around the corner as another pulse blast rocketed into the wall, sending debris and dust flying through the air.

"That *motherfucker* stole my suit!" He yelled as he sprinted for the exit with all he was worth, pain in his side no longer quite so relevant.

"Shut up and keep running!" Myra shouted as she slipped past him.

CHAPTER 20

"Gravity, get ready to cover us." Erich gasped through gritted teeth as he ran towards the exit, "Hangman's in my old suit."

"What!?"

Erich winced as the woman shouted over the comms, "Yeah, it seems it was a little less damaged than I gave it credit for."

It had also apparently more or less survived having a building dropped on it.

In different circumstances he might have taken a moment to take pride in his creation's longevity. As it was, the pain in his side somewhat soured that experience, especially tempered by the knowledge that if his shields hadn't taken the brunt of the shot, he would probably have been smeared all over the hospital walls.

"Michaelson!" Myra shouted through the comms, mercifully cutting off that line of thought, and Gravity's ongoing yelling, "You better have every gun we have trained on those doors when we come out. Even if your guns can't even scratch the suit's paintwork, the motherfucker's bringing plenty of goons with them."

They were? Erich hadn't even noticed. Then again, the sight of his suit, fully intact and bearing down on him, had done quite a good job of commanding his focus.

"Will do, boss." Responded a man, presumably Michaelson. The guy didn't sound happy, but he didn't sound like he was about to flee either. *"The Nazi's are perking up out here, so a few of our people are busy, but we'll have more than enough guns on that door."*

From behind them, they heard the patter of gunfire and then the sound of metal shrieking.

Likely just encountered one of my bots, Erich thought, dismayed by just how little time the drone had apparently lasted. From the sounds of things, Hangman had just smashed the machine aside and kept moving.

So much for his plan to nullify the telepath's mind reading ability by using drones.

Erich and Myra burst out of the hospital and straight into a scene out of a war movie. The smoke had cleared, and fire was being sent every which way as Myra's people blazed away at the Nazi's. The cars that had filled the carpark they had inserted through had all seen better days as they were liberally filled with bullet holes.

Fortunately for his peace of mind, none of Myra's people were using them for cover, given that the vehicles would provide next to no defense from bullets.

"Get over here!" Myra shouted, tugging him towards a set of pillars. Erich was about to complain about being manhandled as pain shot up his side again, but the moment he opened his mouth to speak, Myra's head rocketed to the side as a bullet pinged off it.

That shut him up, and he willingly allowed himself to be shoved into cover, even as his side screamed in protest.

And a good thing too, because the moment he had sunk down behind cover, the double doors of the hospital all but exploded outward as the massive form of his old suit charged out of it.

"Holy shit!" Gravity cursed, unknowingly echoing his own thoughts.

"Light em' up!" Myra shouted as skinheads spilled out of the hospital after the armored telepath.

Erich didn't hesitate, and neither did the rest of Myra's people, as a deluge of fire pattered against the suit's glowing energy barriers. The people to the left and right of it weren't so tough though, and a number of the skinheads that had been caught in the open were minced under the impressive amount of fire-power.

The suit didn't stop though, and Erich had a sudden terrible sense of déjà vu as he recalled his own first outing with the suit.

Only now he was on the other side.

"Scatter!" he shouted as he scrambled out of the way as the suit ran toward them, firing as it advanced.

A few of the White Tigers had heeded his words and dived to the side, but most hadn't heard him, and were sent flying as the wide-angle pulse blasts detonated amongst their ranks.

Erich winced as people were sent sprawling by the energy weapon. The only exception was Myra who had just tanked the blast.

Then Hangman punched her in the face, and even from a half dozen meters away, Erich heard the crack as the purple woman's head snapped back. She swung back almost instantly, but the suit moved with an eerie grace to step around the blow, before hitting her with a body blow.

Erich and the rest of Myra's people fired into the melee, but with every moment that passed, the New Brotherhood goons advanced further out of the hospital, forcing more and more of the White Tigers to change targets.

The mech's fists smashed into the woman again and again. And again and again the bruiser tried to counter attack, only to be sidestepped by the slow-moving suit.

He's pre-empting her moves, Erich noted with a complete lack of surprise.

"Root Command Charlie-Epsilon-Zulu," he shouted, not really expecting a response.

Only, to his surprise, the suit froze mid-movement.

Holy shit... he thought, hope blooming in his chest.

...Then it blasted Myra with its pulse blaster, sending the blood-ied woman sprawling, before turning it's 'eyes' on him.

"Of course," he sighed, as it started advancing on him.

"Voice recognition software, Erich." Hangman said, voice practically oozing smugness even through the telepath's artificial cadence. *"Something you really should have invested in to begin with."*

Erich didn't dignify that with a response as he dodged backwards, blazing away with his remaining weapons.

"Is that half-baked piece of junk really the best you could do, Mechromancer?" Hangman snorted disdainfully as the bullets ricocheted off his defenses.

"Shit. Shit. Shit." Erich cursed, pain flaring in his side as he backpedaled.

"Come on, let's get your sad story over with." The Meta grunted as he brought his guns up, only to grunt in pain as a green aura settled over his limbs.

"Not quite yet," Gravity grunted with gritted teeth.

Erich looked over to see the woman crouched behind a nearby pillar, arms outstretched and glowing.

"Do something Erich." Gravity grunted, sweat streaming down her forehead from the strain of holding the struggling suit in place. "Your ridiculous suit is too fucking strong for me to hold for long."

"Right," Erich nodded, frantically looking around as he dismissed the peculiar sense of déjà vu.

Shields, down. Guns, not worth a damn. Exoskeletal strength, pathetic. Battery, comprom- Ah.

"Arm one, detach weapons system and extract battery." He hissed frantically.

"Acknowledged." The suit said in time with the sound of one of his weapons clattering to the floor. **"Warning: Removing power source will cause catastrophic suit failu-"**

"Root Command, extract battery." He hissed even more frantically.

"Acknowledged." The suit intoned, reaching behind his back to clumsily yank out the compromised power core with a spray of sparks, before freezing as the whole suit ran out of juice.

Lamenting his refusal to install a backup power supply, Erich tried to reach behind himself to grasp the power core, only to grunt with frustration at the fact that the awkward angle left it out of reach.

Which left him looking rather ridiculous as he flailed behind himself.

"Erich!?" Gravity hissed.

"Working on it!" He shouted back in frustration, before jumping up and slamming his back into the floor.

Pain exploded out from his side, and his breath exploded from his lungs as he hissed in pain, but he heard the cracking sound he wanted.

At least, I hope that's the arm cracking, he thought as he considered not just his bones, but the incredibly volatile energy system he was bashing into the floor.

It didn't really matter in the end. Clambering up slowly – a feat made more difficult by the all the dead weight that was his suit – the engineer slammed his back into the floor again.

And again.

And again.

Until finally he heard the snap he had been waiting for.

"Faster, Erich!" Gravity hissed as the suit in front of her audibly whined as its servos strained against her powers, "Whatever you're thinking of doing, he sure as shit doesn't like it."

Erich barely heard her. Drenched with sweat, he sprawled onto his side and scooped up the detached arm; the sparking battery Artificer-Tech battery still held in its feeble grasp.

This is going to suck so fucking much…

He hesitated for just a moment, before he jammed his index finger into the device's insides through it's cracked case. It was like dipping the digit in lava. Biting his lip to stifle the shriek of

279

pain he wanted to let loose as the material of his glove started to adhere to his skin, he found the wire he was searching for and pulled it loose before yanking his hand away.

Well, at least it didn't instantly explode in my hand, he thought as he pivoted.

He had never had much success with ball games. For all his ability to calculate the physics involved in the creation of an ideal throw, his ability to put it into practice was limited. Which was why he was so surprised when he lobbed the battery and his ungainly projectile arced lazily through the air to clang directly against the Hangman's helmet.

Ideally, that would have been the moment his hastily improvised explosive device *did* explode. As it was, it clanged against the helmet and tumbled to the ground with a clatter.

Then it exploded.

Both he and Gravity were thrown from their feet as a vibrant *pink* fireball engulfed the suit. Erich's side exploded with pain *again* - and this time he definitely heard something crack - as he was sent sprawling against the concrete.

Wincing as he clambered onto his elbows, ignoring the litany of aches and pains from his body, he saw that the spot where the Hangman had been was utterly shrouded with smoke.

Oily purple smoke.

"Yeah, let's try and avoid breathing any of that in." Myra huffed as she strode over to him, gingerly clutching her torso, where a blood patch was forming in her shirt.

Seems that bulletproof is not the same as blaster proof, he thought grimly.

Dismissing the woman from his mind, he called out, "Gravity, you still alive?"

"For now." The woman grunted back from wherever she'd landed.

Erich nodded, "Right, well keep an eye out, he might still be-"

As if on cue, Hangman strode out of the smoke, his suit cracked and smoking, but still mobile.

"Motherfucker..." Myra hissed as she brought up her gun, "How fucking tough do you build those things?"

Erich didn't grace that question with an answer as he scrambled behind a nearby car.

From his hiding spot, he saw that the suits barriers were completely gone, as armor plating crumpled or falling away as the heavy duty rounds of Myra's oversized machine pistol slammed into the suit. Internals he was intimately familiar with were exposed to the light of day as the suit raised its arms to deflect some of the firepower headed its way. He saw one of the forward lights spark and fail and realized that the bastard must have tried to use the system's 'flash'.

Not going to happen, he thought smugly as he took in the battered state of the construct.

For just a moment, Erich almost believed that Myra's attack would be enough to finally end the telepath.

But when her clip ran dry the suit was still standing. One of its arms had been completely shredded and he could see blood as well as coolant leaking through the dents in its armor, but the other limb was all but untouched.

Myra didn't even have time to attempt to dodge before she was blasted from her feet once more by a wave of pure force. Her gun flew from her hands as her limp body was sent skidding across the carpark like a ragdoll.

"You people are beginning to get on my nerves." The suit's damaged speakers crackled as the whole machine ominously turned towards Erich's hiding space.

...Shit.

Erich narrowly avoided being splattered across the pavement as the car he was hiding behind was thrown onto its side by a ton of angry power armour.

"Gravity!" He managed to not-quite shriek as he sprinted for his next bit of cover.

Gunfire erupted from behind him as he ran, and almost instantly he heard another blast of force from the suit. Sliding into cover, he glanced out to see the sparking remains of the final outdoor drone lying in the street, while Gravity's yellow helmed head darted between burnt out cars.

Sighing in relief, he glanced over to see that his momentary delay had cost him. Hangman was aiming at him once more.

Time seemed to freeze as he heard the low whine of the weapon's build up, knowing in his heart of hearts that his flimsy piece of cover would provide no protection from the powerful device.

Not like this! He thought, an unexpected rage blooming within his chest as his arms shot up in a futile attempt to protect himself.

The boom that followed was as unexpected as it was welcome.

Erich watched in disbelief as the suit's pulse blaster failed catastrophically, blowing the suit's forearm clean off.

"Argh!" Hangman's pained shriek echoed through the battlefield as he clutched at the mangled mess of metal and wiring that remained of the suit's arm.

Even from this distance, and through his surprise, Erich could see the tell tale tint of vivid crimson blood amongst the hydraulic and coolant fluids dripping from the construct's ruined appendage.

"You!" the suit turned on him once more, cutting off his momentary pang of sadistic joy at the sight.

"Oh, shit!" Erich shouted as the suit charged towards him.

From behind, he saw Gravity fire at it as it moved, but even with its dilapidated state, the suit slipped to the side with only the smallest of movements and continued its sprint toward him.

Fucking telepath, Erich despaired as the Hangman's bullshit power let the suit dodge every shot headed its way.

...Only to trip as a bevy of shots crackled across its side, destroying the right knee joint in a spray of sparks and the sound of crunching metal.

Erich could only watch in dumfounded disbelief as the massive construct hit the floor with a deafening crash and slid a few more inches towards him, before coming to a grinding halt.

"Priority target located," an all too familiar voice announced, shattering the relative silence that followed.

Doing his best impression of a goldfish, Erich glanced over to see one of the drones emerge from the hospital, its leg still sparking and dragging behind it as it gamely limped toward the suit.

Even as his mind tried to keep up with what just happened, he found himself subconsciously tallying the damage.

Frankly, he was amazed the thing was still standing; littered with bullet-holes, it's paint scorched, as if someone had tried to light it on fire, and one of its arms hung limp - forcing it to hold it's cheap Chinese AK knock off in one hand.

But it *was* still standing, and Erich had never seen a more beautiful sight.

He was *not* so dumbfounded though that he didn't think to immediately dash over and yank the gun out of the cheap automata's hand while it went through the robotic motion of reloading.

Or attempted to - given that it only had one arm, it had been failing.

"Weapon lost," it announced, in a manner that might have suggested indignation if it had come from a being capable of the emotion.

Plucking a fresh clip from the drone's belt, Erich left the grasping drone behind and strode over to the downed suit.

"Wait, Jason!" a surprisingly normal, if frantic female voice coughed from within the hunk of metal, "I can help you! Your sister- the organization I'm a part of-"

"Can't move, right?" Erich grinned, before pressing the gun into the suit, honing his aim into one of the cracks in the suit.

"Sucks, don't it?" He said.

Then he pulled the trigger, luxuriating in the kick of it beneath his hands.

When the gun finally clicked empty, he sighed, tossing it aside and collapsing onto his ass, wincing as pain shout of from his side from jarring impact.

It was done.

He'd won.

Now to get back to work, he thought as he took a shuddering breath - luxuriating for just a moment in the acrid taste of gunpowder on his tongue.

"Is Myra still alive, Gravity?" He called out tiredly to the open air, only vaguely listening to the continual pop of gunfire in the background.

"I don't know, *Jason*." The woman in question responded from behind him, "I thought I saw her chest moving when I ran past her."

Erich deliberately ignored her use of his 'real' name. He was too tired to bother with secrets right now.

"And the rest of the New Brotherhood?" He asked as he watched the drone limp over and pick up the discarded gun, woodenly attempting to finish the reloading cycle it had started before he interrupted it.

"Seems they're retreating back into the hospital now that their boss is down." The woman responded dispassionately. "Probably waiting for reinforcements."

"Good." Erich muttered tiredly as he reached into his jacket and grabbed the detonator. "That makes this next part easier."

CHAPTER 21

Erich stared over at *his* suit from his position at his worktable.

It had seen much better days. Hell, one of the arms had fallen off when they finally roused Myra long enough for her to lug it into the van.

Fortunate for us that the surviving White Tigers were still a bit shell-shocked by the hospital's sudden demolition.

He had not been in the mood to argue about it taking up space in the van. Even if the return trip had made the original trip over there seem positively spacious by comparison.

Positive outcome or not, blowing up the hospital from all of a few dozen meters away had not been his wisest move.

Still, he supposed it all worked out in the end as he took another swig of his drink.

...A drink he nearly spilled when Gravity shouted out from behind him.

"Oh, for fucks sake, Erich." Gravity roared, box of belongings in her hands, "You said you were going to get the body out of that thing! You know how hot it is in here? It's starting to stink."

Turning to glare at the woman in question, he scowled, "Can't a man enjoy his moment of triumph for but a few moments?

"Not if he wants to stay a *free* man." Gravity shot back, "We blew up a hospital. Abandoned or not. The cops and the capes aren't going to ignore that. We need to get the fuck out of town."

...and find a doctor, went unsaid, as they were both all too aware of the silent member of their trio. Sarah was currently lying on a rack in the corner of the room, watched over by his one remain-

J. R. Grey

ing sentry drone; who Gravity had had the audacity to name Limpy.

He had wanted to scrap for the thing for useful parts when it showed up at the shop, somehow having managed to limp home from all the way across town.

More resilient design than I expected, he admitted grudgingly.

"How's your side, *Jason?*" Gravity eventually sighed as she slid the box into the van.

Erich winced both at the reminder of his partially spilled secret AND the sensation he had been attempting to dull with sweet, sweet alcohol when she walked in.

"Only really hurts when I breathe," he shrugged, regretting the motion immediately as it sent another wave of fresh agony through him. He also deliberately made no comment on her use of his 'real' name.

Part of him was hoping that if he ignored her use of it long enough it would go away.

Which might have been why Gravity had zero sympathy for him when she responded, "Yeah, well the sooner we get out of this city, the sooner we can find a doctor who isn't too afraid of the Red Squares or what's left of the Brotherhood to treat us all."

"Treat me and Sarah you mean?" Erich muttered with more than a little jealousy.

The gravity manipulator had gotten away from the fight with nothing more than few cuts and bruises.

"Yes, treat you two," the woman said with an audible roll of her eyes, one that utterly failed to hide the hint of smugness beneath it.

"Have we even decided on a destination yet?" He asked, wondering

when it was decided that they were all sticking together, even though there was no real *need* anymore. Their common cause had ended with the death of Hangman.

286

"The West Coast." A new voice interrupted, startling them both and sending Erich's beer tumbling to the floor as he grabbed his gun.

"Who the fuck are you?" Erich muttered though gritted teeth as pain shot up his side - *again* - from the sudden movement, while also ignoring the belated 'Intruder Detected' from the useless security bot in the corner.

"Winter Witch." The armoured woman said from her position at the door, "and I would tell that drone to stand down before it does something... ill advised."

Her tone made it clear that she wasn't going to ask nicely a second time.

"Designation: Limpy, stand down," Erich muttered as he realized who was talking to. He let his gun drop too, but made no move to holster it.

"What would the leader of the Red Squares want with us?" Gravity asked equally wearily as she also let her weapon fall to her side.

"I'm here to thank you for removing my biggest competitor for me," the supervillainess grinned. "After the disappearance of Hard-Light, a few of my people were concerned that we might be next. More than a few suggested that we should launch a pre-emptive attack on this 'Hangman' before he could turn on us."

"Because that worked so well for our crew." Gravity grunted.

"Quite so." The woman said, "I was of the opinion that we should attempt to acquire more information on our foe before doing anything rash. An opinion that was only reinforced when all of my informants within the New Brotherhood went... dark"

Something close to a frown came over her features, before the immaculately polite mask came back on, "After that happened, I suggested that we should let the Brotherhood's little civil war play out first. It wouldn't do for us to remind both factions that they had external enemies, lest they decide to put their own

287

squabbles aside to deal with US. Doing so would give us time to properly mobilize for an all-out engagement."

Erich figured that made sense, if you didn't know that Hangman was using that time to create Nazi werewolves.

"However, you can imagine my surprise and delight," Winter Witch continued, "when before even our preliminary preparations were completed, the situation was resolved for us by the remnants of Hard-Light's organization."

"You're welcome," Gravity said in a manner that suggested the woman was anything but, "but I'm willing to bet the head of the Squares didn't come all the way down to this shit-shack just to say 'thanks'."

Erich couldn't decide whether to be more or less concerned by the fact that Winter Witch seemed more amused than irritated by Gravity's *very ill-advised* attitude. It almost eclipsed his offense at Gravity referring to his shop as a *shit-shack*.

"Quite correct, Olivia," the woman smiled, "you always were rather astute when you choose to be. Rare as it is."

Gravity didn't quite growl, but the noise she made wasn't all that far off.

"So, why are you here?" Erich said before Gravity could say something even more ill-advised.

"Originally, I intended to recruit you," the woman admitted as she turned towards him. "However, that was before I learned exactly HOW you finished off our latest foe."

The ample application of high explosives? He had to admit that without the context of *Nazi Werewolves* it did seem a little... excessive for a gang-war.

"Did you really have to destroy the entire hospital?" the woman sighed, unknowingly echoing his own thoughts. "Honestly, even in his youth Hard-Light was more subtle than that. And the man was quite the beast back then."

Erich shrugged, because it wasn't like he was about to explain that he wasn't so much taking out the Brotherhood as he was attempting to keep the lid on a world sundering new method of creating Metas.

One that he still had no idea how Hangman had come across.

Besides, well, telepathy.

"As a result, things have changed," she continued. "Blur arrived in the city this morning, ostensibly to investigate the recent gang violence. And with one of the Titans in New Granton, you've all suddenly become too hot a commodity to handle. Which means you're both in the unenviable position of being too dangerous to leave alone, and too much trouble to incorporate into the Squares."

"So you want us out of the city?" Erich finished.

"No." Winter Witch shook her head, humour fading as the vicious gang leader came to the fore, "my earlier *suggestion* wasn't a suggestion. The Red Squares want you out of the *country*. You make people nervous."

"You're exiling us." Gravity muttered, spitting the word as if they were toxic.

"Exactly," Winter Witch said unsympathetically, "getting into the West Coast is easy. Getting out is significantly less so. So much so that the Red Squares would feel much more comfortable with you within that madhouse's borders."

Erich was kind of worried that he was growing somewhat numb to

the world crashing down around him.

...and it could be worse, was just about all he could summon up to the idea.

Sure, the West Coast was an anarchic mess, but it was still better than the big brother state that was the European Union these days, or the civil war in the Pan-Asian Alliance.

Those are even the better options as far as the wider world is concerned, he thought grimly.

It seemed that every other week some third-world government got knocked over by one supervillain or another. He was of the opinion that pretty soon there wouldn't be any countries left outside the Big Three that weren't under the iron fist of one Meta or another.

Sure, the West Coast was cesspit, but at least it was a vaguely familiar cesspit.

"If we're such a problem, why not just kill us now and be done with it?" Gravity asked, prompting Erich to sputter as his thoughts ground to a halt.

Gravity snarkily continued, "you wouldn't even have to do it yourself. I'm sure that bitch, Grey Hood, is just begging for a chance."

Winter Witch just shrugged, "the thought certainly crossed my mind, but as I said, I *am* thankful to you for dealing with a problem for me. That means I'm inclined to let you live for now."

"How gracious," Gravity snorted.

Winter Witch's smile was as ice cold as her namesake when she turned towards the younger woman, "It is isn't it... *now get the fuck out of my city before I decided to be less gracious.*"

To Erich's infinite relief, Gravity was smart enough to shut up at that moment.

Satisfied, the woman turned to leave, before pausing at the door, "Oh, and for fucks sake, get rid of whatever body is stinking up the place. I can smell it from here. The last thing I need is for you three to get caught before even getting out of the city."

CHAPTER 22

Lucy looked over the carnage with a frown. Even weeks after the event that had destroyed the abandoned hospital, work crews were still pulling bodies from the wreckage.

Work crew, she mentally amended.

New Granton didn't have the funds to direct more than token effort to the affair.

Or rather, is unwilling to spend anything more than the bare minimum on this neighborhood, she thought as she glanced at the denizens of the area, who were cautiously watching the work from a distance.

As if feeling her eyes on them, a young mother pulled her child closer to her before striding off, ignoring the muffled complaints of her offspring. A quick glance up and down the street had similar results from others.

Not all fled though. Some remained to watch. To glare.

To guard, she thought as she noted the gang colors adorning a number of them.

The 'Red Squares' if she remembered her hurried readings on the trip over here. Apparently they were the dominant force in the city now that the other two factions had been driven out.

They posed no threat to her, or the work crews given that she was present, but it was still troubling to see such a blatant show of force arrayed against a Guild hero.

She didn't know whether it was the norm here, or simply the result of the recent carnage. If it was the former, then the city was even worse off than she feared. If it were the latter though...

Well, it wasn't like she could blame them.

"Shadow Guild." She huffed under her breath as she watched yet another skeletal corpse be dragged from the rubble.

This had their fingerprints all over it.

A newcomer infiltrating a known gang. A brief and violent coup. The systematic destruction of other gangs in the area, and then finally the destruction of the infiltrated gang by law enforcement as the original gang engaged in more and more obvious criminal behavior. At which point the infiltrator would *disappear.*

Or rather, that's the usual way these things go, she thought as she glanced at the carnage.

Clearly someone had thrown a spanner into the works of this particular operation, because it was the 'New' Brotherhood that had been destroyed, and now, rather than a city with a conflicted and fractured criminal underground, there was now one completely unopposed faction remaining.

That would be a pain in the ass to remove.

In fact, she was reasonably sure that taking down the Red Squares would be completely impossible for the beleaguered police force within the city.

The power disparity was simply too great.

"You have no jurisdiction here, Blur." A strident voice called out over the sound of heavy machinery, "This territory belongs to the New Granton Defenders."

And here's the reason why that disparity is so great, she thought with a sigh as she turned toward the newcomer.

Valiant was not a particularly impressive man to look at. For one thing, his vivid red jumpsuit only served to display his rapidly

burgeoning gut, and his lack of a visor meant that she had a clear view of the man's very bloodshot eyes.

Addict.

Behind him, the man's team were equally lackluster - if in different ways.

"The entire country is Olympian territory." She said calmly as she let the stoic mask of Blur fall over her. "We go where we feel we are needed."

"Fuck that." Valiant swore as he stormed up to her, "this is our town. We don't need outside help. Least of all from you gloryhounds."

"Your opinion means nothing to me," she shrugged. "I go where I please."

"You're wasting your goddamn time. I just said that we'll handle this!" Valiant spat as he started to turn crimson.

Behind him, Blur could see his team cringing away from their boss.

Well, at least they aren't total fools, she thought, before turning her gaze on their furious leader. It took a special kind of stupid to argue with a member of the Olympians. Especially the granddaughter of one of the founding members.

Still, it raised questions.

What are you hiding? She thought as she sped up her senses to better catalogue the man's many micro-expressions.

Anger. Indignance. Hangover. Fear... Desperation.

Interesting. Perhaps there was more to this case than simply incompetence. If anything, it only reinforced her belief that the Shadow Guild was at work here.

Pressure from them? They certainly had the influence, but it would be odd for them to act so... blatantly. Why? Her eyes flicked toward the shattered ruins of the hospital. *A result of this operation's failure? Overextended? Exposed? Vulnerable?*

Gradually, she let time resume its normal flow as she came to a decision.

"No, I don't think I am." She said, watching the leader of her fellow hero team carefully, "I think something of note happened here."

Something the Shadow Guild wanted covered up.

And she'd be damned if she'd let that happen. Not when they'd finally slipped up in a manner she could use to expose them.

Her body started to blur and vibrate in the signature fashion that given her the moniker 'Blur'.

Valiant and his cronies rapidly paled, their various powers feebly flickering to life as they got ready for a fight.

"You can't be serious! Fights between Guild members are prohibited! They'll be an inquest! Sanctions!" A young woman called from the back.

Behind her, the relief efforts ground to a halt, as members of the work crew started to notice the impending Meta fight burgeoning not more than a dozen meters away. Some stayed to watch. Most started to run.

Wise, but needless.

She could take down all of these chumps without endangering anyone.

"I know." She said, her voice distorted by her power, as she turned her attention back to the pathetic excuse for a hero team in-front of her. "That's what I'm counting on."

"That's quite enough." Someone called out before either side could make the first move.

Right on time, Blur grinned as she turned toward the newcomer who was confidently striding over, his Guild uniform creased and stained in a manner that suggested long hours and little sleep. *The Shadow Guild's man on the ground.*

As if to reinforce her theory, she could hear the New Granton Defenders exhaling in relief at the man's approach.

All except for one of them.

"Did you see that?" Valiant said as he turned toward the newcomer, "this bitch was about to attack us!"

"Language, Valiant." The man frowned, "you represent the Guild when you put on that suit. Act like it."

"And what about her?" Valiant responded, "I'm pretty sure picking a fight with another hero team is worse than throwing out a few curse words."

"Rest assured, I will speak with Blur." The man said, tiredly glancing toward the glaring Olympian, "in the meantime, you and your team should return to your base. I don't think they'll be anymore need of you tonight."

Valiant looked like he was about to speak up again, but another look from the newcomer silenced him. In the end, the hero was forced to swallow his impotent rage and storm off, his team trailing behind.

Blur didn't bother to watch them leave, her focus was entirely on the figure across from her.

"Shadow Guild," she huffed.

"We are on the same side, Lucy," the man said sadly. "I do wish you would come to recognize that."

Blur's snort of disdain said exactly what she thought of that.

"What are you doing here, Blur?" the man continued.

"Exactly as I said to that pathetic excuse for a hero team." Blur said, "starting my own investigation of what went down here."

"That would be a gross misallocation of your time, given that Guild resources are already present" the man said. "The Olympian's right to intervene in situations across the country was awarded on the basis that it would allow the most powerful members of the Guild to rapidly react to developing situations without the need for excess oversight."

Blur nodded, "which is a right I am exercising here."

"This is not a developing situation," the man shot back. "And certainly not one that requires the presence of a powerful Meta."

"I disagree, I believe that there is more to this situation than a 'conventional' Guild investigation will turn up."

It went without saying that the man in front of her was about as far from a 'conventional' member of the Guild as you could get.

Which was exactly what she wanted to investigate, and both of them knew it.

The man sighed, "I had a feeling you might say that."

As if on cue, Blur's communicator started to ring.

"You might want to get that. Sounds important."

Scowling, Blur did exactly that.

"What's up, Techno?"

"I'm sorry, Blur," her fellow Olympian said, all-but wincing at her tone, "I know you said you didn't want to be disturbed, but we've got a situation developing in New York. It looks like Raider's crew is

getting ready to make a move. We're all getting called in."

Blur resisted the urge to swear as she sent a venomous glance the Shadow Guild operative's way.

"I'm on my way." She spat, cutting the line as soon as Techno told her where transport would be waiting for her.

"Don't think this is over," she snapped as she turned to leave.

"I wouldn't do you the disservice of assuming it was," the man sighed, "though I still maintain the hope that you will come to see that we are on the same side in this Blur."

As if, she thought as she stormed away.

The Shadow Guild was a blight on her grandfather's legacy, and everything the Guild stood for.

Used to stand for, she corrected.

It seemed that with every passing day, the Shadow Guild movement grew in power within the Guild, and she had no idea how deep the cancer spread. The only thing she did know was that someone high up within the Guild's power structure was keeping the faction protected.

Someone with enough powers to get the Olympians redeployed on short notice.

The worst thing was that Shadow Guild wasn't even the root problem. It was a symptom. A result of the fact that the current rules and systems weren't working. *Couldn't* work in a world that was rapidly being overrun by individuals with incredible powers, with no discernable cause or origin.

Shadow Guild wasn't an act of callousness on the part of elements of the Guild. It was one of desperation.

Still, it was wrong. And she wasn't about to compromise on her grandfather's vision by bowing to fear and desperation.

The ends *never* justified the means.

And she wasn't alone in that belief. Just as Shadow Guild had allies, so did she.

"Did you get everything, Techno?" She asked as she fired up her communicator.

"Yep," the young man chuckled from over the line, "I'm sending everything that was on his Omni-Pad and phone to you."

Lucy had to resist the urge to giggle as she saw pulled up her pad to see the files being sent over from Olympian HQ – unimaginatively named Olympus by the general public.

"You're a lifesaver, Techno," she complimented the technomancer, and even through the comms she could hear his blush.

"I try."

Lucy smiled, at the giddiness in her teammates tone. It was like having a little brother again. Albeit one that wasn't quite as prickly as-

No. She shut off that line of thought as a pang of shame ran through her.

"So, what am I looking at here?" She asked, earlier giddiness forgotten as she glanced at the Omni-Pad while walking towards where she was supposed to meet her transport.

She knew she could do a superspeed scan of the document herself, but she'd found from experience that Techno was infinitely better at picking up details that she might miss - and only slightly slower.

Picking up on her sudden grimness, and likely guessing the cause, Techno was kind enough not to comment on it as he started summarizing.

"Not a ton to go on in here. It looks like this operation was a total clusterfuck like we guessed, and the operative they had on the ground was killed before the plan could reach the later stages."

Nothing they hadn't already guessed, "anything we can use?"

"Maybe. I've got the names of a number of villains that keep re-occurring during this report; Gravity, Hard-Light, Mechromancer, Myra and Bronte. Hard-Light went to ground after his initial contact with the Shadow Guild operative, and they have no idea where he went, but we have a general idea on where the others have gone."

"Just tell me where they've gone." Lucy asked as she heard the telltale roar of her transport swooping down from overhead. "With any luck we can get to them before the Shadow Guild does."

"...The West Coast."

For just a second Lucy was glad for the deafening sound of the overhead vehicle's engines, because it served as ample camouflage for her loud, creative and venomous cursing.

Made in the USA
San Bernardino, CA
15 April 2020

67491772R00183